THE DARING MISS DARCY

Lost Ladies of London Book 4

ADELE CLEE

The Daring Miss Darcy
Copyright © 2018 Adele Clee
All rights reserved.
ISBN-13: 978-1-9998938–3-5

Cover designed by **Jay Aheer**

CHAPTER ONE

The black unmarked carriage rolled to a stop on the corner of Longacre, a street north of Covent Garden. Here, so close to the narrow lanes and crooked timber buildings of St Giles, the night was anything but still. Drunken quarrels tumbled out from packed taverns onto the streets. The deep rumble resonated like that of a tenor singing the restless song of the poor. The soprano came in the form of women hawking their wares, of stray dogs whining and children crying.

Ross Sandford, Marquess of Trevane, Vane to his friends and enemies, shuffled to the edge of his seat and extinguished the candle in the lantern hanging from the roof of his conveyance. At night, a man could embrace the cold emptiness filling his heart. And yet the need to rouse a flicker of emotion in his lifeless chest had drawn him out from his house in Berkeley Square to this dirty and dangerous part of town.

Dressed in black, Vane opened the door and stepped down to the pavement. After straightening his coat, he jerked his head to his coachman, Wickett.

"Wait here. Twenty minutes is all I need."

That would be enough time to lure a rogue or two out from the shadows, enough time to heat the blood as it rushed through his veins.

Wickett stared at the fog-drenched street and shook his head. "Ten minutes should be plenty, my lord. Every light-fingered cove in the district will be out on the hunt tonight."

Vane knew that. Why else would he have come if not to practice his pugilistic skills? Pity the fool who thought him easy pickings.

"Strange, I do not recall asking for your opinion."

"If you wanted a simple coachman, you would have hired one from The Dog and Duck." From atop his box, Wickett inclined his head respectfully. "You wanted a man who isn't afraid to take a shot. A man who can sew a wound as good as a French modiste sews silk. You wanted a man who can change your shirt so your sister won't notice the blood, who can tie a cravat—"

"Yes, yes, Wickett. You have made your point."

"Then as a man who's survived these streets and has a need to protect his master, take heed. No more than fifteen minutes else I'll be carting home a dead man."

Vane inhaled deeply as a flash of excitement sparked. Death might bring the answer to the questions plaguing his waking thoughts, and those disturbing his dreams, too. Had Estelle Darcy survived the shipwreck? Was she out there somewhere, living and breathing? Did she ever think of him? Had she cared for him at all?

Vane shook himself and focused on the lithe, athletic figure glaring wide-eyed from the box seat.

"What's wrong, Wickett?"

"Wrong?"

"You have the look of a man waiting to watch his friend dangle from the scaffold. Where is your faith in my ability to ward off an attack?"

"It's no good looking for trouble when your mind's not in the game. Ever since you came back from visiting Lord Ravenscroft, you've not been yourself."

No, he was not himself.

The pledge he'd made to find Estelle Darcy and prove she was alive and well, gnawed away at his conscience like a starving rat with razor-sharp teeth. But he'd abandoned all hope of success. All leads led to naught. The runner he'd hired had sent him on a fool's errand to Canterbury and then to Maidstone. An acquaintance in Whitechapel sent him to a woman on Upper Newman Street. While she had a smart mouth, and had recently returned from France, it soon became apparent that Estelle was her working name.

"Of course I'm not myself. My sister married a blasted pirate."

That was not the reason for his morose mood. Ravenscroft had proven himself worthy. Anyone who saw Fabian and Lillian together could not question the depth of their love. Still, it was as good an excuse as any, and it would stop his coachman's carping criticism, for now.

Wickett bent his head. "You miss Lady Lillian that's for sure, but it's no reason to dice with death at every given opportunity."

Hell, he missed Lillian more than he could say. But after eight years spent learning to live with loss, suppressing pain was not a new concept.

Vane's mind drifted from thoughts of his own sister to the miniature portrait of Ravenscroft's sister locked away in his desk. Why would he want to remember Miss Darcy's likeness when he'd spent an eternity trying to forget her?

"I suppose you think me foolish." Vane tugged his coat sleeves and flexed his fingers.

"It doesn't matter what I think, my lord. I'll never understand the minds of intelligent folk."

Intelligent?

Only an imbecile would enter an alley in this part of town, at this time of night. But he'd rather partake in a fistfight than hover on the verge of consciousness in a laudanum-induced state. Besides, was a beating not a form of self-flagellation, punishment for his incompetence?

Through the thick, smothering cloud, Fate's finger beckoned him, taunted him to step towards the alley.

"If I fail to appear in fifteen minutes, I suggest you come and find me."

Wickett turned his head and muttered something into the raised collar of his driving coat. "Fifteen minutes," Wickett repeated. A weary sigh left the coachman's lips, the white mist joining the thousands of other frustrated breaths that made up this foggy night. "But then I've never been good at telling the time."

"And yet you're always there when I need you."

Wickett tipped his hat. "Let's hope you're in need of my services long after tonight."

"Indeed."

The coachman would continue to complain until Vane returned unscathed.

Squaring his shoulders and cracking his neck, Vane strode towards the narrow passage, pulled by an invisible rope. One thing was certain. Regardless of what happened in the next fifteen minutes, he was guaranteed to feel something.

Vane paused at the entrance.

He strained his eyes and peered through the white mass swirling in ominous shapes towards him.

Danger lurked within.

He could feel it, smell it, taste it.

Like a panther on the prowl, he honed his senses. Three long, sleek steps and he noted movement. Dull, grey shadows drifted into his field of vision. The stench of the streets wafted over him:

4

grime and sweat and stale tobacco. The choking bitter scent of fog.

His heart raced as the need for vengeance coursed through his veins.

Footsteps shuffled closer. The faint shadow before him grew in height and breadth.

"What 'ave we 'ere then?" The rough, gravelly voice echoed in the confined space. "You seem to 'ave lost yer way, guv'nor."

Out of the corner of his eye, Vane noted another figure push out from a doorway to his right and skirt around to stand behind him. Excellent. Two made for a more satisfying challenge.

"Oh, I'm not lost." Vane clenched his fists at his sides. "I know exactly where I am." Arrogance dripped from every word.

"Happen you know what's coming then."

The man stepped forward with the confident swagger of someone who'd grappled on the streets many times before. Upon witnessing the rogue's slender frame, some men might breathe a sigh of relief. But this thug would be light on his feet, fast with his fists.

"And I would wager twenty guineas *you* don't have the first clue what's coming." Vane enjoyed taunting them. Despite offering himself as bait, he refused to throw the first punch.

The rogue flexed his bristled jaw. A line of spittle flew from his mouth to land on Vane's boot.

"Give us yer watch, seal and coin purse, and then you can be on yer way."

A firm hand from behind gripped Vane's shoulder. "Do as 'e says and you might get to keep them shiny boots."

Vane snorted with contempt. "If you want anything from me, you'll have to take it by force. And I suggest you tell your accomplice to remove his hand else I'm liable to break his fingers."

Both rogues chuckled.

"This swell cove has a tongue what would whip the shirt off yer back, make no mistake."

Vane firmed his jaw. When it came, the jab would be quick. "I am simply giving you a choice." Estelle Darcy had not afforded him the same courtesy. She had struck his heart without warning. A blow so swift and sudden he had not seen it coming. "Step aside, or raise your fists."

"This ain't one of yer fancy fighting clubs."

"And this is not the first time I've brawled in an alley."

"Prancing about in stockings and slippers ain't brawling. There ain't no rules on the street."

"Then what are you waiting for?"

A growl signalled the first punch.

Vane dropped his weight, elbowed the man standing behind hard in the stomach, driving him back in order to miss the hit from the rogue in front.

The man behind crumpled to the ground with a groan. Vane dodged another flying fist and followed it with one of his own, a solid smack to the rogue's cheek that whipped the fool's head back.

Damn, it felt good.

The other man scrambled to his feet, swung his arm wide and caught Vane just below the ear. The dull thud rang through his head causing a momentary loss of balance.

Vane's mocking laugh sliced through the air.

This was what he wanted, what he needed. Pain. Physical suffering. Emotional torment. Hot blood awakened every fibre of his being.

God, he had never felt more alive.

"Come on!" Vane cried, beckoning the rogues to take their best shot. "You can do better than that." The burning need for satisfaction proved overwhelming.

The scrawny one took a swipe. Vane ducked and threw all his

weight into a hard uppercut just below the ribs, robbing the ruffian of breath.

"Why, you filthy—" The other man jumped on his back, and Vane reached behind, grabbed the miscreant's neck and flipped him over his shoulder to land on the ground.

Vane could have ploughed into them, finished it there and then. But he wanted his fifteen minutes' worth and so padded lightly on the balls of his feet while he waited for them to recover. Men of their ilk did not walk away.

They gathered themselves, but then a growl from behind forced Vane to glance back over his shoulder. Black eyes appeared through the mist, eyes partially obscured by grey fur. Another growl brought a flash of pointed teeth. A wolf—a hound of sorts—stalked closer.

Both rogues took advantage of the distraction. They lunged forward, tackled Vane to the ground, their jabs lacking skill and precision. Delivering one blow after another, he fought back. The crack of bones reached his ears. Blood dripped from one man's nose onto Vane's cheek.

Breathless pants filled the air.

A manic euphoria flooded his chest.

The wolfhound barked and bared its teeth.

One thug dragged Vane to his feet. "Hit him, Davy, and have done with it. That mangy mutt looks like it ain't eaten for weeks."

Davy looked nervous. Blood stained his lips. One eyelid had swollen to the size of a plum. And yet he found the strength to draw back and release his clenched fist.

The uppercut made contact with Vane's chin, the power of it knocking his teeth together. His legs buckled, and he fell back, smacking his head hard on the ground. The thud echoed in his ears. Spots of light danced before his eyes. A fog of confusion clouded his mind. He couldn't focus. The world swayed.

Loud voices and the clip of footsteps near the entrance caused both rogues to jump up and take flight. The hound chased after them, snapping at their heels.

Strange voices rent the air.

"Turn here, Mr Erstwhile. Turn here. This is Bedford Street. I'm convinced of it."

"Where? My dear, I cannot see the tip of my nose in this dreaded fog."

"There is little point patting the air. Look for a sign, Mr Erstwhile. A sign."

"I fear you are mistaken." The sweet feminine voice floated towards him on a gentle breeze to stir his muddled senses. "We are heading in entirely the wrong direction."

"What did I say?" Mr Erstwhile complained. "Why walk when a hackney cab is by far the better option?"

"In this weather?" came the matron's horrified reply. "Have you seen Mrs Pritchard's leg?"

"Thankfully, I've not had the pleasure."

"*Mangled* is the only way to describe it. Mangled. And how did she end up in such a sorry state?"

"Yes, you have told me five times within the space of an hour. Her hackney mounted the pavement and crashed through the chandler's window."

"Precisely, and—"

"Wait." The feminine gasp sounded so close and yet so distant. The toe of a boot hit Vane's leg. "There's a body … on … on the ground."

"A body?" the matron shrieked. "Good heavens. Come away at once. Lord knows what ails him. Disease is rife in these parts."

Vane blinked to clear his blurred vision. His head felt thick and heavy and while he could hear their words he struggled to form a reply.

A woman wearing a dark cloak with the hood raised came closer, her pretty face and ebony hair framed in a golden halo. It was a face he'd seen before, long ago, a face seared into his memory lest he ever try to forget. It was the face of an angel.

Estelle?

How could it be?

Death really had claimed him this time, and now he lay at the foot of heaven's door. The thought banished the cold from his hollow chest. Contentment settled in its place, so warm, so comforting.

"Leave him be," the gentleman instructed. He stepped forward to tug on the young lady's arm. "Clearly, there's been a disagreement of some sort. We should find a constable."

The lady snatched her arm free and dropped to her knees beside him. Heaven was but an arm's length away. All he had to do was reach out and touch it. The Lord had heard his prayers.

"Ross?" The angelic whisper brushed his cheek.

No one called him Ross—not a single living soul.

It was the name given at his baptism. The name spoken by his parents. The name that once breezed from Estelle's lips when he dared to trace his fingers down the elegant column of her throat and press a tender kiss on her sweet mouth.

"Ross?" she repeated, not Vane, not the manufactured name he used as a shield. Not the name women breathed on a satisfied sigh or men cursed to the devil. With trembling fingers, she cupped his cheek. "What happened to you?"

You happened to me.

Was this the part where he confessed his sins? Were the golden gates about to appear through the mist? Was this to be a glorious epiphany, the moment when he discovered what the hell had happened all those years ago?

"We must leave now." The white-haired gentleman stepped forward, his full beard and curled moustache a clear sign of his divinity. "We cannot afford to linger."

"We cannot leave him here like this," the angel, this beautiful version of Estelle, said.

Footsteps brought another figure: that of Wickett. "Begging your pardon, but I'll take it from here."

The angel straightened and shrank back into the shadows.

Don't go!

Wickett bent down, lifted Vane's lids and moved a bony finger back and forth. Satisfied, he patted Vane's chest, dabbing and inspecting the pads of his fingers, no doubt looking for blood.

Vane groaned when the coachman pushed against his ribs.

"My lord, are you hurt?" Wickett's face blurred and drifted in and out of focus. "Can you hear me, my lord?"

Oh, he could hear him, but why he was still clinging to life when heaven was but a few feet away was a mystery.

"Let's get you into the carriage. It seems you've taken a mighty bump to the head." Wickett stood over him, one foot planted on either side of his chest. He grabbed the lapels of Vane's black coat and hauled him to his feet. "Right you are. Steady now. We don't want you falling and taking another injury."

"I ... I assure you, I am perfectly capable of ... of standing."

The urge to sleep came upon him. The strain to keep his eyes open proved too taxing. He searched for the angel, but she had disappeared into the mist, the beautiful dream lost to him. The gates to paradise barred to him for now.

"Do you need assistance?" Mr Erstwhile stepped forward. "He's too large a fellow for one man to carry."

"Happen you should get yourselves off home, and quickly if you want to keep hold of that tidy watch and walking cane."

"Listen to the man," Mrs Erstwhile said in a mild state of panic. "We must make haste."

"I can take you as far as Piccadilly," Wickett said. "Don't suppose his lordship will mind under the circumstances."

"Well, we would not wish to impose. We only need to go as far as Whitecombe Street—"

"Come, Mr Erstwhile, we shall lose Miss Brown if we linger." The woman tugged her husband's arm. "And I can feel one of my migraines coming on."

"Thank you, but we will walk. My wife finds carriage rides in the fog somewhat unnerving."

"As you please." Wickett firmed his grip on Vane's waist and clasped the arm draped around his shoulder. "Turn left at the end of the street, and you'll find yourself on St Martins Lane."

The couple bid farewell and disappeared into the night.

"This is what happens when your mind's on other things," Wickett complained as he assisted Vane across the road to his carriage. "Count yourself lucky the rogues didn't have a blade else they'd have gutted you like a fish."

"I would have finished them both were it not for that blasted wolf."

"Wolf, you say?" Wickett chuckled. "No one has seen a wolf in England for three hundred years, let alone one wandering the streets of St Giles."

"A hound, then." The haze in Vane's mind was clearing. A large mouthful of brandy would numb the pounding in his head. "The damn animal came from nowhere." Perhaps that, too, had been a figment of his imagination, a symbolic representation of a hound from Hell.

And yet it had all seemed so real.

The Devil's beast had come to claim him. The Lord's angel frightened it away to offer him a better alternative.

But what did it all mean?

Was seeing a vision of Estelle's sweet face a clear sign that all was lost and he should abandon his search? Or was the illusion meant to bring her to the forefront of his mind?

Not that he needed reminding.

The portrait might be locked in a drawer, but her image haunted every cold corridor of his mind, still haunted the lonely chambers of his heart.

CHAPTER TWO

E stelle should run. She should pick up her skirts and run as far away as her legs could carry her. But already her breath came in rapid pants. Her heart raced so fast it hammered in her chest. The acrid fog clawed at the back of her throat. This must surely be the reason her eyes stung.

A tear fell, and then another.

Ross!

So many years had passed since she'd last seen him. He looked the same and yet so different. The same lock of ebony hair hung rakishly across his brow. Those piercing blue eyes still possessed the ability to muddle her mind though they were colder now—distant. Broad, muscular shoulders filled the slender more athletic frame she remembered. The same square jaw marked him as handsome although it held a defiant, rugged edge often common in those with a life blighted by hardship.

But what did Ross Sandford know of hardship?

Despite the changes, one thing remained irrevocably the same. The intense longing for him still burned deep in her core. Eight years apart and still her heart ached.

Oh, this was impossible.

"Miss Brown, wait!" Mrs Erstwhile's concerned voice reached Estelle through the fog. "Wait, else we will lose you."

But Estelle could not wait. With any luck, Ross had failed to recognise her. Why would he when she was a ghost to those she once knew? No doubt he had forgotten her face. No doubt he'd married, and love for another filled his heart now.

A sharp pain stabbed her chest.

Hopefully, he had not thought of her since that fateful day when she'd fled Prescott Hall knowing he was to come and offer marriage. And yet not a minute passed when she did not dream of what might have been.

"Miss Brown!"

Estelle glanced back over her shoulder and quickened her pace. The clip of footsteps chased behind.

Panic flared.

Ross!

What would she say to him? Too much had happened. How could she possibly explain?

Firm fingers gripped her elbow. "My dear, this is not the place one wanders alone." Mr Erstwhile drew her back as he gulped for breath. Being short in stature and large around the middle he suffered easily from exertion. "One wrong turn and we might lose you for good."

One wrong turn had brought the past hurtling to the present. What could be worse than that?

"Heaven knows what unsavoury characters linger in the shadows." Mrs Erstwhile came to stand at her husband's side. She put her hand on her chest to calm her ragged breathing. "You saw the state of that poor gentleman. Beaten and left for dead and all for a guinea."

Estelle considered her options. The Erstwhiles were good, kind-hearted people. She should at least wait until they were home and settled before taking flight.

"Come, it is best we keep to the streets where the lamps are lit." Estelle fell into a slow pace beside them. "I'm certain if we head this way we shall soon reach Leicester Square."

A tense silence ensued.

Every step brought with it the fear of Ross trailing behind in pursuit, of him calling her name, of having to explain to the Erstwhiles that she was not the sweet Miss Brown they believed her to be.

Mr Erstwhile made an odd humming sound. "It just occurred to me that you called that gentleman by his name."

"Did I?"

"You must have seen him before. Has he visited the shop? I'm sure I would have remembered such a prestigious client."

Estelle's pulse fluttered in her throat. "He reminded me of someone I once knew." Someone from a different time, a different place. A love not destined for this life. "A gentleman from the same village, but clearly I was mistaken."

That was enough information. He did not need to know any more, and she did not have the strength of heart to tell him.

Mrs Erstwhile's frantic gaze darted left and right as the clatter of horses' hooves and the creak of rolling carriage wheels drew near. "We're walking far too close to the road." She ushered them to walk in single file away from the curb edge. "Oh, my poor heart cannot stand the strain."

"My dear, if a carriage mounts the pavement, we'll be lucky to escape alive let alone suffer a mangled leg."

A hulking black shadow whipped past on their left.

"No doubt that's his lordship's carriage." Mr Erstwhile came to stand at Estelle's side once again. "It begs the question what was a gentleman from the upper echelons of society doing in an alley near St Giles?"

"Come now." Mrs Erstwhile clutched her husband's arm.

"Many lords court actresses. Where better to find one than a stone's throw from Covent Garden?"

Jealousy roiled in Estelle's stomach. "Why would he court an actress?" She could not hide her disdain. "Such an upstanding gentleman must surely have a wife."

Mrs Erstwhile tutted. "I should think as long as there's an heir it wouldn't matter. The aristocracy fail to adhere to the same moral code we do. Isn't that so, Mr Erstwhile?"

Estelle silently scoffed. While that applied to some lords of the *ton*, Ross Sandford was not the sort to be unfaithful.

"Indeed." He sighed. "Oh, to be an earl."

Mrs Erstwhile coughed to express her displeasure. She coughed again although this time she pressed her fingers to her temple and winced.

"I merely meant it must be exhausting," Mr Erstwhile said with a chuckle. "Keeping one lady happy is a task in itself. Attempting to manage two, would test any man."

"Talking of gentlemen and their interests," Mrs Erstwhile began. "Mr Hungerford's reason for inviting us to dinner had nothing to do with learning more about the way we use St John's Wort in our work."

Estelle groaned inwardly. "On the contrary, I thought he seemed rather keen to discuss the process of making tinctures and tonics."

Mr Erstwhile snorted. "I think he was more interested in why the son of a gentleman works in trade. He asked some rather impertinent questions."

"Trade? You make us sound like market hawkers, husband. It takes skill and dedication to treat those with cramps and agues." Mrs Erstwhile grunted. "Besides, Mr Hungerford has visited the shop three times this week when he could have easily sent a maid."

She had been in many precarious situations during her eight

years in France and knew enough about men to know the glint in Mr Hungerford's eyes stemmed from more than an interest in the apothecary. Not that she would admit to it of course. Mrs Erstwhile needed no encouragement when it came to affairs of the heart.

"I think the man is besotted with our Miss Brown," Mrs Erstwhile continued. "Besotted, indeed, and now his wife has passed, he's free to marry."

Mr Hungerford's motives for entertaining them were of no consequence. Estelle could not remain in London. What if she saw Ross again? Tonight, she'd escaped before he'd regained full use of his faculties.

Returning to France was not an option. Faucheux had men watching the ports, had spies lurking in every dockside tavern. A stone-cold shiver ran across her back. God help her if the smuggler ever found the courage to travel to England.

No. As soon as they reached Whitecombe Street, and the Erstwhiles were tucked up in their bed, she would pack her meagre belongings and go somewhere far away from Mr Hungerford's lustful gaze. Somewhere far away from the clutches of the cruel Faucheux. Far away from Ross Sandford, from the man who would always hold a piece of her heart.

CHAPTER THREE

"Good God, man. Do I look like a matron with failing health?" Vane batted Wickett's hand away as the coachman tried to assist his descent from the carriage. "I took a knock to the head not a lead ball to the chest."

Wickett raised a brow as he scanned the breadth of Vane's shoulders. "Granted. But for a man so strong and robust, you've been mumbling gibberish ever since I carried you out of that alley."

"You did not carry me." Vane stepped down to the pavement outside his townhouse in Berkeley Square. He touched the tender lump on his head and winced. "And if I spoke nonsense, it's because I was momentarily stunned. I would have beaten the life out of both rogues had that blasted dog not thrown me off my game."

A wave of excitement washed over him as he flexed his fingers and recalled throwing a barrage of satisfying punches.

"Dog? I thought you said you were set on by a wolf." A smile touched Wickett's lips. "Happen the fog brings out all sorts of wild creatures."

Vane sighed. "No one likes a pedant, Wickett. I clearly remember using the word *hound*."

"Yes, my lord, you were attacked by a hound and saved by an angel."

"It's called an epiphany." Lord, he knew better than to mention such things to his coachman, but after injuring his head, he'd taken to rambling. "It is a documented fact that, in a rare moment of weakness, one might encounter symbolic representations of one's life."

"Or you might have hit your head and been confused."

For a man dragged up on the streets of St Giles, Wickett possessed more sense than most lords of the *ton*. Still, Vane liked to keep him on his toes.

"During my search for a coachman with a particular skill set, I do not recall adding *brimming with condescension* to the list."

Wickett tipped his hat. "I'm not sure I know what that means. But you asked for an honest man, and that's what you've got, my lord."

"Indeed."

"Now, keeping in mind that I've only got your best interests at heart, I feel it my duty to say you smell like you've been rolling about in a pigpen."

Wickett was right. One whiff and the stench of piss and ale caught in the back of Vane's throat.

"Trust me, over the years I have rolled around in far worse places."

"Would that be with wolves or angels, my lord?"

Vane smiled. "I wish I could say it was the latter."

It was not a coincidence that the vision he glimpsed in the alley, as he hovered on the brink of consciousness, bore a likeness to Estelle. Despite all attempts otherwise, hers was the image he conjured when slaking his lust.

"Talking of wolves, my lord, another lady came to the mews earlier this evening and asked me to pass you a note."

"And I trust you read it and acted accordingly."

His coachman knew to burn all letters inviting him to partake in secret assignations. Still, some ladies continued to risk their reputation. Only last night, he'd glanced out of the window and noticed a woman watching the house from the safety of her carriage.

Wickett nodded. "Your presence was required at a house in Burlington Gardens. Happen it would have involved more rolling around in disagreeable places if you take my meaning." Wickett cleared his throat. "The lady was most insistent, having never met a man with your talents for rousing a howl."

"You have such a way with words, Wickett." Vane laughed but then winced when the pressure hurt his head. "Perhaps you should have gone in my place."

"When a man can't afford coal for the fire, there's no time for lingering atop the bedsheets. Happen a lady of her quality was looking for more than a five-minute fumble in the dark."

"Count your blessings." Vane gripped his coachman's shoulder. "Loose morals bring nothing but trouble. Why do you think I avoid such encounters?"

Vane had believed himself impervious to pain. A tour de force when it came to suppressing emotion. And yet a jealous husband had found the chink in his armour. In ruining his sister's reputation, Lord Cornell had shot a barbed arrow straight through Vane's heart. And by God, the man would pay.

"I'm not sure I'd have your strength of will, what with all the offers you get."

"Now that my sister is married, perhaps it wouldn't hurt to partake in the odd liaison." It would make a change from brawling in taverns and alleys, and yet he couldn't quite muster the enthusiasm.

"I don't suppose you'll have a problem finding a willing partner."

"An excess of willing partners has always been the problem." How ironic that the only woman he'd ever wanted proved elusive.

Wickett's beady eyes moved to a point beyond Vane's shoulder. "Perhaps a wolf followed your scent, my lord." He gestured to the light spilling out from the drawing room window. "Either Bamfield has fallen asleep and forgotten to blow out the lamp, or one of your lady callers has knocked the front door and barged her way inside."

Vane groaned. He was not in the mood for false displays of affection, for women too quick to fondle the bulge in his breeches in the hope of luring him into bed.

"You'd better see to the horses," Vane said with a sigh, "while I dispose of our unwanted guest."

Wickett nodded. "I'll wait here until you're safely inside. Wolves hunt in packs in case you've not heard."

His coachman was full of amusing quips. And yet Vane couldn't shake the sense that someone hid in the shadows, watching him, waiting to pounce.

Bamfield was not asleep. Like all good butlers, he opened the door before Vane reached the top step. Bamfield scanned Vane's attire, his hooked nose twitching as he sniffed out the pungent scent of the streets.

"Good evening, my lord. Welcome home. May I take—"

"Don't ask to take my hat and gloves as you can see I have neither." Excess apparel proved cumbersome when battling beasts across town.

"No, my lord, though might I suggest a change of clothes before you greet Lord Farleigh."

"Farleigh is here?"

Bamfield inclined his head. "His lordship arrived an hour ago and is waiting for you in the drawing room."

The news came as some surprise. His friend had only recently returned to his country estate after his wedding north of the Scottish border. "And his wife and children?"

"Remain at Everleigh, my lord."

Relief coursed through him. Although the house belonged to Farleigh, Vane had no desire to watch fawning lovers while in his current mood.

Shrugging out of his black coat in the hope it would rid him of the smell of the gutter, Vane brushed the lock of hair from his brow and entered the drawing room.

Lord Farleigh sat in the chair beside the fire, cradling a glass of brandy while gazing absently at the flames. The click of the door closing dragged the lord out of his dream-like state.

Farleigh placed his drink on the side table and stood. "Well, have you any news?"

"News?" Vane suspected Farleigh referred to the letter he had sent informing his friend that Lillian had been kidnapped by a pirate.

"Regarding Lillian."

Vane strode to the drinks table. He sloshed brandy into a crystal tumbler, gulped it down and inhaled sharply. "Fabian Darcy kidnapped her." He was not in the right frame of mind for lengthy explanations. Farleigh was an intelligent man, more than capable of filling in the rest for himself.

"Darcy?" Farleigh frowned. "But you were friends and neighbours. I assume it has something to do with him blaming you for what happened to Miss Darcy."

Fabian blamed him for Estelle leaving England, blamed him for her death. Grief did that. Now it was somehow his fault the lady had supposedly survived and had not returned home.

"Fabian believes Estelle didn't drown when *The Torrens* sank off the French coast." It was a ridiculous notion. Vane cursed inwardly as his thoughts drifted to the vision in the alley. Now, as the heat of the brandy soothed his senses, clearly the knock on the head had played havoc with his imagination. For pity's sake, he was a man of logic, not flights of fancy.

"Please tell me you don't believe that. No one survived the shipwreck. They searched for days."

And yet Fabian Darcy seemed certain his sister had. "One of his men is convinced he saw her in Paris. Fabian believes she boarded a ship for England. He wants my help to find her though I expect all efforts will prove fruitless."

"And the fool thought that abducting Lillian might somehow persuade you to offer your services?" Farleigh gave a contemptuous snort. "Clearly the man doesn't know you at all."

"It is of no consequence now. Fabian and Lillian married and are living on an island off the Devonshire coast."

Farleigh cast him a knowing grin. "At least he had the sense to do the honourable thing, though I don't suppose you gave him a choice in the matter. Indeed, I'm surprised you let him live."

Regardless of the scandal, Vane would never force his sister to marry for the sake of propriety. "On the contrary, they married before I arrived." Before Vane had a chance to wring the pirate's neck. "While I was busy courting Estelle all those years ago, Fabian carried a torch for my sister. She says she loves him." Vane shrugged. "What could I do?"

Farleigh gave a weary exhale and dropped back into the seat. "And so it appears my attempts to race here and offer assistance are for naught."

"Not for naught." For once in his life, Vane was glad of the company. "I'm in need of a drinking partner this evening. Someone to share the decanter. Someone to ensure I don't down the entire contents." Vane held up his empty glass. "Time for another?"

Farleigh nodded. "There's little point me riding back to Everleigh tonight." The lord scanned Vane from head to toe. "And clearly I'm needed here as something is dreadfully amiss."

"Why do you say that?"

Vane carried two tumblers over to the hearth, gave one to Farleigh, kept a hold of the other and dropped into the chair opposite.

"You have a bruise beneath your chin and a cut across your knuckles. Though your breeches might be black, they fail to hide the grime of the streets." Farleigh paused as his curious gaze drifted over Vane's face. "And you have the same look about you as when last I came."

"Displeasure is a mask I often wear." Despite Vane's wealth and status, a restlessness consumed him—one that could not be sated. He craved something though knew not what. "As is one of discontent."

"Then you should gaze into a looking glass for it is a far more dangerous expression than that. You have the wild, tormented appearance of an avenging angel. One who seeks to punish the unworthy. One eager for retribution no matter what the cost." Farleigh raised a brow. "Tell me I'm wrong."

Vane had no reason to lie, not to Farleigh. Perhaps it was his friend's name—Christian Knight—that instilled trust and confidence. The name embodied the loyal, upstanding gentleman seated before him. A man whose integrity knew no bounds and friendship had no limits.

"No, you're not wrong."

"Then I would hate to be the man on the receiving end of your wrath."

"Who said a man had roused my ire?" Perhaps he wanted vengeance on a ghost, on an angel.

"You forget how well I know you." Farleigh raised his glass in salute. "You've never given a damn about any of the women who've warmed your bed. And so I ask, who is he? Who is sitting at home oblivious to the fact the Devil is about to come knocking?"

"It is someone you know." Lord Cornell's saggy jowls and sour face flashed into Vane's mind. The man was a snake, a slithering coward who preyed on the weak and feeble. Vane sipped his brandy to calm the raging storm within. "I promised Fabian I would search for Estelle, and I have. I will." It was hopeless. He'd contacted an acquaintance in the rookeries, called at every inn en route from Dover to London, questioned every landlord. How did one go about finding one particular pebble on the bottom of a vast ocean? "But another matter takes precedence."

"One of revenge?"

"Indeed."

"For what?"

"For everything." Bitterness dripped from his words. "Lord Cornell bribed Lord Martin to ruin Lillian." It didn't matter that Lillian was married now, or that Fabian had threatened Lord Cornell to within an inch of his life.

Farleigh frowned. "Cornell? But how? Why?"

"Out of spite and jealousy, and because his wife concocted a ridiculous story, and he believed her. And so he hurt Lillian to hurt me." Vane would not rest until he'd brought Cornell to his knees.

Farleigh leant back in the chair. "Then I must caution you to have a care."

That was the point; he didn't care. Now that Lillian had Fabian's protection, Vane could do as he damn well pleased. Bugger the consequences.

"You place too much faith in Cornell. The man is a coward."

"Agreed. Cornell is a weasel. But it is for your soul I fear. When you have your retribution, what then? Will you be forever chasing those men who want to see you suffer? Will your heart ever be at peace?"

Vane had felt peace once in the last eight years: an hour ago in an alley in St Giles. "I'll be at peace when I'm dead."

"Can you not put this behind you?" Farleigh pressed his point. "Forget Cornell. Take a wife. Sire an heir. Move to the country. Find some semblance of happiness in all that family brings. Love will find you again if you open your heart to the possibility."

"Love?" Love had cast him aside long ago. Vane squirmed in his seat as he searched for his impenetrable mask. The one that showed he didn't give a damn about anything. The one that said he preferred a life of solitude. "Good God, you sound like my sister."

"Then perhaps you should listen to those who know you well enough to offer advice."

"I have always been my own man. My conscience carries the loudest voice, and so I must do what I feel is right."

So why did the wise mutterings in his head speak of finding Estelle, not seeking vengeance? The lady's image lived permanently in his mind. The strange events of the evening had awakened something else in him. A longing he'd suppressed. He'd gone looking for a fight to appease his demons and caught a glimpse of heaven.

"Damn it, Vane, you're the most obstinate man I know."

As always, Farleigh spoke the truth.

Vane considered his options.

Two roads lay ahead. Should he focus his efforts on finding a ghost? Or should ruining Cornell be his priority? Perhaps he should leave it to Fate to decide.

They sat in quiet contemplation, watching the flames dance in the hearth. Farleigh's sighs and incoherent mutterings conveyed his frustration.

"Marriage suits you," Vane eventually said. "You look invigorated."

"Rose suits me. I'm happy to report that true love is all the poets claim it to be."

Vane forced a smile, but jealousy slithered through his veins. In his youth, the love of one particular woman was all he lived for.

"Then what are you doing here when you should be at home in bed, making love to your wife?"

Farleigh swallowed a mouthful of brandy. "Must you torment me? One night away from Rose is akin to spending a week on the rack." When Vane frowned, Farleigh added, "It's the worst kind of torture."

Torture? His friend should try spending eight years pining. "Then why stay? I am quite capable of getting drunk without you."

"Having seen you like this, I cannot leave now. Rose saved me from a miserable, lonely existence. I would not be a good friend if I did not try to do the same for you."

The comment was like an ice pick chipping away at Vane's frozen heart. For a few seconds, the words found a way through the thin cracks. Farleigh was his only friend. But one trustworthy companion was worth more than a thousand fake admirers.

"I'm beyond saving or haven't you heard."

A knock on the door brought Bamfield. "I have taken the liberty of having a bath drawn, my lord, should you wish to change your clothes."

The thought of relaxing his tired muscles proved inviting, but bathing alone gave a man nothing to do but think. Due to the ache in his head, his mind was still somewhat muddled, and all thoughts would invariably lead back to the vision of Estelle.

"Thank you, Bamfield. As always, you seem to know what is best."

Farleigh chuckled. "One only has to sniff the air to know you're in dire need of a wash."

"There is another matter, my lord." The butler glanced briefly at Lord Farleigh.

"You may speak freely," Vane said while offering an indolent wave. "After all, this *is* Lord Farleigh's house, and you are his butler."

He supposed he should return to his own house in Hanover Square. Now that he was no longer responsible for protecting Lillian, it didn't matter if the world knew where to find him. Indeed, a few determined ladies had already made headway in that regard.

Bamfield inclined his head. "Wickett mentioned you received an injury to the head and advised I keep a close watch on you. Would it not be wise to send for a doctor?"

Damn. "And what else did Wickett say?" Perhaps hiring an honest man had been a mistake.

"Wickett said I am to remind you that you were keen to express your gratitude, by way of a letter, to those who stumbled upon you in the alley this evening. That it might ease any fears they may have for your welfare."

Had he said that? He could not recall. But the couple's timely arrival had sent the rogues running. The least he could do was allay their fears.

"Stumbled upon you in an alley?" Farleigh repeated sounding rather amused. "What on earth were you doing there?"

Vane sighed. "An elderly couple lost their way in the fog." He chose not to mention his epiphany, or that he'd thought the white-haired man was the Divine. "The precise nature of events after I fell are still somewhat unclear."

"And where was this alley?"

"St Giles."

Farleigh inhaled deeply. Panic flashed across his face, but he said nothing.

Vane turned his attention to Bamfield. "Wickett mentioned he knew of their direction. Tell him he may deliver a note in the morning, assuring the Erstwhiles of my good health."

From what he remembered they had appeared distressed, and so it was the gentlemanly thing to do considering their advancing years.

"Anyone who encounters you in an alley on a foggy night might think they'd stumbled upon the Devil," Farleigh said.

In truth, he had looked more like a dazed drunkard than anything more dangerous. "The couple should be thankful they missed the wolfhound. The sight of black eyes and sharp teeth pouncing out of the mist would have given them nightmares for weeks."

"Begging your pardon, my lord, but by all accounts, their granddaughter was the most distraught. The lady fled the scene in a state of panic almost as soon as Wickett arrived."

"Their granddaughter?"

Damn Wickett. Vane recalled mumbling something about the angel fleeing. Now the coachman thought to use it as an opportunity to tease him. Perhaps he should replace his man with one who knew his place and kept his opinions to himself.

"According to Wickett, the lady feared you were dead, my lord. And in light of the fact she seemed to know you, Wickett thought a letter might prevent gossip in the salons."

"You think I care about gossip?" Vane rubbed his temple. Something about this whole debacle bothered him. As did the fact he could not recall the event with clarity. But while Vane had granted Wickett permission to speak honestly in his company, he would not dare embarrass his master in front of Bamfield. Which meant one thing. They had both seen the same vision in the alley. "Send for Wickett. I want to see him."

Bamfield blinked rapidly at the sudden request. "In the house, my lord?"

"I don't care about muddy boots, fetch him now."

Quickly masking his brief look of horror, Bamfield retreated.

"What is it?" Farleigh asked as they sat waiting. "Something has set you on edge."

"I doubt you'd believe me if I told you. But when Wickett arrives, you may hear the conversation for yourself."

They fell into a companionable silence.

Vane replayed the events of the evening in his mind. Had he seen their granddaughter and imagined a likeness to Miss Darcy? The thick fog had hindered his vision. The faces of those surrounding him had barely seemed real. Whenever he tried to picture the angel's sweet face, he only saw Estelle.

Bamfield returned. "Wickett is just scraping his boots, my lord."

Wickett appeared and came to stand between the two chairs, much to Bamfield's chagrin. "You sent for me, my lord."

Vane stood and placed his drink on the mantel. "When you entered the alley off Longacre, how many people did you see?"

Wickett frowned. "I saw you sprawled on the ground, and the old couple hovering near your body."

"Anyone else?"

"Only the young woman."

"The angel?" Vane attempted to clarify.

Wickett nodded. "She was a pretty thing, of that there's no doubt. Soft skin, pink cheeks and full lips. Happen most men would describe her as such."

"But not a real angel." Lord, he sounded like a simple-minded buffoon, a bedlamite. "Not a heavenly vision."

Lord Farleigh cleared his throat. "Perhaps Bamfield is right. We should send for a doctor."

"Oh, she was a vision all right. Happen she knew you, though she's not one of them hungry wolves hovering around the mews."

"Wolves?" Farleigh snorted. "In England? It seems your coachman has taken a knock to the head, too."

It couldn't be Estelle. The words echoed in Vane's mind. Fate was not that kind. He was not that lucky. "But you have reason to believe the lady was a relative of the Erstwhiles." Strange how he remembered their name.

"She looked too young to be their daughter."

"Describe her. Describe this angel we both saw."

"Black cloak with a gold lining, hair as dark as night."

Vane caught his breath. "What else?"

"Eyes wide and just as dark." Wickett touched his hand to his shoulder to indicate her height. "Small and slender, light on her feet. Called you by the name of Ross."

Estelle!

Lord Farleigh inhaled sharply. He sat forward in the chair. "No one calls you by that name, not anymore."

"No. They don't." Vane's pulse thudded in his ears. Even his beloved sister, Lillian, called him Vane. "Wait here a moment."

Vane strode from the room to the study further down the hall. Taking the key from the bookshelf, he opened the drawer and ferreted around inside. He tried to ignore the slight tremble of his fingers as he withdrew the miniature portrait.

Resisting the urge to look at the beautiful image encased in the gilt frame, he returned to the drawing room and thrust it at Wickett.

"Is this her?"

Wickett took the picture and studied it. "Looks like her. The lady went by the name of Miss Brown if I remember rightly." When Wickett returned the portrait, Vane caught a glimpse of silky black hair before placing it face down on the mantel. "At first, I thought she was a maid or companion," Wickett continued, "but she spoke proper, just like the elderly gentleman."

"And you have their direction?"

"They were heading to Whitecombe Street, my lord."

"And the number?"

The hour was late. Sleep would elude him tonight if he did not discover the truth for himself. In those dark, restless hours, he would replay every word spoken, every kiss he'd ever shared with Estelle Darcy. He had to know. And he had to know now.

Wickett raised a shoulder. "The gent didn't say."

A sudden sense of despair filled Vane's chest. He would knock on every door, drag exhausted folk from their beds until he found the right house.

"If I had to guess I'd say Mr Erstwhile makes tonics or perfumes. He had that odd smell about him ... sweet like flowers and herbs ... and something sharper, almost bitter."

"Take me to Whitecombe Street. You have fifteen minutes to ready the carriage." Vane turned to Bamfield. "Call Pierre. I require a change of clothes, preferably black."

The next fifteen minutes passed by in a blur. Vane bathed quickly, lost his temper with Pierre when he insisted on fussing with his cravat. In the end, Vane dressed himself. The same fiery excitement he'd experienced earlier in the evening surfaced again.

"You're convinced it is her?" Farleigh said as Vane climbed into the carriage and settled into the seat opposite. His friend insisted on coming for fear Vane might venture to St Giles again, worried that another knock to the head might mark the end of him. "I find it hard to believe."

"You heard Wickett. It is her."

Hope sprung to life in Vane's chest. Soon he would have the answers he thought lost to him. Why break a promise? Why profess to love a man only to abandon him the next day?

"But surely Miss Darcy would have sought her brother out." In the dark confines of the carriage, Farleigh's gaze searched Vane's face and lingered on the bruise beneath his chin. "Forgive me if I sound cynical but if Miss Darcy survived the shipwreck why wait eight years before returning to London?"

"Well, we will soon know."

Vane struggled to sit still.

In his mind, he imagined what he would say to her, although he would not give her the satisfaction of telling her she'd ruined his life.

Wickett slowed the carriage as they turned into Whitecombe Street and drew to a stop outside Marselles Perfumery. Beneath the light of the streetlamp, one could see the ornate walnut caskets in the window. The boxes were lined with burgundy velvet and held a glass bottle of unique design.

Vane rapped the roof. From what he remembered, heavy perfumes made Estelle sneeze, and so he doubted she lived there.

When the conveyance rolled to a stop opposite the apothecary shop, Vane's heart lurched. Mr Erstwhile's name was painted in gold above the door.

Vane sat there for a few minutes and stared at the facade.

What would he do if Estelle was inside?

What would he do if she was not?

"Is this the one?" Farleigh said, peering through the carriage window.

"This is the one." Nerves pushed to the fore. Good God, what the hell did he have to fear? He had done nothing wrong. "Wait here. I doubt I'll be more than a few minutes."

Vane threw open the carriage door and stepped down. Candlelight filtered through the shop's bow windows. Two figures busied about inside. Vane straightened his shoulders and inhaled deeply, ready to confront the ghost of his past.

CHAPTER FOUR

All hopes Estelle had of fleeing London were dashed upon her return to Whitecombe Street.

In their absence, someone had entered the apothecary shop through the back door, smashed glass bottles and emptied the drawers of dried herbs over the floor. The sweet aroma lingered in the air to irritate her nostrils. A bookshelf lay upturned, the precious pages of text ripped from their bindings and strewn about the room. And yet amid the chaos, there seemed something orderly about the mess, something structured, purposeful.

"Oh, Mr Erstwhile, who would do such a terrible thing?" Mrs Erstwhile swayed as she struggled to stand.

Estelle fetched a wooden stool and guided the woman to the seat lest she collapse into a distressed heap. "Sit for a moment and catch your breath."

"Whoever did this has no heart, no conscience." Mr Erstwhile brushed a hand through his mop of white hair and sighed. "If I find out Mr Potter had something to do with it, I'll … Lord knows what I shall do."

Guilt flared. Estelle could not help but picture one particular cold and callous Frenchman. In all honesty, she hoped she was wrong and that Mr Potter was the man responsible. The apothecary despised competition and was forever spreading lies to cause mischief and steal Mr Erstwhile's customers.

But what if Faucheux had come?

Estelle's stomach roiled at the prospect. She mentally shook herself. They were eighty miles from Dover. What need had a smuggler to come so far inland?

"We cannot open tomorrow, not with the shop in such dreadful disarray." Mr Erstwhile bent down, scooped a handful of herbs and brought them to his nose. "See if you can find the drawer for rosemary."

Estelle took the lamp from the counter and scanned the labels on the drawers scattered about the floor. She found the one he needed and handed it to him. "We should do as much as we can tonight." So much for her plan to leave. The Erstwhiles were good people. They'd given her a place to stay, and a means to make a living when she'd had barely five shillings to her name. The least she could do was offer her help. "We should save what herbs we can."

Mr Erstwhile stared at the pools of liquid on the floor amid the remnants of broken glass. "It would be wise to wait until daylight. No doubt most things will need replacing."

As the son of a gentleman, and one who had dedicated his life to curing ailments, Mr Erstwhile had funds aplenty. A day or two at most and he would be back in business again.

"I can visit Mr Broom in the morning and place an order for provisions." She had a good mind to call in on Mr Potter to gauge his reaction upon hearing the news. The skills she'd learnt in France meant she could read the involuntary tics of a liar, could hear the hitch in the voice of the guilty.

"Take yourselves off to bed," Mr Erstwhile said. "I'll secure the back door and then follow you upstairs." He rummaged underneath the counter, withdrew the metal cash box and opened it with the key retrieved from his waistcoat pocket. "One thing is clear. This was not the work of an opportune thief with ten starving mouths to feed."

Estelle stepped closer and examined the box. The gold sovereigns shone in the dim light. If money was not the motive, then that left jealousy or revenge. The Erstwhiles were not the sort to be cruel or unkind. And so she couldn't help but think this vile act was in some way connected to her.

"What a dreadful end to what was an entertaining evening." Mrs Erstwhile attempted to stand but wobbled and dropped back onto the seat. "Help me, Miss Brown, won't you? My head is spinning, and I have a peculiar pain in my stomach."

"Of course." Estelle wasn't sure if the woman's sudden illness was a consequence of finding the shop in such a shambles. She offered her arm. "Hold on to me, and I'll escort you to your bedchamber."

Mrs Erstwhile gripped Estelle's elbow. "Thank you. Had I not given Gwen a few days off to visit her sister I would call on her to assist me."

"Perhaps it is best Gwen wasn't here." Had the culprit been watching the premises? Did he know the house was empty?

"You're right." Mrs Erstwhile clutched her stomach as she hobbled through to the hall. "Good heavens. I cannot recall the last time I felt so queer."

These strange symptoms had taken the woman suddenly. Mr Hungerford's servants were plagued by a similar malady, so he'd said. Or could Ross have been suffering from a contagious illness? Had he been taken unawares, just like Mrs Erstwhile, and had no choice but to collapse in the alley? But then she recalled the bruise beneath his chin. Had he been robbed, or attacked by a jealous lover during a row?

Shaking all thoughts of Ross Sandford aside—for what did it matter when she was leaving London in a few days—she assisted Mrs Erstwhile into bed. Estelle left the woman cuddling a chamber pot and returned to the shop to speak to Mr Erstwhile.

Lost in thought, he was staring at nothing of any consequence. Although he'd suggested they leave tidying the shop until the morning, Estelle sensed he had no desire to go to bed. And so she lit a few candles, picked up a wooden drawer and placed it on the countertop.

"I should go and find a brush and scuttle."

It took a moment for the gentleman to reply. "What? Yes, perhaps that is wise."

"A few hours of hard work and you may still be able to open tomorrow."

"Oh, I intend to, my dear. I just needed a moment to recover from the shock." He slipped out of his coat, folded it neatly inside out and placed it on the end of the counter. "Help me straighten the bookcase."

Gathering her strength, Estelle gripped the old bookcase and hauled it upright. Most of the books beneath lay untouched, and so she picked one up, blew off the dust and placed it back on the shelf.

"What are your thoughts regarding what happened here tonight?" she asked. "If not a thief, then who do you think did this and why?"

Mr Erstwhile rolled up his shirtsleeves. "Time will tell. Liars are found out eventually. They are often so wrapped up in untruths they forget what is real."

A hard lump filled her throat. She wanted to explain that not all deceivers were black of heart.

"But you do not think money is the motive?"

"No, my dear, I do not." He handed her another book. "Only a man with evil intentions desecrates the written word. Even those of the lower classes understand the value of books."

"And how do you propose to discover the identity of this devil?"

The old man smiled. "I do not need to do anything other than continue as if nothing has happened. Courage and resilience are the weapons of the gods when fighting evil." His intelligent blue eyes searched her face. "But you already know that."

Estelle's heart skipped a beat. Did this kind and generous man possess the ability to read her mind, to see into her soul?

"When we met on the ship to Dover, and you offered me employment, not once did you ask about my past. Why?"

He smiled. "I have learnt that regardless of where a person has been, what matters is where they are going. Besides, I know goodness when I see it. I know when a lady deserves a helping hand."

Oh, if only her father had been as compassionate, as understanding. If only she had possessed these weapons of the gods when she'd needed them most. How different life would be.

"No words will ever express the depth of my gratitude." How could she run now? How could she disappoint them? Was she destined to leave destruction and misery wherever she went?

"I do not need to hear the words. The truth is in your eyes. Over the years I have become adept at deciphering the unspoken. That is how one discovers what truly ails people."

Estelle blinked rapidly, hoping the horror of all she had experienced didn't linger there. "Wh-what do you see when you look at me?" She did not need his diagnosis to know what caused her pain.

Mr Erstwhile sighed. "I see a wealth of loss and sadness all hidden behind a helpful manner and a sweet smile."

This man's insight unnerved her.

"That is in the past," she said softly. Who was she trying to fool? "Know that I am on a new path now."

They fell silent while they examined the drawers and returned those undamaged to their rightful place.

"A wise scholar from the Orient once told me that the road to acceptance eventually leads to happiness," Mr Erstwhile said. "Marriage to Mr Hungerford may bring the contentment you seek. It is only a matter of time before he makes you an offer."

Marriage to anyone was impossible when her heart was not her own.

A loud rap on the front door made them both jump.

Mr Erstwhile peered through the gloom at the large shadow hovering outside. "Good heavens. If that is Mr West looking for more laudanum, then the man has a problem. If the fellow cannot wait until morning, what hope is there?"

The apothecary made his judgement based on the height and breadth of the night-time caller. Standing over six feet tall and with shoulders almost too broad to fit through the door, Estelle was relieved that he appeared too robust to be Mr Hungerford.

The impatient visitor hammered the door this time.

"Yes, yes," Mr Erstwhile cried. "I'm coming."

Estelle touched the old man's arm as he passed. A deep sense of trepidation filled her chest. "Is it wise to open the door after all that has occurred this evening?"

"We often have midnight callers. You know that."

Out of hours visitors were usually women with sickly babes, drunkards who had tripped over their own feet and sprained an ankle, or those who knew Mr Erstwhile was skilled at pulling out rotten teeth.

Estelle shrank back as she watched the apothecary unlock the door. He opened it ajar, not wide enough so that she might put a name to the shadow. She heard the rumble of a deep voice, the timbre familiar enough to prickle the hairs on her nape.

"Ah, my lord, may I say you look much improved since last we met." Taking a small white card, Mr Erstwhile squinted as he examined it. "Please, come in out of the cold and tell me how I might be of assistance." He gestured to the damaged items littering the floor behind him as the figure hovered on the threshold. "Forgive the mess and watch where you place your feet. I'm afraid someone sought to cause mischief while we were out this evening."

"Then I shall not keep you long." The rich drawl reached her ears clearly this time. Nervous tremors rushed through her, stealing her breath, leaving her dazed and somewhat unsteady on her feet. "I merely wish to thank you and enquire as to the condition of your companion. My coachman mentioned that the *young* lady appeared most distressed."

"Getting lost in the fog is a harrowing experience. But rest assured, Miss Brown has fully recovered." Mr Erstwhile stepped aside. "It has been a strange night I don't mind telling you."

"Miss Brown?"

"My assistant. The young lady you mentioned."

Ross Sandford stepped into the light.

Good Lord, no!

It could not be. Not now. Not so soon.

The room spun.

Her heart thumped.

Anyone else entering the shop would look at the floor to avoid stepping on broken glass. With wide eyes, they would scan the disorderly room, shocked to see such a state of disarray.

But not Ross Sandford.

His piercing blue eyes settled on her instantly and did not falter, not for a second. A dangerous energy filled the room. Ragged breathing invaded the tense, oppressive silence. His hard stare proved unnerving, but she deserved no less.

The urge to run came upon her, but it was a coward's choice, she knew.

The crunch of glass beneath Ross' feet signalled his move

towards her. With slow, purposeful strides, he came to stand but a few feet away. Broad shoulders filled her line of vision. The firm, arrogant tilt of his jaw conveyed his displeasure. Controlled anger emanated from every fibre of his being.

"May I present Miss Brown, my lord?" Mr Erstwhile introduced her as a grand matron would a debutante. Bless him. Like her, the old man gave no consideration as to what was deemed *de rigueur.* "My assistant."

What could she do other than plunge into a curtsy? "My lord."

Nausea took hold. Her stomach flipped.

The gentleman had inherited his father's title, that much she knew. The name Marquess of Trevane suited the strong, powerful figure of the man standing before her. Estelle scanned his face, looking for a sign of the benevolent gentleman she once knew. But her search was in vain.

"Miss Brown." The words were cold, hard, tinged with contempt. Ross inclined his head though his gaze remained fixed on her, his target—his prey. Casting Mr Erstwhile a brief sidelong glance, his countenance softened slightly. "While eager to ease your distress after the unfortunate events of the evening, my primary reason for calling at such an improper hour is because I believe Miss Brown and I are acquainted."

Mr Erstwhile gasped. "How interesting. Miss Brown thought you seemed familiar but dismissed the idea as folly given the circumstances. Then Miss Brown must have lived in the village close to your country estate."

"Indeed, though that was many years ago," Ross said sharply. "One might easily be mistaken."

Heat rose to Estelle's cheeks, hot and scorching. He despised her. That much was evident. The last time she'd seen him, other than in a dank alley in St Giles, his smile had stretched from ear to ear. Alone in the orchard, he'd picked her up, swung her around until she laughed so hard she couldn't breathe. He'd caressed her cheek, ran the pad of his thumb over her lips. Kissed her so deeply and with such tenderness, her heart melted.

He had loved her then.

Oh, Ross!

The muscles in her throat tightened. Tears welled, but she refused to let them fall.

Estelle lifted her sagging shoulders. "Would you mind, Mr Erstwhile, if I had a moment alone with his lordship?" There was no time to answer all of his questions now. How did one explain eight tragic years in a matter of minutes?

Mr Erstwhile frowned. Suspicious eyes moved back and forth between them. But one did not refuse a marquess anything.

"I will go upstairs and check on Mrs Erstwhile." He turned to Ross. "My wife has taken ill. The shock of it all, you know." The man inclined his head. "I shall return presently." He said no more, but with every retreating step Estelle's heart thumped harder against her ribs.

With his eyes flicking briefly to the door, Ross waited to hear the creak of the stairs before taking one last step forward.

Estelle braced herself for the barrage of questions, for the words that conveyed disdain for liars and deceivers.

The oppressive silence proved suffocating. Feeling compelled to speak, she said, "You look well, Ross. Considerably better than you did earlier this evening."

"And you survived the shipwreck." The stone planes of his face showed not the slightest sign of emotion. Clearly, he no longer cared.

So why had he come?

"Fate intervened, though I've come to learn it can be cruel as well as kind."

"Personally, I have yet to witness evidence of the latter." Ice-blue eyes settled on the neckline of her simple forest-green dress.

Why did he speak so calmly? Why did he not rip her to shreds and leave her in a tattered heap? At the very least she deserved a scathing reprimand, a dozen lashes of his tongue.

"Why did you come?" She had to say something to move the conversation towards the real crux of the matter.

"For proof you exist, nothing more."

"And are you satisfied?" She waved her hand down the front of her dress. Disappointment flared. Though her mind knew better, in her heart she'd often imagined him pulling her into an embrace, telling her nothing mattered other than the fact she was alive and well.

What a fanciful fool!

"Not nearly satisfied yet." He closed the gap between them. His large hand settled on her waist, searing her skin even through the layers of fabric. "There is something I must see."

He reached out and traced a finger from her chin down the column of her throat, leaving a burning trail in its wake.

"Wh-what are you doing?"

"Discovering the truth for myself. You may hide behind a false name, but you cannot hide the mark of your birth."

She knew what he spoke of. "You distrust what your eyes tell you is true?"

"I did not say that." Skilled fingers followed the edge of her neckline, skin-to-skin, stroking her flesh, the soothing, caressing motion teasing her nipples to peak.

Estelle stood frozen to the spot as his fingers dipped between her breast and bodice. Her breath came in ragged pants. She wanted him to fondle her, to claim her mouth, to hike up her skirts and give life to this empty shell of a body.

"Well?" The word left her lips on a sigh. It took every effort not to arch her back and push against him.

Estelle gasped when he tugged the material to reveal the upper curve of her breast. When his gaze settled on the small brown birthmark, he inhaled sharply through his nose.

She waited for him to say something, but he whipped his hand away and stepped back. Lust and love flowed through her veins. Disdain and abhorrence radiated from him.

"How could you?" His clipped tone sliced through the air and yet for a moment she saw something other than controlled anger. She saw pain flash in those fierce blue eyes.

I never meant to hurt you.

Estelle opened her mouth to speak, but he raised a hand to stop her.

"Do not waste your breath. I am in no mood for explanations. Nothing you could say would ever tempt me to forgive you."

Without another word, Ross turned on his heels and marched towards the door, kicking away the broken bottle in his path. The sound of the overhead bell preceded his departure.

Tears swam in her eyes. Her heart ached with regret, with the throbbing pain of an old wound never healed.

Estelle hurried to the window. She wiped away the mist caused by her heavy breathing, pressed her face to the glass and watched Ross stride towards his black carriage. Without warning, he came to an abrupt halt. Fog swirled around his legs, clawed at his body. He looked up to the heavens, cursed the Lord and punched the air.

And then he gathered himself, shook his head and squared his shoulders, climbed into his conveyance and slammed the door.

The vehicle jerked forward, quickly gathered momentum and disappeared into the blanket of fog.

CHAPTER FIVE

"Do not say a word."

"I'm not a fool." Lord Farleigh sat back in the dark confines of Vane's coach. "You look ready to unleash the Devil's wrath upon anyone who glances your way."

Vane gritted his teeth. An intense rage burned in his chest, heating to a roaring inferno. Hot pulses of energy throbbed in his fingers. He needed to punch someone, needed to release the pent-up emotion.

After all these years, Estelle was alive.

It meant only one thing. She cared nothing for him when she ran away, cared nothing for him now. He was an easy man to find. So why had she not come knocking? Why had she chosen to work for an apothecary rather than ask for his help?

Disappointment filled his chest as did a crippling sense of inadequacy he rarely encountered. *Damnation*. Rage he could deal with, but this nauseating feeling of failure he could not.

Memories of his sister's ruination entered his head. He'd been helpless then, too, had sworn no one would ever hurt him in the same way again.

Anger resurfaced at the thought.

For eight blasted years, he believed he was somehow responsible for Estelle leaving, responsible for her death. Not once had she come to ease his misery. God damn, the woman hadn't even bothered to send a note.

Unable to control himself, he punched the roof, the pain bringing temporary relief. Any other coachman would have slowed the horses believing the sound a signal to stop. Wickett knew better.

Farleigh sighed. "Rather the roof than you pounce across the carriage and take your frustration out on me."

"From my reaction, I'm sure you can guess the outcome of my visit."

"Then it is as her brother suspected." Farleigh paused. "Miss Darcy is alive."

"Oh, she's alive." Vane had felt the rapid beat of her heart as he caressed the soft mounds of flesh, had heard the hitch in her breath when he exposed the damning mark. "Estelle Darcy is working as an apothecary's assistant no less."

Farleigh knew him well enough to know what this sudden revelation meant. The belief that Estelle was dead had shaped Vane's life, his attitude, all relationships, his reputation.

"She's working for a living?" Farleigh seemed more shocked by that fact. "Then she never married?"

The comment sent Vane's stomach shooting up to his throat. "How the hell should I know? I'm just the fool she abandoned. I'm the fool she cared nothing for, the one she left and never thought of again."

"Clearly the lady has fallen on hard times. Perhaps there's more to the story than that. After all that happened at Everleigh, I know only too well things are often not what they seem."

"Good God, do not defend her actions."

"I'm not. I am simply saying that until you're in possession of the facts, you cannot make a qualified judgement."

"Let me understand you." Vane gave a snort of contempt. "You suspect a terrible event kept her away from her friends and family. One so terrible she let everyone believe she'd died on *The Torrens*. Why did I not think of it before? Poor Miss *bloody* Darcy."

"There is no point talking to you when you're like this." Farleigh turned away abruptly and stared out of the window.

A tense silence ensued.

Vane tried to sit back, tried to close his eyes and pretend he didn't give a damn. But a restlessness consumed him, one he'd gone to great lengths to suppress with loose women, brandy, and fistfights in the narrow lanes of St Giles.

Farleigh glanced at him numerous times before eventually saying, "Will you see her again?"

"Who?" Vane knew to whom Farleigh referred and was merely stalling.

"Miss Darcy. What did you say to her when you left?"

Damn right he'd see her again. While the voice in his head screamed *never*, his heart demanded an explanation, craved justice.

"I paid her the same courtesy she did me and left without a word. Once assured of her identity what more was there to say?"

"I see." The corners of Farleigh's mouth twitched. "Do you think you might still be in love with her?"

Panic shot through him.

Having spent years battling to exorcise the memory of Estelle Darcy, no other woman had ever made him feel the way she did. Oh, he'd sated his lust, but the tremors were superficial, failed to ease the clawing hunger within.

"Haven't you heard?" Vane's tone brimmed with mockery. "The only person I am in love with is myself."

Farleigh laughed. "According to the law of the land the majority rule, so it must be true." He paused. "What will you do now? Will you go home and drain the decanter? Will you wander the alleys hoping a rogue might beat every ounce of emotion from your chest?"

Vane thought for a moment. To go home would mean a sleepless night pacing the floor, replaying every pathetic moment of the young fool who'd chased Estelle to Dover only to discover she'd boarded the boat with another gentleman.

"Why go home when I am in the mood for mischief?"

Farleigh groaned. "Why do I get the feeling the evening is about to take a turn for the worse?"

Nothing could be worse than discovering the dead walked. "Perhaps I need to broaden my horizons. Colonel Preston has returned from his expedition to the Antarctic Peninsula. Preston's benefactor is holding a ball this evening to celebrate the explorer's findings. We shall go there."

"We?"

"If I go alone, there is every chance the night will end with a dawn appointment. Besides, don't you want to hear of Preston's whale sightings? They say it's fascinating."

Farleigh narrowed his gaze, but then recognition dawned. "For a second, I thought seeing Miss Darcy had softened your brain. But clearly I'm mistaken. Lord Cornell sponsored Preston's trip did he not? We are going so you may taunt the gentleman."

Vane could not prevent a grin from forming. "So you will come?"

"If only to ensure you don't end up in Newgate."

Lord Cornell's townhouse in Bedford Square was a two-minute walk from the British Museum. The peer liked to think of himself as an intellectual. A man whose mental faculties compensated for his saggy jawline and portly stomach. If Vane's sources were to be believed, the lord spent many an afternoon debating the form of classical sculptures and examining Egyptian antiquities.

"You didn't tell me the ball was at Cornell's house." Farleigh grabbed Vane's arm and brought him to an abrupt halt at the bottom of the steps.

"Cornell is Preston's patron. Where else would it be?"

"Then I doubt you have an invitation," Farleigh whispered.

"Why would I need an invitation?"

Farleigh shook his head. "Is it not advisable to return to Berkeley Square and change our clothes?"

Vane glanced down at his boots and grinned. "So we're not wearing stockings and shoes. There's not a gentleman here brave enough to throw us out, not a servant foolish enough to refuse us entrance. And I do so enjoy causing a stir."

They stepped aside to allow two ladies to pass. Both women tittered and nudged each other. From the blush touching their cheeks, their interest in him had nothing to do with his unconventional attire. One almost tripped over the hem of her gown as she craned her neck to lock eyes with him.

"Come. We shall follow those ladies inside. By now, everyone will be too busy drinking and dancing to bother with latecomers."

"Tell me you're joking. Every woman in there will sense your presence." Farleigh sighed. "Oh, life is so much simpler in the country."

"If not a little dull."

"Trust me there is nothing dull about spending the day conversing with one's wife, the nights nestled—"

"Spare me the details. Unless you want to dig your blade a little further into my wounded heart."

"Is it wounded? Most people say you have no heart."

Vane shrugged. This was not the conversation he wanted to have while preparing to confront Lord Cornell.

"What is it you want me to say, that I'm envious of what you have with Rose?"

"Are you?"

Damn right he was.

With his skill in the bedchamber, something he'd mastered in the hope he might feel something more meaningful, he'd earned a reputation as a scoundrel. A label far removed from the real man buried beneath the facade.

Choosing not to reply, Vane mounted the steps, offered the butler his calling card and simply said, "Marquess of Trevane and Viscount Farleigh," before moving past the flustered servant.

Within minutes of entering the ballroom, gentlemen directed shocked and scornful glances their way, appalled at their inappropriate choice of dress.

"The disrespect of it," one gentleman muttered while sucking in his cheeks.

Some ladies cared not and drew closer, using the language of their fan to convey many messages: follow me, touch me, kiss me, do anything you damn well like to me.

It did not take long for one of them to pounce.

"Lord Trevane." Lady Barlow, a young widow of some notoriety, curtsied in such a way as to offer up her bountiful breasts. "What a pleasure it is to find you here." She moistened her lips. "I fear the evening has been rather tedious so far. That is unless you enjoy hearing tales of sea monsters and frosty nether regions."

"Sea monsters and frosty nether regions," Vane repeated in a slow drawl. "I'm afraid both are foreign to me. But I shall see what I can do to create some excitement tonight." He meant in taunting Cornell, but the lady took it to mean something far more salacious.

"Should you wish to take some air and explore nature's offerings, I'm told the garden has a couple of delights to behold."

Farleigh sighed and feigned interest in those dancing the quadrille.

"There's a hothouse," Lady Barlow said in a seductive lilt as she continued trailing a finger along the neckline of her gown. "You may want to *slip* inside and experience its pleasures for yourself."

"Thank you, Lady Barlow. I shall bear that in mind. Of course, a man must first pay homage to the host before he partakes in the entertainment provided."

A coy smile played on the lady's lips. "Then you'll find Cornell in the library examining etchings with a host of other ancient bores."

Vane inclined his head, and the lady sauntered away. He turned to Farleigh. "Will you wait here while I speak to Cornell?"

"Lord no. At the rate ladies approach you, it will take an hour to cross the room unless I hurry you along."

Clearly, Farleigh despised these events just as much as Vane.

The library door was open. A group of men stood huddled around a large walnut desk, their heads bowed as they stared and pointed at a creased map. Cornell neglected to notice them at first, and so Vane cleared his throat.

"Good evening, gentlemen. Forgive the intrusion, but I wonder if I might ask a question?" He did not wait for a nod of approval. "Did Colonel Preston sight the Peninsula or was he fortunate enough to dock and set foot on land?"

Cornell swung around, affronted at the interruption until his insipid grey eyes settled on Vane. The snake's skin slithered over his jaw as he struggled to decide what expression to wear.

"I only ask," Vane continued, "as my brother-in-law commands numerous vessels and is keen to capture overweight mammals with a view to exploring how they might survive away from their natural habit."

Vane and Lord Cornell were the only men in the room who

knew that Fabian had kidnapped the plump lord in the middle of the night, stripped him naked and tied him to the railings as a warning never to harm Lillian again.

A gentleman with a tiny mouth and wiry white hair stepped forward. His dry skin and red nose led Vane to conclude this was Colonel Preston. "The question we should ask is how do these large mammals behave in their own environment?"

"I imagine all species are alike." Vane stared down his nose at the quivering Lord Cornell. "The males are manipulated by the females. Those males not considered the alpha of the species must resort to cunning tactics to get what they want."

Preston rubbed his jaw while considering Vane's point. "What you describe are human traits. I am not certain the same applies to all levels of the animal kingdom."

"Weak animals will always look for ways to fool their predators. It is a case of kill or be killed. Do you not agree, Lord Cornell?"

Cornell's eyes widened. "Well … yes."

"Problems arise when the alpha grows wise to these tactics and knows he must act quickly to put the runts in their place." Vane ran his tongue over his teeth. "Usually with a bite to the jugular."

Cornell gulped and fiddled with the gold fobs on his watch chain.

"But please forgive the interruption." Vane inclined his head to Colonel Preston. "I came merely to congratulate the colonel on a successful voyage. Good evening, gentlemen."

Vane strode from the room. Once out in the corridor, he stopped and sucked in a breath.

"Well, I'm impressed," Farleigh said, grabbing a glass of champagne from a passing footman. "I expected you to drag the lord out by his fancy cravat and beat him to a pulp."

Oh, it had taken every ounce of strength he possessed not to pick up the letter opener and drive it through Cornell's black heart.

"Perhaps I want him to suffer, to live in fear for a while." The bastard had made Lillian suffer for months, years. "I want him to lie awake at night wondering when I'll strike. For me, the thrill of the chase makes the prize more rewarding."

"Then I thank the Lord I'm your friend and not your enemy."

Vane smiled, but the hairs on his nape prickled to attention. He turned to find Lady Cornell watching him from the end of the corridor. Her golden hair was styled in an elaborate coiffure adorned with flowers and ridiculous trinkets to make the young woman appear comely.

"Another admirer craving your attention?" Farleigh said with some amusement. "How on earth have you abstained since your return from Italy?"

Lady Cornell trailed her fingers over her collarbone, her eyes still trained on Vane, urging him, begging him to approach.

"During all my dalliances, it never occurred to me that Lillian might be the one who would get hurt." The pain of discovering that Lord Martin had taken his sister's virtue and discarded her so cruelly still lived in his chest. "No loving brother would continue to behave in the same manner."

"But you're a man. You have needs. Why not take a wife as I suggested and be done with this whole charade?"

Farleigh's advice was flawed when one considered the lord had recently married for love. But his friend meant well, and the last thing Vane wanted was another conversation about Estelle Darcy.

"I'll settle for nothing less than what you have with Rose. You know that."

Vane studied Lady Cornell's voluptuous form. Her soft breasts bulged out from the neckline of her vibrant red gown. Once, her pretty pout may have conjured an image of full lips sliding up and down his cock—and yet it did nothing to spark lust in his loins now. How could it when only one woman dominated his thoughts? Only one woman could rouse emotion in his chest.

Tired of waiting for him to approach, Lady Cornell came forward. Vane's initial reaction was to give the woman the cut direct, punishment for her wicked lies and tawdry tales. Then again, perhaps she might prove useful in his quest to bring Lord Cornell to his knees.

"Lord Trevane. I must say you're the last person I expected to see this evening." She thrust her hand at him leaving him no option but to press his lips to her silk glove.

"Lady Cornell," Vane said, straightening. "May I present Lord Farleigh?"

The lady was obliged to offer Farleigh her hand. "My lord." Farleigh barely had a chance to greet her when she snatched her hand away and turned her attention back to Vane. "Are you interested in learning of the colonel's southern exploration or have you come to conduct one of your own?"

Farleigh cleared his throat, no doubt tired of hearing veiled attempts at seduction. "Excuse me, but I shall await you in the ballroom." He bowed and left them alone.

Good.

It would serve Vane's purpose if Cornell chose that moment to venture from the library. He might even consider putting a hand on the woman's waist, trailing a finger seductively down her bare arm if it would rouse Cornell's ire.

"Well, my lord?" Lady Cornell continued. "Are there any uncharted regions you have yet to probe?"

"It might surprise you to learn that I am weary of exploring pastures new." Two years ago, he would have taken Lady Cornell, hard and quick, over her husband's desk, hoping she possessed the power needed to banish the ghost of Estelle. And yet now he found the thought abhorrent. "Perhaps the time has come to marry, to invest all efforts on one particular lady."

Panic flashed in the woman's eyes. "But you … you can't." Her chin trembled, and she shook her head to gather her composure. "A gentleman with such strong passions could never be happy with a simpering miss."

"Then perhaps I shall wed a courtesan, a woman with immense skill in the bedchamber," he said merely to observe the lady's reaction. "Besides, as a peer I must marry, eventually." The lie fell easily from his lips. He did not care about siring an heir, not anymore.

Lady Cornell's eyes widened. "Of course you must, but perhaps you should wait a while longer."

"And why is that?" What was this woman about?

"Because an option may soon present itself. One you may not have considered before."

"How so?"

Was she implying he might marry *her*?

The lady had conveniently forgotten bigamy was a crime punishable by death. If she cared so little for her pretty neck, perhaps she was of a mind to murder her husband while he slept in his bed. And to think she had once been on a list of eligible ladies his father suggested he might wed.

"A young woman marries an old man for one reason only." She stepped closer and placed her hand on his chest. "Would you not like to bed me, Vane? You would not be disappointed. Like my mother, I do possess some talents of my own when it comes to pleasing men."

"I'm sure you do."

From what he recalled, her mother had many lovers over the years, including one particular favourite though she took that secret to the grave.

"I'm more than happy to demonstrate if only you'll give me a chance." Her hand dropped to the waistband of his breeches. Concealed amid the folds of her gown, her fingers ventured down to stroke the length of his cock.

Damnation!

Vane gritted his teeth and stepped back. "Your husband may have something to say about that." Cornell was craven. Revenge was something he concocted behind closed doors.

"Cornell is old. One never knows when one might end up a widow."

Lord, the woman was just as cold-hearted as her husband. The urge to offer a disparaging remark took hold. But he would bide his time. Impatience be damned. Experience had taught him that the most painful blows came unexpectedly, catching the victim unawares.

"Your point is moot. This is a conversation to be had at some other time." If she killed Lord Cornell, it would save him the job. And yet he found he wished Cornell a long and sufferable life. Death was not nearly severe enough. "And so I shall bid you a good night."

He needed to leave, needed to be away from these unbearable people.

"Wait," Lady Cornell whispered, gripping his upper arm, but he turned on his heels and strode away.

A hundred pairs of eyes followed him through the glittering ballroom. A few ladies stopped him and boldly suggested more than a dance. He'd come to learn that people adhered to strict modes of propriety only when it suited them. Hypocrisy was the ton's true god.

Vane eventually found Lord Farleigh leaning against the iron railings outside, smoking a cheroot as he gazed up into the foggy night sky.

"Thinking of Rose?" Vane said as he approached.

"Who else?" Farleigh offered him a smoke. Vane obliged. He

drew on the head and let the woody essence calm him. "As much as I enjoy your company, Vane. There is only one place I want to be tonight."

Vane blew a ring of white smoke into the crisp air. There was only one place he wanted to be, too—an apothecary shop in Whitecombe Street.

CHAPTER SIX

"Thank you, Potter." Mr Erstwhile inclined his head. "It is good to know we can count on our friends and colleagues in times of great need."

Estelle observed the exchange with a degree of admiration. The world would be a better place if everyone was as forgiving as Mr Erstwhile, or as quick to admit to their mistakes as Mr Potter.

"Miss Brown may call and collect the provisions you need. It will serve you until you restock the shelves. Poaching customers is part of doing business, but I want you to know I had nothing to do with what happened here."

After living with smugglers, Estelle knew the traits of liars and thieves. In her expert opinion, Mr Potter appeared genuine.

"People like to cause mischief," Mr Erstwhile said. "More often than not for ridiculous reasons. Perhaps a frustrated customer took his anger out on the bottles."

"Then we must all be on our guard." Mr Potter doffed his hat. "Now, I shall leave you to your work. You'll want things tidied and ready to open tomorrow. Good day to you."

Mr Erstwhile hurried around the counter and opened the door for his competitor. "Good day, Mr Potter." The bell stopped ringing long before Mr Erstwhile released the handle. The poor man had spent the morning assessing the damage and had fallen prey to lengthy bouts of silent reflection.

"Well, I think that puts paid to the theory that Mr Potter hired someone to break into the shop out of spite or jealousy," Estelle said, as she continued sweeping up the remnants of broken glass.

After coming face-to-face with Ross last night, she had been in no fit state to do anything other than lie on the bed and sob into the pillow. Like a true gentleman, Mr Erstwhile did not pry but simply offered a handkerchief, a nip of port, and a few wise words that tomorrow might be a better day.

Equally, she had never asked why a gentleman of his standing and education worked for a living, although she knew it had something to do with following his heart and with Mrs Erstwhile's lower status.

"Hmm. I must say I am surprised by Mr Potter's visit." Mr Erstwhile stroked his white beard. "Surprised yet overjoyed. How strange it is that in our darkest days we often find a ray of sunshine."

"Perhaps that is because you have the one thing most people lack."

"Oh, and what is that?"

"Faith." Estelle expected the worst and was never disappointed. "You believe in goodness. Your heart is full of love and gratitude. You're a man of strong convictions, and I admire that."

Mr Erstwhile dabbed the corner of his eye. "My dear, you will make an old man cry if you continue to shower me with such praise."

Estelle propped the brush against the counter. She came to stand at his side and placed her hand on his sleeve.

"It is deserved, sir. And I shall be forever in your debt for the kindness you have shown me."

Mr Erstwhile covered her hand with his own and patted it gently. "We were never blessed with children. But had we been so fortunate, we would have wanted a daughter exactly like you."

Estelle's throat grew tight. She did not deserve their good graces. The Erstwhiles made her want to be kind and loyal, to be honest and true regardless of how frightening the thought.

"Then I shall try not to disappoint you." Gathering herself, she sucked in a breath. "Now, I should go to Mr Potter and collect what we need. Mrs Erstwhile is still weak from this sudden bout of sickness, and I would like to be here when she wakes."

"Did she drink the ginger tea you gave her?"

Estelle nodded. "I sat by her bed until she'd emptied the cup."

"Then go now. I can—"

A knock on the door preceded the turn of the handle and tinkle of the bell.

Mr Hungerford entered the shop and paused in the doorway. "For a moment, I feared you weren't open today. The sign says you're closed." His curious gaze drifted to the display cabinet, to the empty shelves and missing drawers, to the neat pile of herbs and shards of glass on the floor. "Good Lord, has something happened here?"

Mr Erstwhile ushered the gentleman inside and shut the door. "A slight mishap that is all. Someone broke in through the back door last night and made a dreadful mess."

The colour drained from Mr Hungerford's face. His green eyes flicked to Estelle and scanned her from head to toe. The nervous flutter in her stomach spoke of unease, not admiration.

With golden hair and a pleasing countenance, she considered him a handsome gentleman. Dressed smartly in a claret coat and hat, green waistcoat and beige breeches, he had the air of a man running an important errand. Oddly, she had a reason to be thankful to the intruder. Mr Hungerford would have to be without feeling or conscience to make a romantic declaration today.

"I trust no one was hurt by this dreadful fiend?" Mr Hungerford's gaze never left her.

"Thankfully, it happened while we were dining with you, sir," Estelle replied.

The gentleman appeared stunned. "Then I cannot help but feel somewhat relieved that you were not at home. Although I doubt the villain would have had the courage to enter had he noted the glow of candlelight streaming through the window."

"Who can say?" Mr Erstwhile said. "Time spent contemplating what might have been is time wasted."

After seeing Ross Sandford, Estelle wished she could embrace that particular pearl of wisdom.

"Indeed." Mr Hungerford removed his top hat and placed it on the wooden counter. Tugging at the fingers of his gloves, he removed those, too. "Now, tell me how I can be of assistance."

"Oh, no, no." Mr Erstwhile held up his hands. "We are almost done here, and I cannot have you dirtying your fine clothes on my account."

"But the sooner things are put right, the sooner you can return to normality."

"What is normality but merely a figment of the imagination?" Mr Erstwhile replied cryptically.

The comment gave Mr Hungerford pause. The gentleman struggled to form an appropriate reply. "There must be something I can do," he eventually said.

"The door is fixed, the shop tidied, and Miss Brown is off to collect provisions."

Estelle groaned inwardly.

For a man so wise, Mr Erstwhile rarely spoke without thought. Did he share his wife's opinion? Was he as eager to thrust her into Mr Hungerford's path, just as keen to see her wed and settled?

"Then I shall accompany Miss Brown on her errand." Mr

Hungerford's eyes sparkled to life. One corner of his mouth curled up into a satisfied grin. "With my assistance, she can collect twice the provisions."

Mr Erstwhile walked over to the window and stared out into the street. "Hmm. You're walking today I see."

"I make it a point to take regular exercise. Good health must be a priority. As you know."

Mr Erstwhile turned back to face them. A knowing smile played on his lips though it left Estelle baffled. "Then I have no objection unless Miss Brown would prefer to go alone."

What could Estelle do other than nod and thank Mr Hungerford for his thoughtfulness? She would not embarrass Mr Erstwhile by offering a curt reply even though her employer seemed to have lost the gift of intuition.

"Thank you, Mr Hungerford." Estelle forced a smile. "But I should like to hurry. Mrs Erstwhile has a list of things for me to do this afternoon." It was more of an exaggeration than a lie, but she did not feel an ounce of guilt for it.

"We will work together to ensure you're back in plenty of time."

His congenial manner failed to express the sudden predatory hunger in his eyes. Thank heavens they would be walking along a busy street and had no need to wander alone through the warren of narrow lanes.

"Then I shall fetch my bonnet and jacket."

Estelle left them alone, although Mr Erstwhile still seemed preoccupied with something outside. When she returned, the men were deep in conversation. Mr Hungerford had asked about her background numerous times, mentioned her eloquent elocution and education, had struggled to hide his frustration when she became evasive.

"Ah, there you are, Miss Brown." Mr Hungerford straightened. He offered his arm. It mattered not that she worked for a living and he received an income of almost a thousand pounds a year. A fact he'd been quick to mention over dinner. "Shall we head out?"

"Certainly." With a deep sense of dread, she placed her hand in the crook of his arm. Mr Erstwhile opened the door, looking almost pleased by the prospect of them spending time together. How odd he should offer encouragement when he was an advocate of true love.

They left the shop, had taken but ten steps when Mr Hungerford could no longer suppress his impatience. Barely contained excitement coloured his cheeks. Indeed, he was like a valet whose master had given him a diamond cravat pin for Michaelmas.

Mr Hungerford stopped abruptly, forcing her to turn and face him. "I came today hoping to have a quiet word with you alone."

"Oh, and why is that?" The incident at the shop had not deterred him, and so it was better to deal with the matter quickly.

"It cannot have escaped your attention that I admire you greatly, Miss Brown."

The man's wife died four months earlier. Clearly, he belonged to the club where women were considered a necessary accoutrement. Mr Hungerford had no children and so should be in no rush to marry. Then again, perhaps she was jumping to conclusions. Perhaps he wanted a mistress, not a wife.

"If I've learnt anything these last few years," he continued, "it is that life is too short not to act on one's feelings. Although Miriam passed so recently, her illness forced us apart long before."

Estelle swallowed down her apprehension. "Mr Hungerford, I must tell you that—"

"Please, Miss Brown, allow me to speak before nerves get the better of me." Mr Hungerford reached for her hand and clutched it tightly.

"Sir, you have forgotten yourself. Has it slipped your attention that we are standing in the street?" Estelle glanced left and right, frustrated that the few passers-by paid them no heed.

But then something caught her eye: a black carriage parked further along on the opposite side of the street. A figure stood watching them intently beneath the brim of his top hat as he leant against the door, his muscular arms folded defiantly across his chest.

Ross?

Locking eyes with her, he pushed away, tugged on the cuffs of his dark blue coat and stalked towards them like a wolf on the prowl.

Good Lord!

Mr Hungerford gripped her hand. "Miss Brown, when a man has something important to say he does not care who raises a disapproving brow. I know we have only known each other for a month, but—"

"I beg you, say no more, sir." Panic infused her tone. Her heart flew up to her throat. "I fear now is not the time for declarations."

She looked up as Ross mounted the pavement.

How could she ever have thought him the same man she knew in her youth? A dark and dangerous energy radiated from every fibre of his being. Ross Sandford's hard, unforgiving expression could frighten the Devil. Perhaps he *had* risen from the fiery pits of Hell, for the sight of him ignited a scorching heat deep in her core.

"Miss Brown." Ross offered a graceful bow. There was something sleek and seductive about the simple movement. Ice-blue eyes settled on Mr Hungerford and then fell to their clasped hands.

"Lord Trevane." Estelle swallowed in an attempt to catch her breath. She tugged her hand free from Mr Hungerford's grasp. "I must say I'm surprised to see you. Do you have business in Whitecombe Street?"

"I do now."

A tense silence ensued. As the higher-ranking gentleman, it was up to Ross to make an introduction.

"We are on our way to collect provisions for Mr Erstwhile." Estelle forced a smile.

Ross' belligerent gaze journeyed over Mr Hungerford. "We?"

Estelle gestured to the gentleman at her side. "Lord Trevane, allow me to present Mr Hungerford."

Mr Hungerford inclined his head, but before he could open his mouth to speak, Ross said, "Goodbye, Hungerford. I shall escort Miss Brown to wherever it is she needs to go."

Mr Hungerford blinked rapidly. His mouth opened and closed but he could not quite form a reply.

While Estelle wanted to place some distance between herself and Mr Hungerford, what gave Ross the right to think he could storm into her life and assume control?

"I'm afraid I have already accepted Mr Hungerford's offer of assistance, my lord."

Mr Hungerford cast her an affectionate smile. Heavens. Now the man would think she held him in high regard.

"Leave, Hungerford." Ross ignored her comment and squared his shoulders. "Leave now else I shall make it my business to remove you, physically if necessary."

Since when had Ross Sandford turned into an obstinate fool? "Arrogance is a rather unbecoming trait," she blurted.

"As is dishonesty," Ross countered.

"I have never lied to you."

Ross rubbed his chin. "Do you want to discuss the nature of your deception here, *Miss Brown*?" He turned a contemptuous eye to the stunned gentleman at her side whose mouth hung agape. "Are you still here, Hungerford?"

"People are beginning to stare." Estelle glanced at Mr Hungerford, waiting for him to say something, but the fellow simply stood there stupefied.

"Perhaps I should leave you to deal with this matter." Mr Hungerford stepped away, the tremble in his voice a sign of his unease. While some might think him craven, Ross looked ready to pounce, ready to rip Hungerford's throat out with his bare teeth. "Clearly, you are acquainted and have something of great importance to discuss. Unless, of course, you insist I stay."

Estelle considered the gentleman's offer.

She knew why Ross had come. He wanted answers, explanations. He wanted to know why she'd left him, how she'd survived.

Did she have strength enough to relive eight years' worth of nightmares?

Spending time in Ross' company was sure to open old wounds. Even now, while annoyed at his brash manner, the urge to feel those large arms surround her, to hear his whispered words of comfort proved unnerving.

But she could not run forever. She cared for the Erstwhiles and did not have the heart to disappoint them. Even so, how could she stay?

Oh, what was she to do?

Estelle turned to Mr Hungerford. "Thank you for your kindness, sir. And you're right as always. My brother and Lord Trevane were childhood friends, and so I must address his lordship's complaint."

Already she had revealed too much, but this shameful situation did nothing to quell Mr Hungerford's heated gaze as he studied her face. Indeed, he looked pleased at the prospect of having to compete.

"May I call on you this evening? I believe we, too, have much to discuss."

Ross muttered something unintelligible. She noted his hands clenched into fists at his sides.

"Of course," Estelle quickly agreed, eager to be rid of him before Ross unleashed the anger brimming beneath the surface.

Ross did not wait for her to say anymore, nor did he pay Mr Hungerford the courtesy of acknowledging him. No, he simply took hold of her wrist, turned on his heels and forced her to march along Whitecombe Street.

"Stop this," she whispered through gritted teeth as he barged past several people going about their business. He had not bothered to ask where she was going, but from the determined set of his jaw, he had another place in mind. "You're hurting me."

Ross released his hold on her wrist and gripped her hand instead. People gaped and stared. In their youth, such scandalous behaviour would have seen them married within the week. But she was a lady no more.

"You're walking too quickly." Estelle had to break into a jog to match his pace. "Where are we going?"

"Somewhere quiet," he snapped. "Somewhere away from prying eyes."

Oh, she could not be alone with him.

They passed a coffeehouse.

"What about here? We could find a table."

He stared straight ahead. "Since when has a coffeehouse been a quiet place?"

They turned into Coventry Street, continued north of Leicester Square.

"We could sit in the square near the statue. No one will disturb us there." And she would not be inclined to stare at his mouth, or long for his fingers to delve down into her bodice.

Two ladies and their maid stopped walking and watched them stride past. The fair-haired one moistened her lips. "It seems one lucky lady has captured Vane's attention. If only it were me."

"You will be the talk of the salons tomorrow," Estelle complained.

No one knew her in town. The ladies could pry and probe their peers, but no one would come up with a name. But an aristocrat with such a commanding presence captured everyone's interest.

"Do you think I give a damn what these people have to say?" They turned into St Martins Lane and entered the courtyard of The Golden Goose coaching inn.

Panic flared as she noted numerous carriages crammed with passengers. They navigated the luggage and wicker baskets strewn around one conveyance. Stray dogs ran wild. One unusually large wolfhound raced over to her, almost knocking her off her feet.

She clutched Ross' arm, both hands settling over hard muscle. "Good Lord." The comment expressed her surprise at the size of the dog and her companion's impressive physique. Ross had always been of athletic build, but now there was so much more of him.

Wearing a frown, Ross' head shot to the hound. The animal came up to him and rubbed its furry head against his leg.

"I think he likes you." For the first time in days, Estelle smiled with genuine amusement.

Ross raised a brow. "I would wager the hound is a she, not he. I seem to attract the wild ones, those of a mind to wander, those quick to deviate from the moral path." One corner of his mouth twitched, though she could not tell if he was angry or amused.

Was he describing her? She didn't think so. And yet she had strayed so far from the path she would never find her way back. What would he say if he knew the extent of her crimes?

Perhaps he was speaking about a lover or a wife. She had to know. "And what would Lady Trevane say about you bringing a woman to a coaching inn?"

"My mother died ten years ago or have you forgotten that, too?"

"I was speaking about your wife."

Jealousy ate away at her heart like one of Mr Erstwhile's caustic solutions. Estelle imagined a lady with exquisite taste in fashion, a lady who oozed sensuality, one who knew how to please a man like Ross Sandford.

Ross' expression darkened. Had her comment roused a hidden pain? Had his wife died in childbirth or in a dreadful accident?

"There is no Lady Trevane. There never has been."

"I see." A wave of sadness washed over her. She should have been Lady Trevane. Once they had been equals. Noble blood flowed through their veins. Now they were worlds apart. "Is it not your duty to marry?"

Ross clenched his jaw and glared at her beneath hooded lids. "Do not dare lecture me on one's duty." He grasped her hand again, pulled her into the inn and through the common room to where the landlord stood behind his counter. "I want a room. Any will do." Dropping her hand to reach into his coat pocket, he retrieved a handful of coins and slapped them onto the wooden counter.

The landlord brushed a wispy lock of hair over his bald head. He pushed his spectacles up to the bridge of his nose and studied her face.

Ross removed a calling card and slid it across the worn surface. "That should suffice."

Bony fingers lifted the card. One quick scan of the name inscribed and the man reached under the counter and plonked a key on top.

"Two hours enough time for you, my lord?"

"Plenty."

"Up the stairs, third door on the right."

Ross nodded.

"And I'll want to see the lady afore she leaves," the landlord added. No doubt he was used to men using his rooms for distasteful purposes.

"I shall make sure she reports to you directly."

Ross cast her a sidelong glance. Perhaps he expected to see fear or shock marring her brow. When it came to the perverse appetites of men, nothing surprised her anymore.

Without protest, she followed Ross upstairs. Amidst all the hustle and bustle, no one paid them any heed. Doors opened and slammed. People barged past, shouting for their companions to hurry, fearing they might miss the mail coach.

Ross stopped outside a door and examined the brass disc attached to the key. "Number twelve. How apt."

She took a moment to recollect the number's relevance. "You speak of the day I left Prescott Hall."

He thrust the key into the lock but did not look at her. "I speak of the day and the month."

"I'm surprised you remember."

"Trust me. I wish I could forget."

A whiff of stale sweat hit her as soon as she entered the room. Dust clung to every surface and clawed at the back of her throat. Ross closed the door, and she heard the clunk of a key turning.

Was it not enough that they were alone?

Now he had barred the exit to prevent her escape.

Nerves pushed to the fore. Estelle swung around to face him. "Now that you have me here what is it you want?"

He stepped closer, towered over her, so large and commanding. His gaze flicked briefly to the double bed. "What do you think I want?"

Desire unfurled deep in her core. Would she allow him to take what should have rightfully been his? The answer swept through her—yes. To love Ross Sandford, to hear him pant her name in the throes of passion … it was the dream of a lost and lonely woman.

But she had suffered enough humiliation and so squared her shoulders and said, "You want to know about the past?"

"I want to know everything." Ross removed his hat and threw it on top of the chest of drawers. "But you can start by telling me how the hell you survived the shipwreck when more than a hundred people lost their lives."

"It's a long story." One she did not care to repeat.

In a sudden move that made her gasp, Ross clutched her hands. His touch sent her heart skipping up to her throat. He pulled her towards the bed. How she wished she could erase the last eight years, wished that they could slip between the sheets, that she could show him what he'd meant to her then, what he still meant to her now.

But everything had changed.

They were not the same people. No longer a perfect fit.

"We have the room for two hours." Ross forced her to sit on the bed. He dragged the chair from the corner and sat opposite her, their knees almost touching. "I think that's plenty of time for you to tell your tale, don't you?"

CHAPTER SEVEN

T he old adage that passions cool with time was a fallacy.

Vane sat on the chair in the shabby room, his eyes fixed firmly on Estelle. The task proved difficult when his traitorous body urged him to look at the bed, called for him to consider the possibility of slaking his desire for this woman and have done with it.

"Very well." She lifted her chin defiantly, unfastened the ribbons on her straw bonnet and placed it next to her on the bed. "Where shall I begin?"

She could begin by undressing, straddling him on the chair and begging for his forgiveness. "Were you on *The Torrens* when it sank?"

Estelle pursed her lips and nodded. "When the storm hit, I thought the world was ending. I've never seen waves like it. Mountain high. Of biblical proportions." She put her hand on her stomach and winced. "The wind was so strong it blew men ten feet into the air. The ship careened to one side, the sea swamping the deck. Don't ask me how I survived, although many times I wish I had not."

Her eyes filled with tears and Vane felt like the worst of

rogues for making her relive what was clearly a painful memory. Still, she owed those who loved her an explanation.

"And what of your lover? Did he survive?" The words sliced through the air like the crack of a whip—harsh and unforgiving.

He knew the answer of course.

Mr Peterson's bloated body washed ashore and was claimed by relatives. Vane had spent a week pacing the beach looking for Estelle while Fabian scoured the beaches in France.

Little did she know that Vane had boarded one fishing vessel after another, had sat amongst the stench of festering fish guts watching every ripple in the water, praying for a miracle. The men had laughed and joked, shared family stories, while he had sat silently, filled with despair.

"My lover?" Estelle's voice brought him back into the room, though the ache in his chest remained. "What on earth are you talking about?"

"There is no point denying what I know is true." Why else would she leave him if not to elope with another man? "You boarded the vessel with Mr Peterson. People saw you dining together in a dockside tavern."

A groan resonated from her throat. She shook her head, her frown disappearing only to be replaced by an arrogant grin.

"And so because a gentleman offered me sanctuary that means we were conducting a liaison? Maudette never left my side, not for a second." Estelle closed her eyes briefly and whispered, "Poor Maudette. She did not deserve such a fate."

"What do you mean Peterson offered you sanctuary?"

"Some men will assist a lady without demanding certain rewards in return. Three drunken bucks made a wager—which one of them would have me first. Mr Peterson punched the tallest one. He told them I was his sister and would shoot anyone who so much as looked at me in the wrong way."

Anger burst to the fore—hot fury for the bastards who thought to take advantage of an innocent woman. Shame quickly followed, for presuming to think he had all the answers.

"Forgive me. Under the circumstances, I could not help but think the worst."

If she'd not left him for another man, then what had he done to lose her favour?

He thrust his hand through his hair. The flurry of mixed emotions unsettled him. He preferred to feel empty, to feel nothing. The devil on his shoulder forced him to look at the bed, and whispered, "*Take her and have done with it*."

"To assume such a thing means you think I'm a liar. That when I told you how much I—" She stopped abruptly and sighed. "It doesn't matter now."

Vane came to his feet. He turned to the window and watched people climb in and out of the coaches. Part of him did not want to hear any more. But knowing the truth was the only hope he had of putting the past behind him.

"And so how did you manage to reach the shore?"

A tense silence ensued.

"French smugglers found me one night while they were rummaging through the wreckage looking for anything of value."

Smugglers!

A host of unwanted images flooded his mind. "Did … did they hurt you?" He closed his eyes while he waited for her answer, but lacked the strength to turn around and face her.

"Monsieur Bonnay led the men. He lived in a cottage in Wissant and took me in. His wife treated me like a daughter, and so no man dared lay a hand on me."

Relief flowed through his veins to calm his racing heart. "How long did you stay with them?"

"Four years."

Vane swung around unable to contain his shock. "Four years! Why the hell didn't you leave sooner?"

Why did you not come home?

Estelle sat with her head bowed, her hands clasped in her lap. "I tried, many times, spent sleepless nights planning my escape. But I knew too much. Though Madame Bonnay became my protector, the men would have killed me rather than take the risk I might pass information to the authorities."

All the time he'd been carousing the ballrooms, bedding women who took his fancy in the hope of banishing this woman from his mind, she was living in squalor, doing heaven knows what to stay alive.

The thought roused a crippling sense of inadequacy.

"Did you commit any criminal acts?" Vane almost scoffed at his own question. No smuggler would give her board and lodgings without asking for something in return.

"I acted as a lookout, distributed contraband. Once, I dressed as a laundress and took receipt of a couple of kegs of spirits hidden beneath newly washed linen while the revenue officers sat a few feet away supping ale." She looked up at him, sadness brimming in her eyes. "And so the answer is yes, Ross. I have lied, cheated and stolen. I have bribed men to turn a blind eye to my crimes."

Vane dragged a hand down his face. "You did what you had to do to survive."

Damn, he wished she'd not told him.

Now the small part of him that so desperately needed to despise her swelled with admiration for her strength and courage.

A sudden noise from the room next door captured their attention. The loud groan could well have been the sound of a weary passenger relieved to have reached his destination. The creak of the bed may well have conjured an image of the poor fellow collapsing with exhaustion, but the groans became grunts. The banging grew louder, more insistent.

Vane met Estelle's gaze, the flush of her cheeks reminding

him of the innocent young woman who'd captured his heart. She had been so full of life, so vibrant and vivacious. Now a deep sadness lingered behind those wide eyes. She may not have lost her life on *The Torrens*, but she had lost something of herself that day.

"May I ask if you've seen my brother?" she suddenly said over the amorous din. "Is he well? Is he happy?"

"Fabian lives on an island off the Devonshire coast," Vane said, as eager as she to mask the intimate sounds coming from the room next door. "He commands a fleet of merchant ships and has made quite a name for himself."

A woman's cries of pleasure rent the air though they were fake. He could tell.

Vane swallowed deeply. "Fabian and Lillian married recently. He kidnapped her in the hope it would persuade me to search for you. As it turns out, they're in love."

Estelle blinked. "Good heavens, I don't know which piece of information to address first." She fell silent, lost in her own thoughts. "I'm glad he's happy."

"Oh, he is happy beyond words." Vane could hear the thread of jealousy in his tone. "But since his man Mackenzie spotted you in Paris, Fabian has not stopped looking for you. He will be relieved to know you're safe and well."

She clutched her hands to her chest and closed her eyes briefly, looked every bit the serene angel who'd come to save him in the dank alley.

"You cannot tell him I'm alive. Fabian must forget about me." The words *as must you* echoed in his head though they never left her lips. "I'm not the same person. Too much has happened. Society would never accept me."

Vane gave a mocking snort. "Society does not look favourably on any of us. Your brother is in trade. A rogue ruined my sister years ago. And as for me … well …"

"But you're the Marquess of Trevane. People will make allowances. At some point, you must take a wife of noble birth else the ancestral line will stop with you."

After a quick bolt to the finish line, the wild activities next door came to an abrupt end.

"I am not the marrying kind, regardless of my title and position. When I'm dead, I'll not give a fig who sleeps in my ancestors' bed."

"You never used to think that way."

"Too much has happened," he said, repeating her words. "I'm not the person you remember."

"No, there is rather a lot more of you." Something akin to admiration flashed in her eyes. She scanned the breadth of his shoulders, absently moistened her lips. "One thing is certain."

"What is that?"

"Neither of us smile like we used to. We have turned into morbid cynics during our years apart. Life has lost all meaning."

He was about to tell her that things would have been different had she not abandoned him, but pride kept him from opening his mouth.

A suffocating silence pressed heavily upon him.

He couldn't bring himself to sit in the chair for it brought an intimacy to the moment, a level of civility, he was trying desperately to avoid.

"And so you escaped the smugglers," he said to distract his thoughts, "and found work in Paris." Fabian would want to know the details.

"Madame Bonnay died. Not long after, her husband was found dead in the woods. With both of them gone I had no choice but to escape, though I doubt I shall ever stop looking over my shoulder."

"But you've not seen the smugglers since."

"No. After that, I spent two years working as a maid but—"

Her eyes suddenly filled with tears. A few drops landed on her porcelain cheeks. She shook her head and sucked in a deep breath. "After leaving there, I moved to—" A choking sob escaped.

Vane saw a multitude of emotions pass across her face: grief and shame and sorrow. He closed the gap between them, took her hand and brought her to her feet.

"Sometimes it is better to cry than to bury the pain inside." He was a hypocrite. Every negative emotion he'd ever felt lingered in the hollow cavern of his chest.

Tears came in a constant stream now. She seemed so small and helpless, not at all the wicked vixen he'd painted her out to be. The sight of it tore at his heart. He cupped her cheeks, wiped away the evidence of her misery with the pads of his thumbs.

"Oh, Ross, I cannot tell you how dreadful it has been."

"Hush now." Against his better judgement, he drew her into an embrace. Almost instantly her essence penetrated the fine fabric of his coat. The strange energy that had always bound them together flowed between them as though the last eight years had never existed. "You're safe now. You're home."

"I will never be safe. I have no home." She wrapped her arms around him, pressed her forehead to his chest and cried until there were no more tears left to shed. It was the sound of someone devoid of all hope.

No matter how many women he'd taken in his arms, no matter how many he'd taken to his bed, no one touched him like Estelle did. Despite the gravity of her situation, despite all that had happened, the urge to hold her and never let go almost knocked him off his feet.

And then she looked up at him, all lost and forlorn, those wide doe-like eyes swollen and red.

He bent his head, brushed his lips once across hers and whispered, "I'm sorry for all you have been through."

She looked into his eyes, yet it felt as if she'd found the secret door to his soul, opened it and stepped inside. When she came up on her tiptoes, he froze.

"I'm sorry, too." For what, she did not say. But she closed her eyes and kissed him. One chaste peck led to another and another, each one more daring than the last. Her breathing grew short and shallow. Small hands skimmed his waist and drifted up over his chest to clutch the lapels of his coat. "Oh, Ross," she gasped against his mouth. "I have been alone for so long."

The comment resonated with him. Yes, he had kissed women but never truly tasted them. He had entered their willing bodies but never made love to any of them. A man could count a hundred lovers and still be lonely. He could lie next to a warm body at night and still be frozen to his core.

"Won't you kiss me?" she whispered. "Just once, like you used to."

He wanted to deny her and yet found he could not. She wanted the sweet, tender kiss of a young man but she would get the sinful kiss of a scoundrel.

Vane crushed her to his chest, covered her mouth and devoured those plump, wet lips. She tasted as he remembered: of rightness, of hope, of something infinitely addictive. The carnal need for more, the need to satisfy the clawing hunger, led him to tease her lips apart and enter the only place in the world he'd ever wanted to be.

Estelle met him with equal enthusiasm, letting her tongue tangle with his. Her pretty moans conveyed delight in the erotic dance. Their desperation to explore, to sate their lustful urges was yet another thing they had in common. A whimper resonated in the back of her throat. One of pleasure, not pain.

Liquid fire burst through his veins. Dangerously hot. Wickedly sensual. His pulse galloped. His desire spiralled. Their passion ignited like a blinding fury: wild, intense, uniquely satisfying.

With his large hands settling on her buttocks, he shuffled forward until she had no choice but to collapse on the bed. He followed her, covering her body as he'd always planned to do.

They were lost in their heady kisses, panting as their bodies writhed to an ancient rhythm.

Years of practised skill in the steps of bringing a lover to a bone-shattering climax abandoned him. While his fingers fumbled with the hem of her dress, dragging it up past her thigh, his mind rushed to the denouement. They were fully clothed, but he imagined them naked, pictured the moment of bliss when he entered her body.

Good God, he was liable to spend himself long before then. The thought was sobering as was the sudden banging and moaning again from the occupants next door.

Was this what he wanted?

To take his dream and turn it into something soiled and sordid. Eight years of pining, of heartache, reduced to a quick fuck in a coaching inn. Everything he touched bore the Devil's mark. Would he ruin the one thing he'd always held sacred? The only truth in his life: his feelings for Estelle.

He tore his mouth away and scrambled to his feet. His hard cock throbbed against the material of his breeches, the ache for satisfaction muddling his thoughts. The need to dominate surfaced, too. He could kneel between her legs, taste her arousal with his tongue. Suck and lick her into submission. Give everything, take nothing. Show her the pleasure she had denied herself long ago.

Vane looked down at her—the angel of his dreams, the devil of his nightmares. During all the solitary moments when he had played out this scene, he was strong, commanding, knew his mind. But in reality, he did not know what the hell he wanted anymore.

"We should leave," he heard himself saying, "before we both do something we may well regret."

He turned to the window, desperate to look at anything other than her swollen lips and bed-tousled hair.

The people outside were busy going about their business, oblivious to his inner torment. All except one woman who stared up at him intently. She stood too far away for him to distinguish her features. Perhaps it was a coincidence or a consequence of his strained nerves. Suspicion flared when she turned and hurried away from the courtyard.

A creak and a weary sigh drew his attention back to the room and led him to conclude Estelle had stood, too.

The tension in the air was palpable.

"Emotions are running high," he continued. "We still have much to discuss, but we shall leave it until another day." Did he want to know what prompted her to leave Prescott Hall, to leave him? He wasn't sure.

"You're right," she said weakly. "No doubt Mr Erstwhile will wonder what happened to me, and he has enough worries at the moment."

Vane turned to face her and wished he hadn't. Sadness filled those dark brown eyes. He preferred seeing the fire of passion alight there.

"You speak of the theft at the shop."

Estelle patted down a few stray locks of hair and gathered her bonnet. "The intruder stole nothing. He left the money box full of sovereigns and only sought to cause unnecessary damage."

"Then it is not the mark of a thief but of someone with a point to prove," Vane said, grateful that someone else's problem distracted him from his own. "Has Mr Erstwhile upset anyone?"

"I highly doubt it." She brushed her hand down her dress to

remove the creases. "There is not a kinder more honest man than Mr Erstwhile."

"How did you come to work for him?"

"We spoke on the crossing to Dover. He has a way of seeing what other people cannot, of understanding a person's secrets without a word passing from their lips."

"Like a seer? Like a man renowned for his moral and spiritual insights?"

A brief smile brightened her face. "Yes, exactly like that. I owe him a debt of gratitude."

"Then I shall escort you on your errand to gather provisions." Part of him wanted to return to Berkeley Square, to put this woman from his mind and concentrate all efforts on ruining Lord Cornell. Part of him needed to remain at her side, to know she was safe, to discover more about this Mr Hungerford. "It's the least I can do after dragging you away from your errant knight."

She frowned. "Errant knight?"

"Mr Hungerford. Clearly, the gentleman has designs on securing more than your company." The thought roused Vane's ire.

"He is just a lonely man who cannot function without a wife."

The cryptic comment proved intriguing. "And you believe he has marked you for the role?"

Estelle shrugged. "When it comes to understanding the motives of men, I am often left baffled."

"Likewise, I gave up trying to understand a lady's motives eight years ago." He spoke of the way Estelle had professed her love only to flee on a ship heading to France.

A howl of satisfaction from the adjoining room brought another blush to her cheeks. "Now I know why the landlord insisted I visit him before leaving. The sounds of pleasure and pain are often the same."

Never had truer words been spoken.

"Then I shall meet you downstairs in a moment."

She looked at him with some confusion.

"The landlord will want to see you alone," he added. "To ensure your opinion is your own."

It was not a lie but an exaggerated truth. Vane needed a minute to gather himself. The mask he'd held in place these last few minutes needed adjusting, repositioning.

Estelle nodded. "I shall wait for you downstairs."

Vane watched her unlock the door and leave the room, then he sat on the chair and buried his head in his hands.

The day had been enlightening on many levels. He'd discovered something of her savage life, of the woman she'd become in his absence, of the criminal things she'd done. He sensed there was much more to tell, most of it equally harrowing, deeply unpleasant.

For his sins, his own mind was a muddled mess of confusion. He'd lost count of the conflicting emotions tearing through him: anger, pity, raging lust, and another indeterminable feeling hovering just out of reach. In short, Estelle Darcy had managed a feat beyond the capabilities of any other woman.

She had made him *feel* something.

And yet amid all the chaos one frightening thought remained constant.

He would never stop wanting her.

Nothing she could say or do could banish the intense longing burning inside of him. No other woman would ever compare, and so he was destined to live a vapid life of meaningless liaisons.

Fate had marked him unworthy of love, marked him to live a lonely, empty existence.

CHAPTER EIGHT

Head bent over a ledger, the landlord of The Golden Goose scrawled away with quill and ink as Estelle approached the counter. Sensing her presence, the man glanced up, dispensed with his writing implement and straightened his spectacles.

"Everything all right, miss?" Doubt lingered in his voice as he scanned her face and figure as if searching for a sign of distress.

"Thank you," she said, sniffing away her tears. "Everything is fine."

Everything was far from fine.

The pain in her chest had nothing to do with reliving her nightmares. Nor did she allow herself the luxury of feeling anything when it came to her brother, Fabian. She'd come to terms with the fact she would never see him again. Knowing he was happy made the decision much easier to bear.

No.

Spending time alone with Ross was her mistake. Her heart felt like it was breaking all over again. More unshed tears choked the back of her throat. Her body trembled. She could still feel the heavy weight of him pressing her down into the mattress. The intimate place between her legs still burned with need. She moistened her lips. The spicy masculine taste of him coated the delicate skin.

"Pardon me for saying, but you don't seem all right." The landlord glanced at the stairs with curiosity. "Is his lordship remaining behind?"

Estelle shook her head. "No, he sent me down to see you and will join me shortly." Did he think her a servant girl done away with her deviant master? "I have not hit him over the head with the chamber pot if that is what you're thinking."

"Stranger things have happened."

"I assure you he is alive and well."

The landlord raised his chin in acknowledgement. "Gentlemen of his quality enjoy playing games with us lesser folk." No doubt he'd made his judgement about her class from the simple style of her clothes, coupled with the fact a lady did not accompany a man to a coaching inn, let alone spend an hour alone with him in a bedchamber. "Made you false promises has he?"

The need to defend Ross pushed to the fore. "I'm afraid you're mistaken. I am the one who has led him a merry dance. I hoped he'd put the past behind him. But clearly he has not."

Why she blurted her business to this man, she had no notion.

He glanced at the stairs once again. "Men like to hold a grudge."

"And women thrive on malice and spite," she countered.

"But not you," he said, seeming to know her after nothing more than a brief conversation.

"No. Not me."

The heavy thud of booted footsteps on the stairs alerted her to the gentleman in question.

Ross strode over to join her. "I assume all is in order?"

"Aye, my lord." The landlord inclined his head. "Although you have paid for another hour."

Ross raised a brow. "Perhaps you might offer an extension to the couple next door. I imagine they might make better use of the time."

Heat warmed Estelle's cheeks. Just like those in the adjoining chamber, they too had almost fallen prey to their desires.

Part of her wished she had known Ross' body, wished that she had an erotic memory to cling to when she lay alone at night. But this man was dangerous beyond measure. Just being in his company fed her addiction for him. Lord, he approached kissing with the skill and mastery of a great painter: varying his strokes, applying different degrees of pressure, bringing a vibrancy to life that touched her deeply.

"Where is it you need to go?" Ross' voice broke her reverie. With a hand at her elbow, he guided her away from the counter and towards the door.

Estelle blinked in confusion and looked up at him. "Excuse me?" Where could she go? The ends of the earth were not far away enough to escape this man.

"You said you need to collect provisions for Mr Erstwhile."

"Oh, yes." She straightened. "I must call in on Mr Potter. He has agreed to lend Mr Erstwhile a few herbs and tonics so he may open the shop."

"Then I shall be your escort." Ross seemed colder now, a little distant.

They left the coaching inn and made their way along St Martins Lane to Mr Potter's shop on Castle Street. The apothecary had packaged the necessary items, but Estelle did not have an opportunity to mention the intruder.

Ross carried the parcel as they headed back to Whitecombe Street. While his outward manner was that of any considerate gentleman, she could not shake the thought of how savagely he'd claimed her mouth.

She cast him a sidelong glance, wondering what emotion lay behind the stone planes of his face. At some point, he would ask her the only question that mattered. Why had she left Prescott Hall instead of marrying him? To tell him the truth would only confuse matters. The prospect of a life together vanished the day she left. They were different people now, on different paths. And the sooner she put some distance between them the better it would be for both their sakes.

"May I ask something of you?" She had no right to expect anything from him, and yet somehow, she knew he would not refuse her request.

Ross glanced at her. "That all depends on what it is."

"Don't tell my brother you found me."

"You want me to lie?" A weary sigh left his lips, and he turned from her to focus ahead. "I gave Fabian my word. That may mean nothing to you, but it does to me."

Oh, if only he knew why she'd left he would not be so cold.

"I am not asking you to break an oath. I am merely asking you to delay."

"Why, so you can run again?"

"Yes." What was the point of lying? "You do not understand. Fabian will want to hear everything, every detail of my life. He will want to punish those who have harmed me, want to seek vengeance. All I ask—"

Ross came to an abrupt halt and swung around to face her. "What do you mean those who have harmed you? Do you speak of the smugglers?"

She could not risk telling him about Faucheux, or about the merchant's son, Monsieur Robard. "A woman alone is an easy target. You know that."

A growl rumbled in the back of his throat. Just like the landlord, he scanned her body as if signs of her mistreatment were still evident there.

"You're avoiding my question. I suggest you tell me what happened now or there'll be hell to pay."

87

"This is precisely the reason I do not want you to tell my brother." Estelle turned away from him and marched along the street.

Ross caught up with her in two strides. "Is it wrong that people care what happened to you?"

"No, it is not wrong. But I do not want my brother consumed with guilt or thoughts of revenge when he should focus on being happy."

The same applied to Ross. Her love for both men had set her on her course all those years ago.

A tense silence ensued as they navigated the crowded pavement.

As soon as they turned into Whitecombe Street and the crowd dispersed, Ross suddenly blurted, "Did you marry while away in France?"

The question shocked her. How could she ever marry anyone else when she loved him?

"No, though one smuggler asked me many times." Faucheux would never stop looking for her. The rogue always got what he wanted.

"Good God, your brother is a baron. Why the hell would you marry a smuggler?"

"My brother may possess a title"—she paused, glanced back over her shoulder and lowered her voice—"but I consorted with criminals, Ross. I have worked in a tavern, and as a maid and governess." She closed her eyes briefly at the memory. "The lady you once knew died on *The Torrens* and you would be wise to remember it."

A darkness passed over his features. "You're wrong. Your kindness and devotion to others is still evident in the way you are with the Erstwhiles. The gentleman speaks of you like a daughter, not an assistant."

She couldn't help but smile when she thought of Mr

Erstwhile. "He knows nothing about my past and places value only on the present."

Ross' bright blue eyes focused on her mouth. "Then perhaps I should seek to do the same."

For a moment, she imagined being drawn into his embrace, imagined telling him that they could be friends, share dinner, take trips to the theatre. But he deserved to hear the truth.

"I cannot stay in London."

"You're leaving?" All the colour drained from his face, and he took a few deep breaths. "When will you go?" The hard exterior melted away, leaving a voice tinged with sorrow.

"Soon."

"Then in light of your earlier request, I ask you pay me the same courtesy. I ask that you delay your departure, at least for the time being."

"Why?"

He shrugged and diverted his gaze. "I wish I knew."

Every moment spent with him was torture. She wasn't sure if she had the strength to last the week. "I cannot give you my word, but I shall consider what you have said."

He swallowed visibly numerous times. "You cannot know what it is like to wake in the morning with one's heart bursting with happiness. To go about your day with a false sense of rightness, to have everything you hold dear ripped away without a word or explanation."

Lord help her, did he think her so cold? She knew what it was like to lose the love of her life.

"All I ask," he continued, "is that you spare me the discomfort of calling at the shop to find you have upped and left suddenly during the night."

Discomfort?

Of course, that was all this was to him now. A mild annoyance. A slight inconvenience. Her throat grew tight at the thought. She wasn't sure she could answer without him hearing the hitch in her voice.

"Come." She cleared her throat. "Mr Erstwhile will wonder where I've got to, and he has enough worries at the moment."

Ross inclined his head. Although she sensed he had more to say, he pursed his lips and remained silent. Unspoken words were often the hardest to bear.

Despite returning from France, there would always be a vast sea between them. She would always be the selfish one who ran away from her problems. He would always be the strong, intrepid hero who deserved better.

While Ross tried to maintain an indifferent air as he escorted Estelle back to the apothecary shop, his heart pounded so hard in his chest it robbed him of breath.

When will you go?

Soon.

Those words replayed over and over in his mind. God damn. He wished she'd never stumbled upon him in the alley. He wished he'd never pursued her. Time was a great healer, so the philosophers said. Ballocks. The same excruciating pain pierced his soul. And still, he could not bring himself to swallow his pride and demand to know why she had left.

Hell, he needed a distraction.

He needed a fight.

As they drew nearer to their destination, Ross noted Wickett sitting dutifully atop his box seat, his head bowed. The poor man had sat there for hours and had no doubt taken the opportunity to catch much-needed sleep. Only when Wickett turned the page, did Vane realise the coachman held a book. Ross snorted. Nothing Wickett said or did surprised him anymore.

What did knock the wind out of Vane's sails, and almost forced him to make an abrupt detour, was the sight of Lady Cornell and her maid standing outside the apothecary shop.

Ross gritted his teeth. "I swear that damn woman makes it her business to know where I am at all times of the day."

"Do you refer to the lady in the garish pink bonnet lingering outside Mr Erstwhile's shop?" Estelle spoke calmly.

"Indeed."

"Oh, they followed us to the coaching inn. Numerous times they pretended to look in shop windows in the hope we wouldn't notice them."

Ross raised a brow, impressed at her observation skills. "You saw them?"

Estelle cast him a confident grin. "When one has spent years acting as a smuggler's eyes and ears one notices such things."

"And you did not think to mention it?"

"But then you would have looked over your shoulder. The lady would have abandoned her spying, and you would never know the full extent of her intentions."

Intrigued by Estelle's insight, he asked, "And what are her intentions?" Lady Cornell made no secret about what she wanted, but Estelle did not know that.

"If I were you, I would be cautious. The lady walked the length of three streets, lingered near the entrance of a coaching inn full of unsavoury characters. The fact she is standing outside the shop tells me she followed you here. *Desperate* doesn't begin to describe her actions."

They were but a few feet away now, too close to tell her about his dealings with Lord Cornell.

"I think the woman wants to antagonise her husband in the hope I'm forced to kill him. There's no time to explain the details. But if what you say is true, she witnessed us spending an hour alone in a coaching inn. It would serve me greatly if she continues to believe we're lovers."

Estelle glanced up at him and frowned. "You want me to pretend I'm in love with you?"

"Indeed. She must think there is more to this relationship than an hour spent romping beneath the bedsheets."

"We were not romping beneath the bedsheets."

"On top of the bedsheets then. Both of us lost our heads for a moment."

"Indeed." Estelle stared at his mouth. "You cannot tell her who I am."

Vane had no time to answer. Lady Cornell locked eyes with him. She batted her lashes in a look of utter shock.

"Lord Trevane, good day to you." Lady Cornell offered a hand encased in a pink kidskin glove. "What brings you to Whitecombe Street?" The impertinence of the question conveyed more than a need to pry.

"Lady Cornell." Vane held the parcel by its string and with his free hand gripped her fingers and bowed. "In answer to your question I find that it's the perfect place to spend a pleasurable afternoon."

As if on cue, a flush crept up Estelle's neck to bring a rosy glow to her cheeks. She looked up at him as she had done many times in the past when they'd stolen away to the orchard for a secret rendezvous. It was a look that said he was her world, one that made him feel like a god amongst mortal men. It was a look that cradled his soul, that sang a sweet and soothing melody to chase ways eight years' worth of hurt and misery. Transfixed by the beauty of the moment he could not tear his gaze away.

"Lady Cornell," he eventually said, "may I present my dear friend Miss Brown."

Estelle turned to the woman and inclined her head. "My lady."

The gesture roused Vane's ire. Estelle should have been his

marchioness. She should not have to bend and scrape to the likes of this woman.

Lady Cornell smiled through drawn lips. "Miss Brown? Major Brown's daughter?"

The woman knew full well Major Brown had never married. Vane cursed. It was selfish of him to put Estelle in such an awkward position.

"Oh, no," Estelle said with bright eyes and a warm smile. "I'm afraid I cannot claim to have friends or family in elevated circles." The lie fell easily from her lips, and Vane wondered what other lies she'd told in order to survive.

"Can you not claim *me* as a friend, Miss Brown?" Vane said in a rich drawl.

Estelle raised a coy brow. "Well, yes, but are we not a little better acquainted than that?"

Vane bit back a chuckle. In the guise of Miss Brown, Estelle cared nothing for her reputation. His amusement faded. Why would she care when she had no intention of remaining in London?

Lady Cornell cleared her throat. "So, Miss Brown, are you new to town? I would be happy to take you on a tour of all the interesting places."

"Thank you, my lady. But my work with Mr Erstwhile takes up most of my time." Estelle gestured to the apothecary shop. "And Ross—" She stopped abruptly. "Lord Trevane commands every spare minute at my disposal. As I'm sure you're aware, he can be quite a demanding gentleman."

Vane captured Estelle's hand and brought it to his lips. "And I appreciate the patience it takes to put up with me."

Lady Cornell's gaze journeyed over Estelle's clothes, face and plain bonnet. Jealousy oozed from the woman like a poisonous green mist in danger of choking all those in the vicinity. Vane could see it, could feel it contaminating the air.

"Then I should have a care, Miss Brown." The lady's tone held a hint of amusement that belied her unpleasant sneer. She forced a little titter and added, "Some men go to great lengths to avoid marriage. Society ladies expect so much more from their *friends* you see."

The lady could not hide the grin of satisfaction at her veiled putdown.

"Or is it simply a case that unconventional men seek unconventional partners," Estelle said. "After all, what lady of the *ton* would dine in the common room of a coaching inn? What lady of the *ton* could speak on topics that might interest a man with such a voracious appetite for conversation?"

From Lady Cornell's flustered expression, clearly, she had never been challenged by an intelligent woman. She struggled to catch her breath as she floundered in these uncharted waters.

"Well," she eventually said. "I have an appointment with my modiste and must not delay." Beneath hooded lids, she looked up at Vane and said in a husky tone, "Will I see you tomorrow night, my lord? I hear Lord Cranbourne's ball is to be the crush of the Season. And you know what that means."

Oh, he knew only too well. A lady might easily slip away without her husband's knowledge, only to return an hour later without ever being missed.

"I'm afraid not. I am engaged to dine with Miss Brown tomorrow evening."

Estelle quickly masked her sudden look of surprise. "Indeed. I am certain we will have plenty to discuss."

Lady Cornell sucked in her cheeks. "Should your plans change, know you will also have a *friend* at the ball." She inclined her head to him and flounced away, giving Estelle the cut direct.

After a brief moment of silence, Estelle sighed. "Well, you are certainly in demand, my lord." Did he detect a hint of jealousy in her voice? "Now I know why you insisted I pretend to be in love with you."

You were in love with me once. Do you remember? Do you ever think of me?

The words echoed from the empty chambers of his heart. How was it a man made of stone and steel became as fragile and flimsy as silk in her company?

A chuckle escaped Estelle's lips dragging him from his reverie. "Do you remember when the Reverend Moseley's daughter used to follow you around the village? Did she not hide in your stables once hoping to catch sight of you?"

"She did." What Estelle did not know was that he'd been forced to tell the girl that another woman had claimed his affections. The one who stood before him now. The one who still lived and breathed inside him no matter how many times he'd tried to rid himself of the affliction. "I believe Miss Moseley married Captain Rogers' son in the end."

"How wonderful." Her smile faded. "It is good to know she found happiness."

The comment drew his thoughts to the reason Estelle had left him. This was the perfect opportunity to broach the subject. In his mind, he tried to phrase the only question that mattered. And yet he couldn't quite bring himself to form the words.

He knew why.

It had nothing to do with pride. He could stand in a dank alley and taunt men wielding blades, could stand opposite a scoundrel pointing a pistol at his head, and feel nothing. And yet, thinking of Estelle's answer filled him with fear and dread.

Ask her, damn it. Ask her now!

"Sadly, we are not all as fortunate as Miss Moseley." Vane mentally shook himself in a bid to stop the raging voices demanding more than he could give.

A solemn silence hung in the air between them.

"Well, I should take the package to Mr Erstwhile. He has had his nose pressed to the window for the last five minutes."

Vane forced a smile though he was somewhat relieved she had changed the subject. "May I call on you this evening?" The question left his lips without thought. Damnation. Never had he sounded so eager, so desperate.

"Have you forgotten? I promised Mr Hungerford he could call."

Anger erupted deep within. How the hell he kept it at bay he would never know. "Are you aware as to the nature of his visit?" What he really wanted to ask was what the bloody hell Hungerford wanted.

Estelle glanced at the ground before looking up into his eyes. "Mr Erstwhile thinks Mr Hungerford will offer marriage. We dined with him last night, and he has been most attentive of late."

"Does Hungerford have children?" Did he hold Estelle in high esteem or did his motive stem from necessity?

"No."

"Does he know anything about your background?"

"No, and I have no intention of telling him anything."

"You will have to tell him if you agree to his proposal." He was trying to be magnanimous, trying to be a man who had let go of petty resentment.

Something akin to disappointment flashed in her eyes. "I do not intend to accept him, Ross. How can I when … when I intend to leave London in a few days?"

"You said you would delay your departure."

The shop bell tinkled, and Mr Erstwhile appeared at the threshold. "My lord, good day to you." He gestured to the parcel in Vane's hand. "I trust those are my provisions. Mr Potter must have been extremely busy to have kept you waiting."

"Forgive the delay," Estelle said. "It wasn't Mr Potter's fault. Lord Trevane and I had much to discuss."

"Indeed." Mr Erstwhile ushered them into the shop. "Mr Hungerford appeared most inconvenienced to be overthrown as her chaperone, and so easily, too."

Vane wasn't sure if the old man was admonishing him for shoddy manners. He handed him the parcel. "I'm afraid I did not give Hungerford much choice in the matter."

"No, I don't suppose you did. There is much at stake is there not?" Mr Erstwhile raised a knowing brow.

"More than you know."

A smile touched the old man's lips. "Any worthy gentleman would have put up a decent fight," he said. "If there is one thing I cannot abide it is a man who fails to stand up for his beliefs no matter what the cost."

Vane inclined his head in agreement. He could feel Estelle watching him. "I share your disdain for such things."

Mr Erstwhile placed the parcel on the counter. "Would it surprise you to learn that, in all my years, I know of only one gentleman who has sacrificed his position in society to follow his heart?"

Vane might not be as wise as this man, but he knew to whom Erstwhile referred. "No, it does not surprise me. I only hope I have your strength of will when it matters."

"You are extremely astute, my lord."

"Not always." He had not been shrewd enough to prevent Estelle's hasty departure and had made many assumptions that had since proved foolish.

"Well," Estelle said with a sigh. "We have much to do, and so I shall bid you a good day, my lord."

That was his cue to leave, and yet he wanted to stay. He imagined shrugging out of his coat and helping Mr Erstwhile with his bottles, listening to his philosophical advice on life. He pictured sitting in a cramped parlour, eating stew, watching every expression playing on Estelle's beautiful face.

Vane inclined his head. "Good day, Miss Brown." He stared into her dark eyes and in his mind whispered, *Dream of me.*

"Might we see you again, my lord?" Mr Erstwhile asked though from his tone the man already knew the answer.

"Undoubtedly."

Mr Erstwhile walked over and held open the door. "A wise woman once told me that wealth and position are merely a means to appease one's pride. That the heart needs no such adornments."

Vane glanced up at the ceiling. "Would I be right in assuming you married that woman?"

Mr Erstwhile smiled and raised both brows. "Good day, my lord. No doubt we will see you again tomorrow."

CHAPTER NINE

Upon witnessing Vane approach the carriage, Wickett closed his book and placed it on the box seat next to him. He straightened, gathered the reins in his gloved hands and sat awaiting a command.

"What were you reading?" Vane asked, grateful for an opportunity to tease his coachman. "Advice on how to deal with an obstinate master? Or how best to respond when one's employer spouts gibberish?" Perhaps it was a book on witty quips to tease the upper classes. That's what came of hiring a coachman who could read.

Wickett shook his head. "No, my lord. It's one of those gothic novels all the ladies are talking about … *Nocturnal Visit*."

"*Nocturnal Visit*?" Vane snorted. Wickett enjoyed testing his patience. "Let me guess. It's about a man who gets lost in the fog at night and is ravaged by a wolf instead of an angel."

Wickett shook his head. "I've got to the part where the lady realises her friends only like her when she has money. And now some fancy nabob has come and is turning her head with his flowery words and pretty talk."

"Sounds rather like a night in a London ballroom."

"That's why the lady chose it. Happen there's a message in the title as well as on the inside page."

What the hell was Wickett talking about? "Are you referring to the plot?"

Wickett frowned. "No, my lord, I'm talking about the lady who came and asked me to pass on the message."

"You mean the book really is entitled *Nocturnal Visit*?"

Gripping the reins with one hand, Wickett grabbed the book, reached down and gave it to Vane. "See, take a look for yourself."

Vane examined the words embossed in gold on the spine. "They say Regina Roche is more popular than Ann Radcliffe." He flicked to the first page, to the feminine script suggesting the sender make a late-night call to his house on Berkeley Square. It was signed in a delicate flourish. The lady wanted him to be in no doubt as to her identity.

"The lady's maid was most insistent I accept the gift, my lord."

"Burn it once we're home." Lady Cornell was quickly becoming a nuisance. "On second thought, I'll keep hold of it for now." He had no intention of granting her request but might need to use it as leverage at a later date.

Wickett nodded. "Are we to head back to the square?"

Vane considered the question. His time should be spent thinking of a way to ruin Lord Cornell—a legitimate way that would shame the fool. He should pry into the lord's affairs, look for anything to use against him. But all thoughts turned to Estelle and her meeting with Mr Hungerford.

"Take me to Mr Joseph in Whitechapel."

Now that Estelle had made a sudden appearance, Vane would give the runner another task to occupy his time. He wanted to know everything about Mr Hungerford. Specifically, why a gentleman of his status was keen to court a shopgirl?

Vane found Joseph in The Speckled Hen tavern, tucking into a meat pie. He sat at his usual table in a dingy corner next to the hearth. The man's hard, sculpted jaw looked capable of taking more than a few punches. His eyes made him handsome in a rugged sort of way. They were an intense shade of blue, as inviting as a warm sea to a woman, as cold as ice should anyone rouse his ire. While he had once worked in Bow Street, now he worked for himself, conducted his business from the tavern, and paid the landlord handsomely for the privilege.

The low beamed ceilings proved difficult to navigate for a man of Vane's height. With a slight stoop, he made his way to the bar, paid for two tankards of ale and instructed the serving wench to bring them to the table.

Witnessing Vane's approach, Joseph gestured to the chair opposite. "My lord. We don't often see you around these parts during daylight hours."

The rotten smell of open gutters permeated the air, banishing the scent of sweat and unwashed clothes.

Vane gestured to the open window. "Do you mind?"

Joseph snorted. "You get used to it," he said, reaching up and pulling the window shut. "I've had no luck finding the lady. Seems you're right about her perishing on that ship."

"There's no need to keep looking. The lady found *me*."

Had Fate thrown them together? Had Destiny a hand in their reunion? Had he learned whatever cruel lesson the Lord intended and so seeing Estelle again was his reward?

The landlord, a man with a dirty complexion and unkempt side whiskers, came with their drinks. He scanned Vane's immaculate attire and eyed Joseph in such a manner as to enquire if he needed assistance.

"Nothing to worry about, Fred," Joseph said, accepting the tankards.

With a suspicious frown which looked to be a permanent

expression, Fred shuffled away as if expecting to lose the soles of his shoes.

"So you have no need for my services now you've found her." Joseph shovelled a forkful of pie into his mouth and washed it down with a swig of ale.

"There is something else I need you to do. I want you to find out everything you can about a Mr Hungerford."

"Hungerford, you say? Shouldn't be too difficult what with it being an unusual name." Joseph wiped his mouth with the back of his hand. "Do you know where I can find him?"

"You'll have his address tonight." Vane decided he would venture to Whitecombe Street this evening, purely with the intention of spying. "His wife died recently, so I'm told." Vane thought back to the night Estelle and the Erstwhiles stumbled upon him in the alley. They had not walked far. "I'd wager he lives somewhere in the vicinity of Longacre. Perhaps begin your search for his wife with the records at St Clement Danes. I imagine that's the closest church."

Joseph nodded. He withdrew a notebook and pencil and took down the information. "I'll send the nod to Wickett when I find something of interest."

Vane retrieved a few sovereigns from his pocket and slid them across the crude wooden table. "I'll pay you ten pounds when you've found out what I need to know. And you can keep the money I gave you to find Miss Darcy."

The runner grinned. "If only all fine folk were as generous. I'll ask around the area, see if anyone knows him while I wait for his address. I've a man who can slip in and out of a house without the owner never knowing he was there."

It was suddenly apparent why he no longer worked for Bow Street. Vane proceeded to give Joseph a description of his quarry, one that incorporated the words *fop* and *coward*.

"How soon do you want the information?" Joseph scratched

his head with the end of the pencil. "It will help to know how many men to put on the job."

"Find something of interest within the next twenty-four hours and I shall double your pay."

The man's eyes flashed with excitement. "By something of interest am I to take it you mean something shady?"

"Any information that might make a lady shun his company."

Joseph took a swig of ale from his tankard. "Anything else you need me to do?"

Vane was about to say no, but another idea entered his head. "Do you still have a man in France, in Calais?"

Joseph nodded. "Like I said before, he ain't cheap. And it won't be a quick job for obvious reasons."

"Do I look like a man who cares about money?" Vane paused. "The men I want him to track down are of a criminal element. I expect it will be dangerous."

"Dangerous you say. Do I look like a man who cares about that?" Joseph narrowed his gaze. "Are we talking smugglers then?"

"Find out everything you can about Monsieur and Madame Bonnay from Wissant. The woman died four years ago, and they found the man dead in the woods not long after. I should like to know who took over the smuggling operation. Find out if they have any family."

One of the smugglers had offered to marry Estelle, or so she'd said. Was that part of the reason she moved from place to place?

Vane pushed out of the chair and stood. "If you need to know anything else, send word to Wickett. Oh and have a man watch Lord Cornell's house in Bedford Square. I would like to know where he goes and what he does." Before Joseph could respond, Vane added, "I don't care how many men it takes or what the cost."

Joseph gave a curt nod. "At this rate, I'll be able to afford a fancy carriage of my own."

It was almost five o'clock when Vane returned to Berkeley Square. Bamfield greeted him at the door and with some reluctance informed him of the new arrival.

"His lordship is upstairs," Bamfield said with mild indifference. If butlers were as honest as coachmen, he might have added *making love to his wife.* "Lady Farleigh desired a change of clothes after the long journey."

The long journey? Everleigh was but twenty miles away.

Vane considered grabbing his hat and marching out of the door. Was this to be further punishment for his licentious past? Was he to spend a sleepless night listening to the sounds of true love knowing every encounter he'd ever had fell hopelessly short?

"I shall be in the drawing room for the time being. But ask Pierre to pack the necessaries. I intend to return to Hanover Square this evening."

He could not avoid his home forever. But it was the lesser of two evils. He would rather be tormented by painful memories than sit and witness exaggerated displays of affection.

Bamfield's expression remained impassive. "I shall convey your message at once, my lord. Might I ask if you will dine with Lord and Lady Farleigh this evening?"

The question drew his mind back to Estelle's meeting with Mr Hungerford. "No. I shall dine at my club." Vane doubted Farleigh would leave his bedchamber for the rest of the day. Besides, he had no intention of spending the night at home, not when he hoped to spy on Estelle.

The sweet sound of feminine laughter filtered down to the

hall. Lady Farleigh appeared on the top stair, accompanied by her besotted husband. Happiness radiated from her like a brilliant beacon. Farleigh looked different, too: content and thoroughly satisfied.

"Lord Trevane," Rose said as though pleased to see him. She came forward with graceful poise, grasped his hands and held them tightly. "Christian has been telling me all about your poor Miss Darcy. But isn't it wonderful that you've found her?"

Vane was about to offer a customary reply, but the sudden swelling of his heart gave him pause. *Wonderful* did indeed describe recent events. Painful but wonderful all the same.

"And I cannot tell you how thrilled I am to hear Lillian is wed," Rose continued. It seemed she had an ability to use one concise word to convey his feelings. He was just as *thrilled* for Lillian, too. "And it's good to know Lord Ravenscroft is not really a pirate."

"Indeed" was all Vane managed to say.

"Come," Rose said with some excitement, "let's sit in the drawing room and you can tell me all about Miss Darcy."

Vane glanced at Farleigh who mouthed a silent apology.

Rose threaded her arm through Vane's. "Oh, I know that's the last thing you want to talk about, but it might help to have a lady's perspective."

She was right. His thoughts and feelings were his own, and he had no intention of sharing them with anyone. But in the space of two minutes, Rose had proved to be remarkably perceptive. Perhaps she could offer useful advice to help him persuade Estelle to share her secrets.

"Rose shares my view," Farleigh informed, "that something untoward must have forced Miss Darcy to flee Prescott Hall."

"Indeed." Rose's gaze drifted over his face. "What reason could a lady have for not wanting to marry you?"

"I can think of a few."

Rose shrugged. "Yes, you can be quite frightening when in one of your morbid moods. Can't most men?"

Vane cleared his throat. "That wasn't what I had in mind but thank you for drawing my attention to an obvious flaw in my character."

Rose blushed. "Forgive me, I only meant—"

"I am teasing you," he said. "When it comes to flaws, patience is not a skill I have mastered. Nor do I have the ability to remain calm when anger burns hot inside."

So much for keeping his thoughts and feelings to himself. This lady possessed an ability to draw out the truth without him even putting up a fight.

Vane glanced at Farleigh as Rose led him into the drawing room. A smile formed when he noted his friend's crumpled cravat. The lord had obviously dressed in a hurry for he'd missed a button on his waistcoat, too.

While Farleigh visited the drinks table to pour them both a glass of brandy, Rose settled into the seat by the fire and gestured for Vane to sit opposite.

"I have decided to return to Hanover Square," Vane said before Rose brought up the subject of Estelle. Making the announcement aloud made it more difficult to change his mind.

Decanter in hand, Farleigh stopped pouring and glanced over his shoulder. "You're leaving here? May I ask why?"

Rose sat forward. "I don't suppose it feels like home when we arrive unannounced."

"This is your home, not mine," Vane said humbly. "You're free to do as you please and I'm grateful to Christian for providing an alternative place to stay when we returned from Italy."

The thought of going back to Hanover Square filled him with dread. The same frightful memory played over in his mind. Dawn approached as he ambled up the steps after a night spent in the company of Lady Monroe. The scent of exotic perfume clung to his clothes as did a whiff of stale tobacco. His butler, Marley, had long since gone to bed, and so Vane had let himself in with a key.

It was dark but not quiet.

The sound of whimpering drew him to the hunched figure sitting on the cold marble stairs. Upon hearing the door close, Lillian looked up. He would never forget her swollen face, blotchy red cheeks, and sad eyes ringed with black shadows. She jumped up and hurried down to the hall, flung her arms around his neck and sobbed as she told him of her ordeal.

It was his responsibility to protect his sister. But he'd been too occupied with trying to find a cure for his malaise, trying to cure the mental and physical discomfort that plagued him since losing Estelle.

"I am to blame," Rose said, dragging Vane from his reverie. "But with us being so recently married you see, I just couldn't stay away." She glanced at her husband, and one could not miss the sensual undertone in her smile.

From experience, Vane distrusted the look of love, but all those around him seemed determined to prove him wrong.

"No one is to blame," he said. "The time has come for me to return. I cannot avoid the place forever."

"The ghosts of the past only haunt us if we let them." Farleigh handed Vane a glass of brandy and moved to stand behind Rose. "I should know." He put a hand on Rose's shoulder, and she covered it with her own.

"Has Miss Darcy explained what prompted her to leave home and journey to France?" Rose spoke softly as though somehow lessened the impact of such a blunt question.

Vane cleared his throat. "I have yet to ask her."

"I see." Rose sat back in the chair.

Damnation. Despite having told this woman far too much

already, he had no intention of admitting he was too terrified to hear the truth. He should leave now.

"We all have our crosses to bear," Rose continued. "My father made life impossible, a living nightmare. Perhaps Miss Darcy's father did the same."

"Lord Ravenscroft was a kind-hearted man, too trusting of character." Vane's father had lured him into a mining venture that had little hope of success. Ravenscroft's losses were heavy. "But he loved his daughter."

A look akin to pity flashed in Rose's eyes. "Forgive me, but what we believe and what is true are two very different things. Let me tell you that a young lady does not leave her only means of security, be it emotional or financial, unless the consequences of staying outweigh the danger of leaving."

What the hell was she saying?

"So, Estelle would rather risk her life on a perilous voyage than marry me?" He had thought the same for years. But the way Estelle had looked at him, the way she'd kissed him at the coaching inn, convinced him she felt something.

Perhaps the injury to his head had muddled his mind.

"What Rose is trying to say," Lord Farleigh interjected, "is that perhaps another factor affected her decision. One that made it impossible to stay. Perhaps her father insisted she marry someone else. You told me once before, your father practically ruined Lord Ravenscroft. Perhaps he held a grudge. Perhaps you were the last person in the world he would permit his daughter to marry."

Vane shook his head. "Lord Ravenscroft was just as hurt and confused by Estelle's sudden departure." Her father blamed himself, rambled on about reading the signs, about misplaced trust.

"Then perhaps she doubted your loyalty."

Farleigh's comment struck like a sword to the heart.

"I would have done anything for her," Vane said fervently.

The immense power of the words filled his chest. Give him twenty rogues in an alley, and he could beat every one of them. He sat forward. "I would have given away my birthright, sheared sheep, farmed the land." His love for Estelle burst free of its shackles to flood his body with a warm glow. "She was my life, my love, my everything."

God damn. He'd not meant to say that aloud.

A pained silence filled the room.

Farleigh stared at him with pursed lips, although his solemn expression was soon replaced with a weak smile. "It's about time you were honest with yourself. Perhaps you can salvage something from this. Perhaps it's not too late."

He wanted to say that too much had happened, that they could never reclaim what they once had. He wanted to contradict any words spoken in pride, to say that a part of him would still sacrifice his life to save her.

Vane placed his drink on the side table and stood. "Thank you for your time and your hospitality." He took Rose's hand and bowed. "But I must see if Pierre is ready to leave. I have an evening appointment that I cannot miss."

Farleigh strode over to the drinks table and placed his glass on the tray. "I'll walk with you."

Vane was venturing as far as the hall, not heading out on a pilgrimage to Rome.

Once out in the hall, Farleigh stopped and put his hand on Vane's shoulder. "You're always welcome here and at Everleigh. I shall remain in town for a few days. Perhaps we might meet for supper tomorrow evening?"

Vane cared for this man like a brother. "What so you can press me to speak to Miss Darcy?"

"No, I thought I might challenge you to a game of chess. It is the only pastime I know of where I stand a chance of beating you." Farleigh offered a mischievous grin before adding, "But while we're on the subject of Miss Darcy, all I ask is that you open your heart to the possibility that she is still *your everything*."

Vane's throat grew so tight he could barely breathe. He tapped Farleigh on the upper arm. "Your wife is waiting. If anyone deserves happiness, it is you. All I ask is that you make every second count."

They parted ways. Vane did not wish to linger and so decided Wickett could return for Pierre. As he settled into his carriage, all thoughts should have been on his secret mission to spy on Estelle. Equally, he should have been imagining the multitude of ways he would hurt Lord Cornell.

But one feeling dominated all others.

He had never felt more alone in his entire life.

CHAPTER TEN

"Finish your broth, and then you must rest." Mr Erstwhile sat beside his wife's bed and stroked her brow.

Estelle had passed the open door on her way downstairs to wait for Mr Hungerford. She stopped to listen merely to gauge if they were keeping something from her and if Mrs Erstwhile suffered from a more serious illness than a fever and upset stomach. But the love and devotion expressed between the couple touched her heart, and she felt compelled to watch.

"I'm so weak," Mrs Erstwhile said. "It has been years since I felt so helpless."

Mr Erstwhile brought his wife's limp hand to his lips and pressed a kiss on her pale skin. "You will get better, my love. But you must believe it will be so. Besides, what on earth would I do here without you?"

A lump formed in Estelle's throat. In her experience, only a lucky few shared such a special connection.

"Do you remember the day we met, when you walked into the drawing room to lay the fire?" Mr Erstwhile said, feeding his wife a spoonful of broth. "You looked so nervous."

She swallowed down his offering. "I was terrified. It was my first day working for your father, and I tripped over the rug. You helped me to my feet." A warm smile lit up her face. "Always the gentleman."

"In that moment when our eyes locked something wonderful happened—something truly beautiful. It was as though I had finally come home."

"I remember."

"Then just as our love was worth fighting for, so you must fight to regain your strength."

"I will."

"Promise me you will try."

"I promise."

Estelle crept away but returned to her room instead of heading for the stairs. Once inside she settled on the bed, curled into a ball and hugged her legs to her chest.

Oh, Ross!

Once, her heart swelled with the same soul-deep love Mr Erstwhile spoke of. But she had made a terrible mistake. One that had cost her everything she held dear. While the Erstwhiles had the strength to fight for what mattered, she had been too weak to battle with two patriarchs. Too easily coerced and manipulated.

If only she could go back to that fateful day.

Yes, she had made the ultimate sacrifice for Ross, and for Fabian, too. And yet not a day passed when she wished she had thought of herself. But it was too late. A marquess did not marry a criminal no matter how blue her blood.

Tears welled in her eyes.

Why could she not forget? Why could she not learn to live in the present, instead of dwelling on the past? Those thoughts echoed through her mind until sleep brought her temporary peace.

Estelle woke to a knock on her door. Mr Erstwhile called out, "Miss Brown?"

"Yes" came her drowsy reply.

"Mr Hungerford is here."

"I'll be down in a moment."

The last thing she needed was to hear Mr Hungerford's declaration. The gentleman could be quite determined when he put his mind to something. If he refused to accept her answer, she could always catch the next mail coach heading north. Running away from Faucheux had saved her from a truly terrible existence. If she had the strength to refuse the Frenchman, she had the strength to do anything.

After washing her face and changing her dress, Estelle hurried downstairs.

Mr Hungerford stood in the shop conversing with Mr Erstwhile who was still obsessed with spying on those in the street. Perhaps he suspected the intruder was still watching the premises, waiting for another opportunity to strike.

"Mr Hungerford." Estelle approached and offered a smile.

The man looked pristine in his blue coat and mustard waistcoat. This evening he carried a silver-topped walking cane, though she doubted he had the courage to swing at Ross should the lord threaten him again.

"Miss Brown." He inclined his head. "You look delightful."

The gentleman was easily pleased. She wore a plain sapphire-blue dress that matched his coat to perfection and had tied her hair in a simple knot at her nape.

"Thank you. Will you stay for supper?"

"I thought we might go out for an hour. There's a new coffeehouse on St Martins Lane that seems quite popular."

"Will we get a seat? I imagine it will be rather crowded."

"I'm sure we will."

How different this man was from Ross. The thought drew her mind to Ross' insistence they be alone, to the intimate way he held her close, the scandalous manner in which he kissed away her tears. She could never embrace Mr Hungerford in the same way.

"Are you certain you do not wish to remain here, sir?"

A smile touched his lips. "Mr Erstwhile may accompany us if you'd feel more comfortable."

"Thank you for the offer," Mr Erstwhile interjected, "but I must sit with my wife this evening."

Mr Hungerford frowned. "I trust she is well."

"Just suffering from a touch of fever," Mr Erstwhile said with a smile, although Estelle noted the slight flash of fear in the poor man's eyes. "I would rather not leave her alone if it's all the same."

"Of course." Mr Hungerford turned to Estelle. "We shall walk to St Martins Lane, and if we cannot find a seat, we will return posthaste."

Estelle suppressed a sigh. Perhaps she should force a confession from the man now, but Mr Erstwhile had enough worries without upsetting his best customer.

"Then give me a moment to collect my jacket."

The sun was setting as they left, and still, the knife grinders and orange sellers were out touting for business.

They took a leisurely stroll to St Martins Lane. The slow pace meant but one thing. Mr Hungerford did not plan on remaining at the coffeehouse long. Indeed, it soon became apparent that their discussion was to take place during the journey.

What she found most odd was that he had made no mention of the incident earlier in the day, had not enquired how she knew a man as prestigious as the Marquess of Trevane.

"What has Mr Erstwhile told you about my late wife?" the

gentleman asked, suddenly changing the topic of conversation from that of tinctures and tonics to one of a more intimate nature.

"Only that she died four months ago, and that she had been ill for two years or more." No one mentioned the cause of the illness. "Was a diagnosis ever made?"

Mr Hungerford cast her a sidelong glance while walking. "As I know you will treat whatever I say with the utmost discretion, I must tell you that it was a condition of the mind as well as the body."

"Oh, I see." Estelle wasn't sure what to say. To ask questions might bring painful memories to the fore. "It must have been a worrying time."

"Indeed." He fell silent for a moment. "Do you like children, Miss Brown?"

The muscles in her abdomen tightened. Like carefully manoeuvred pieces on a chessboard, this line of questioning would eventually lead to the subject of marriage. Estelle suspected that regardless how she answered, he would agree with her opinion and find a way to turn it to his advantage.

"Who does not love children?" she said with some reservation.

"I hoped to be blessed with a large family and dreamed of moving to Bath where the air is clean and the streets much quieter." He sighed. "Alas, as the years pass I feel the dream slipping away."

"One must never give up hope, sir." The words left her mouth before she engaged her brain. It was the advice of a hypocrite.

"Do you like Bath, Miss Brown?"

"I have never been."

"Would you like to visit?"

"I can't say that I have given the matter much thought." Oh, the muscles in her shoulders ached from holding her body so tense, so rigid. "Besides, the Erstwhiles have been kind to me and need my assistance in the shop."

"Forgive me if this upsets you, but they will not be around forever. What will you do then? You owe it to yourself to plan for the future. A man as wise as Mr Erstwhile would expect nothing less."

Oh, Mr Hungerford had a way about him that made it impossible to contradict his opinion. Had she underestimated this affable, somewhat timid man?

"I deal with matters as and when they arise. Mr Erstwhile says that when one always looks to the future one misses the real beauty of life." Thank goodness for Mr Erstwhile's discerning gems.

"There is that I suppose." His tone revealed a reluctance to concede.

They walked a minute in silence. When they came upon Brandersons coffeehouse, it was clear from the queue at the door that any attempt to wait for a seat was futile. A raucous din burst from the packed premises whenever anyone opened the door. A lady would struggle to hear her internal voice let alone an expected proposal.

"It seems you were correct, Miss Brown." Mr Hungerford did not seem too disappointed. He waved his cane at a point further along the street. "Let us walk for a few minutes more. There is another place we might try."

A knot formed in Estelle's stomach. Were it not for the Erstwhiles' admiration of this man, she would have insisted they return to Whitecombe Street.

And so, against the nagging feeling in her chest, she continued to walk beside him.

To distract her mind, she started a conversation about the weather. The sun had set bringing a chill to the air made sharper by the sudden breeze. She mentioned the descending fog though he seemed unperturbed by the dangers it presented for those wandering the streets. For one so concerned with his health, he cared not that the odd spots of rain might lead to a downpour. Nor that the distant growl overhead threatened far worse. Indeed, at the first opportunity, he directed the conversation back to discovering more about her background.

"Do I recall you saying you had a brother, Miss Brown?"

She paused and swallowed down her reluctance to reply. "We are estranged and have been so for some time."

He appeared pleased by this snippet of information. "Either way, you strike me as a woman who does not need to ask for her brother's approval." He removed his pocket watch, squinted at the white face and then slipped it back into his waistcoat. "You know your own mind, and I admire that."

"Not all men think as you do," she said, hoping to steer the topic away from marriage.

"I'm a man who values his wife's opinion as much as his own."

Was that because he lacked the courage to make decisions? she wondered.

"If I have gained anything from my association with Mr Erstwhile," he continued, "it is that marriage works best when it is a partnership."

Marriage worked best when two people were in love.

A few fat droplets of rain landed on her sleeve. Mr Hungerford suddenly stopped near the narrow alley leading from St Martins to Castle Street. He drew her closer to the entrance, despite the yellow fog obscuring their vision.

"Would it be a terrible inconvenience if I escorted you home and accepted your generous offer of supper?" Mr Hungerford glanced behind him. "The weather is closing in, and it was foolish of me to insist we keep walking."

Estelle suppressed a groan at the thought of spending a few

more hours in his company. "Is it not a little late now? Mrs Erstwhile is ill, and I imagine they are settled for the evening. Perhaps we should hail a hackney cab and rearrange our outing some other time."

Mr Hungerford failed to hide his disappointment, tuts accompanied his muttered mumblings. "Oh, I have made a dreadful mess of everything."

"You cannot blame yourself for the sudden turn in the weather."

He removed his hat and turned to her. "Miss Brown, I know this is not the ideal place to speak so intimately, but I must tell you that I admire you greatly. Know that my intentions are honest and I fear I cannot delay. I wonder whether you might consider the possibility of becoming my wife." He released a lengthy exhale.

Estelle groaned inwardly. It was destined to be an uncomfortable journey home once she'd refused him. She braced herself in preparation to give the only response her conscience could allow.

A strange shuffling from somewhere in the alley forced her to glance back over her shoulder, and yet she could see nothing behind but a blanket of fog. The hairs on her nape prickled to attention which she imagined had something to do with the awkward situation.

"Mr Hungerford, I am truly flattered—"

He stepped closer and placed a gloved finger on her lips. Notes of expensive cologne reached her nostrils, the smell sickly as opposed to inviting. Nothing like the intoxicating scent of Ross' skin.

"Do not answer now. Take a few days. Imagine a life of contentment in Bath. I can make you happy, Miss Brown, if only you will let me."

Being cocooned in Ross Sandford's arms was the only place

she felt real joy.

Estelle nodded. When she returned home, she would pen a note explaining that she could not possibly accept.

An unexpected grunt from behind made her jump.

Someone grabbed her jacket and pulled her backwards. She opened her mouth on a scream, but a chubby hand smothered the sound. The sharp tip of a blade pressed into her back as the smell of ale and rotten breath breezed past her cheek.

The heavens opened then, and the rain pelted the pavement in an angry roar.

"Give me your purse, Monsieur, and then I shall let this pretty lady go." The thug spoke in a thick French accent, too deep to be Faucheux. Was he one of Faucheux's men?

Lord help them. Mr Hungerford was the sort to oblige rather than fight. Indeed, he reached into his coat pocket and retrieved a small pouch.

"Release her, and you shall have your prize."

"Throw it over now else you will be carrying home a corpse."

Hungerford did as the rogue requested. "Now release her at once." He seemed surprisingly confident, not the stuttering fool who had floundered under the weight of Ross' frigid stare.

The rogue sneered. "Perhaps I should have a little fun with the lady first, no?"

"The hell you will." Hungerford drew the sword from his walking cane and swiped the air, the action more like the exaggerated moves of an actor than a true buccaneer. "Perhaps you would care to fight me for the pleasure."

Mr Hungerford did not sound at all like himself. He possessed the courage of a drunken sot and yet hadn't had so much as a sip of coffee. But then his self-assured grin faded and his eyes grew wide, fearful.

The atmosphere changed.

A dark and dangerous energy pervaded the narrow space.

The rogue gasped and then a choking gurgle resonated in his throat.

"May I offer another suggestion?" Ross' charismatic voice drifted towards her. "Release the lady now else I shall cut your throat from ear to ear."

The clatter of metal hitting the ground gave Estelle the strength to rush forward. Once safely out of arm's reach, she whipped around to see her hero dressed head-to-toe in black. He stood behind the rogue, his expression as menacing as the Devil. A trickle of blood ran from where Ross pressed his knife against the rogue's throat. Rain lashed down upon them. Droplets dripped from the lock of hair hanging rakishly over Ross' brow.

"Let me at him," Mr Hungerford suddenly cried. "It is *my* honour he called into question."

"This is not about restoring honour," Ross chided. "What are you going to do? Challenge him to a duel?"

Hungerford slid the sword back into the sheath and handed the cane to Estelle. "I shall challenge him to a fistfight for the insult he has shown to Miss Brown."

"Good God, man, he dug a knife into her back. Bow Street is the only place for him. After we've had a little scuffle, of course, where I will be forced to break his nose."

"*Non*! Please, Monsieur," the rogue blurted. "It is not my fault. I did not—"

"Be quiet, you devil." In a shocking and highly uncharacteristic move, Mr Hungerford darted forward and slapped the rogue about the face. "We have no interest in anything you have to say."

Ross dropped his hand and stepped back. "Then have at him if it eases your conscience." The rogue raised his fists but then turned on his heels and fled the alley. A muttered string of curses left Ross' lips. "Damnation. Now I've no choice but to chase after him."

"I shall go. This is my fault after all." Mr Hungerford snatched back his cane and darted off in pursuit before Estelle could catch her breath.

Estelle stared at Ross for a moment. From the frown marring his brow, he appeared equally confused by Mr Hungerford's odd behaviour. "Were you following me?"

"In a manner of speaking, yes." He slipped his blade back into the sheath tucked into his boot, brushed the wet lock of hair back off his brow and came towards her. "No doubt you're rather glad I did."

"I have never been more pleased to see you." Her bonnet shielded her eyes from the rain, but water dripped from the tip of her nose.

He cupped her cheek with his bare hand, used the pad of his thumb to wipe the rain from her chin. "Are you all right?"

"I'm fine. The rogue wanted money that's all."

"Perhaps."

"Are you going to tell me what you're doing here?"

"Isn't it obvious?"

"Not to me."

A satisfied smile played on his lips. He looked so sinfully handsome. Lord help her. Would she ever be able to look at him and not feel love in her heart, or lust in her loins?

"So you did not see me stalking you?"

In truth, she had been so focused on avoiding the subject of marriage she had thought of nothing else. "No, I did not see you."

They stared at each other, ignoring the rain. She wondered what he was thinking, wondered why he had come.

"I should get you home before you catch your death of cold." Ross gestured to a point beyond the mist. "My carriage is waiting on Castle Street."

"But what about Mr Hungerford? We cannot leave him." It

suddenly occurred to her that the poor fellow might have caught the Frenchman. "What if he's lying injured in the gutter?"

"I can assure you he will return unharmed."

Ross sounded so confident. Perhaps he knew something she didn't. Perhaps Mr Hungerford was more skilled with a sword than she'd given him credit.

As if on cue, the clip of booted footsteps reached her ears. Mr Hungerford appeared at the entrance to the alley. He stopped, gripped the wall and bent his head as if all the air was spent from his lungs.

"Mr Hungerford." Estelle rushed to his side. "Are you well? Did you catch the rogue?"

"I … I'm afraid not," he gasped. His cheeks were berry-red, and his chest heaved at far too rapid a rate. "The scoundrel was too … too light on his feet, although I whacked him on the back with my cane."

"You hit him with your stick?" Ross mocked. "How brave."

"He was too quick for me. The man is skilled in the art of fleeing a crime."

Ross folded his arms across his broad chest. "Perhaps we should visit Bow Street, recount the event and describe the culprit."

With a quizzical expression, Mr Hungerford inhaled deeply and said, "I cannot remember much about him. All thieves look the same. Besides, Miss Brown is soaked to the skin. I should see her home before she catches a chill."

"*I* shall escort Miss Brown home," Ross insisted.

"I would not be a gentleman if I neglected in my duty to deliver Miss Brown directly to her front door."

Ross straightened. "Perhaps you suffer from an impediment and did not hear me the first time."

"Enough of this," Estelle said with some frustration. "Do not speak about me as if I were not here." Considering the sodden state of their clothes, the inclement weather and the late hour there seemed to be only one solution. "Lord Trevane has his carriage and will see us all safely home."

A smile touched Ross' lips accompanied by a look that suggested he had expected her to come to that conclusion. "After suffering at the hands of that scoundrel, we should adhere to Miss Brown's wishes."

Mr Hungerford sighed. How could he refuse? "Very well. Lead the way."

When they exited the alley into Castle Street, Wickett was loitering on the pavement, the collars of his coat raised to shield him from the rain. He opened the carriage door and waited for them to climb inside. "Where to, my lord?"

"We will take Hungerford home first." Ross settled into the seat opposite Estelle as Mr Hungerford had already claimed the seat beside her. Ross stared at the gentleman in question. "What is your direction?"

"Perhaps we should take Miss Brown home. She is cold and still shaken after her ordeal. I can walk from there."

"I am perfectly fine, sir. I assure you I have a robust constitution." Heavens, she had lost count how many times the smugglers had fought each other with knives. She'd lost count the number of times she had to run and hide from the revenue men knowing they would string her up if they got their hands on her.

Ross clenched his jaw. "My conscience demands I see you to your front door. You chased the attacker, and I would know you arrived home safely."

Estelle considered Ross with some suspicion. He didn't give a damn about Mr Hungerford, which meant he had an interest in discovering where he lived.

Intrigued by Ross' sudden interest, and despite it being somewhat rude, she answered for the gentleman. "Take us to James Street. Mr Hungerford lives at number twenty-eight."

CHAPTER ELEVEN

The carriage rattled along Castle Street on its way to take Mr Hungerford home. Vane sat back in the dark confines of his conveyance and let the immense feeling of satisfaction wash over him.

First, he had followed Estelle without her noticing him. A skill he'd acquired while navigating the backstreets of St Giles looking for a fight.

Even more satisfying was the fact he knew of Hungerford's game. Vane would wager everything he owned that Hungerford was acquainted with the Frenchman who had set upon them in the alley. Indeed, the man was as craven as Lord Cornell, and yet he'd chased the scoundrel through the fog-drenched streets without a second thought.

To add to Vane's bounty, he now knew Hungerford's address and in a matter of minutes would boot the coward out onto the pavement and leave the rest to the runner, Mr Joseph. The true prize of the night was having Estelle to himself on the journey back to the apothecary shop.

Vane glanced at the lady in question. With her gaze fixed firmly on the window, she watched the rain trickle down the pane.

Mr Hungerford sat sulking. Anger brimmed beneath his affable facade but he wouldn't know what to do if he ever found the strength to unleash the devil.

They turned into James Street and the vehicle jerked to a halt beside a row of townhouses. Mr Hungerford's abode was of modest proportion, three floors high although too narrow by Mayfair's standards. Vane could not imagine Estelle living here. She loved riding across open countryside, loved painting in a natural habitat, loved picnics in the orchard and strolling through buttercup fields.

"Should you change your mind about visiting Bow Street, Hungerford, do let me know." Vane couldn't resist ruffling the man's feathers.

"As I said, I see little point in wasting their time," Hungerford replied. "The blackguard will be long gone by now." He turned to Estelle. "Perhaps we could take a picnic to the park tomorrow, Miss Brown."

"What, in the rain?" Vane mocked.

"If the weather is fine," Hungerford added. "If not, then we could return to the coffeehouse." The man was persistent. Vane would give him that. "Perhaps you might be inclined to discuss my proposal."

Estelle cast Vane a furtive glance before considering the fop seated next to her. "Call into the shop tomorrow, and I shall let you know then." One would have to be blind to miss the reluctance in her eyes, and the rigid reservation in her bearing.

"I'll see you safely inside, Hungerford." Vane threw open the carriage door and stepped down to the pavement. Rain lashed his face and bounced off his boots.

Hungerford muttered something incoherent. "I am quite capable of walking, my lord, quite capable of fending off an attack."

"Oh, I don't doubt it." Vane followed the dandy as he hurried under cover of his portico and waited while he retrieved his key from his coat pocket. "But now we're alone is there not something you wish to ask me?"

Hungerford turned to look at him, but his green eyes flitted back and forth nervously in their sockets. "There ... there is a matter I would discuss, but your position demands I keep my lips tightly buttoned." His cheeks flushed as red as the ridiculous claret coat he'd worn.

"Then allow me to assist you. You want to know of my intentions towards Miss Brown." Vane glanced at his conveyance to witness Estelle staring back at him.

"Well, I imagine *my* intentions are obvious, though yours are baffling. Miss Brown possesses too much integrity to be any man's mistress."

"You think I want her as my mistress?" It was a fair assumption given his position.

"Don't you?" Hungerford raised a brow. "I have seen the intense longing in your eyes when you look at her."

"Perhaps I want her for my wife." Vane spoke merely for the thrill of annoying the gentleman. And yet he was surprised to find the idea had already taken root and the first buds were beginning to appear on this new tree of hope.

Hungerford scoffed. "A marquess does not marry a shopgirl."

"Neither does a gentleman."

"Miss Brown is unlike any woman I have ever met."

"In that, we are agreed."

Vane did not bother to offer a parting greeting but simply turned and strode back to his carriage. He informed Wickett of their direction and the message he was to pass to Mr Joseph when they arrived in Whitechapel. Once inside, Vane settled into the seat opposite Estelle, dragged his hand down his wet face and waited to hear the question ready to burst from her lips.

"What did you say to Mr Hungerford?"

"Nothing." The sodden sleeves of his coat stuck to his shirt, the cold seeping into his skin. He sat forward and shrugged out of the garment. "You should remove your jacket before you catch a chill."

"You clearly said something. I watched your lips move."

"Hungerford wanted to know what my intentions are where you're concerned."

Vane tugged at his shirt sleeves as the material was plastered to his arms. He could feel the heat of her stare drifting over him, caught her ogling his biceps as they strained against the restrictions of the fabric.

"And what was your reply?" Lacking dexterity, which he attributed to cold fingers, she managed to unfasten the buttons on her jacket. She slipped it off her shoulders and placed it on the seat next to her.

Vane ignored the question. He wasn't ready to address his feelings just yet, and fear of rejection forced him to remain silent.

He rubbed his hands together to banish the cold. "Had I known it would be this bitter, I'd have had Wickett heat the bricks. There's a blanket in the box beneath the seat should you need it."

"Did you threaten him?" She removed her bonnet and shook off the droplets of rain.

"Who?"

"Mr Hungerford." Her tone carried more than a hint of frustration.

"Why would I do that?"

Estelle shrugged. "How should I know when I haven't the faintest idea what you're thinking? I haven't the faintest idea where you're taking me, either, though I know it is most definitely not Whitecombe Street."

Vane liked that she found him unreadable, unpredictable. "I need to make a slight detour. Wickett has a message to deliver to my man in Whitechapel. But have no fear, we shall remain in the carriage."

That meant he had her alone for at least thirty minutes, more if he instructed Wickett to take his time. And he would rather travel the foggy streets than return to the empty house in Hanover Square.

Silence ensued.

She did not press him on the subject of Mr Hungerford, nor did he ask if she would accept the man's proposal. The answer was abundantly clear.

"Well," she began, "if we're here for a while it seems foolish to sit in silence. What would you like to discuss?"

Numerous questions flitted through his mind. None of them drew his thoughts away from the vibrant energy that thrummed in the air whenever they were alone. None of them captured his attention like the rise and fall of her breasts, like the full lips formed into a pout.

Hell, this woman had a power over him even he could not comprehend.

"So, you're keen to satisfy my voracious appetite for conversation." He imagined she could please him on many levels.

The corners of her mouth twitched. "I have the feeling nothing could satisfy you, my lord."

You could. You're the only woman who can tame me.

"Then ask me a question, Estelle. Allow me to put your oral skills to the test."

She swallowed audibly as her breath came a little quicker.

Excellent.

"Very well." She straightened as if preparing for battle. "Why have you never married?"

"Do you want the truth?"

"Of course."

"Because after what happened eight years ago I could never

trust another woman. And you know my feelings on marriage and fidelity." He would have been faithful to her as long as he lived. And therein lay the irony of the man he'd become.

She placed a trembling hand on her collarbone. "But you have had relations with women?"

"I'm not a monk. I've not taken a vow of celibacy." *And I thought you were dead.*

"No," she whispered. "I didn't expect you had."

Vane leant back against the squab as one question suddenly burned within. "And what about you? You say you never married but have you ever had relations with a man?" It was an impertinent question, one a gentleman would never dare ask a lady. But he felt he'd earned the right to know.

She looked to her lap and sighed—and there was his answer.

The blood in his veins turned ice-cold. She was his, always had been, always would be. To know she'd given herself to another was like a cleaver hacking at his heart. God, if there was one thing he despised it was his own damn hypocrisy.

"Did you love him?" he heard himself say, though he was still rolling on a metaphorical floor, writhing in pain, twisting in agony.

She grew suddenly restless, refused to look at him as she rocked back and forth in her seat. "This was a mistake. Stop the carriage. I want to get out." She reached for the handle.

"Wait!" Panic flared. "You'll fall to your death."

Her hand settled over the metal.

Vane lurched forward and grabbed her wrist. "You can't get out here."

"I don't care." Tears filled her eyes as she tried to wriggle out of his grasp. "Let me go."

He grabbed her around the waist and pulled her across the carriage and into his lap. She fought him at first, kicked the side and tugged the curtain on the viewing window.

And still, Wickett did not take it as a signal to stop.

Vane wrapped his arms around her and held her close. "Whatever it is, you can tell me." It would kill him to hear her story, but her needs had always come before his own.

She squirmed in his lap and punched his chest, the hollow sound drowned out by her sudden sob. "I can't."

Fear turned to anger. When she'd mentioned someone hurt her, surely she had not meant— He shook his head to banish the thought from his brain.

"Tell me what happened, Estelle." How he kept his voice calm, he would never know. "Confide in me."

"I was a fool … a fool who forgot how some men treat their maids," she blurted. "I thought he was a friend."

"Who?"

"Philipe Robard." She gulped for breath. "The … the merchant's son."

Vane kissed the top of her head to bring her comfort, and to stop him from raising the roof with a barrage of vitriolic curses. "Are you telling me he forced you?"

"It all happened so quickly." She curled into his lap and pressed her cheek to his chest. "I hit him with a chamber pot, ran down the stairs and out of the house and never looked back."

Philipe Robard was a dead man. He just didn't know it yet.

One question filled Vane's mind. The words stuck to his tongue like a bitter taste that he desperately needed to expel. "Was … was there a child?"

Please say no.

Her head shot up, and her red, puffy eyes settled on him. "Heavens, no."

Relief coursed through his veins.

"I hit him almost as soon as—" She cut off abruptly but he did not need to hear any more.

"And where will I find Monsieur Robard? In Paris?"

"Find him?" Estelle blinked in surprise. "Why?"

"Why do you think?"

"No, Ross." She shook her head. "I want to forget about Robard. I want to pretend the incident never happened."

He would not forget. At some point in the very near future, he would travel to Paris. Once there, he would find the scoundrel and beat him so severely he would never regain the full use of his manhood.

"Please, Ross." Estelle put a hand on his cheek, and he resisted the urge to close his eyes and relish the connection. "There was nothing you or I could have done to prevent it. I told you because you asked and because you were honest with me. But please, put it from your mind."

"You ask the impossible."

"Can you not understand?" Both dainty hands cupped his face now. "I want to leave all of that behind me." Her face was so close he could feel her sweet breath breeze across his lips. "How can I do that if you won't let me? Please, you must allow me to move on."

"When you say *move on* what you really mean is *run away*." Vane stared into her sad eyes. "Will you ever stop running, Estelle?"

She fell silent for a moment. "How can I? How can I stop when I don't have the courage to face the truth?"

Vane wasn't sure what she was referring to, but she gazed longingly at his mouth as her thumbs stroked his cheeks. He knew enough about women to know she wanted him and so he took a leap of faith.

"And what is the truth? Do you regret leaving Prescott Hall?"

Do you regret leaving me?

She swallowed visibly. "I regret it more than you will ever know."

"Why?" They were finally getting somewhere.

131

"Because I lost the respect and friendship of someone dear to me." She bent her head and pressed her lips to his in a chaste kiss. "I lost you."

Had Estelle been sitting opposite he might have asked questions, probed her for more information. But her soft buttocks were but an inch away from his throbbing cock. The mere touch of her lips roused his desire, and he was lapping her comment up like a thirsty dog did a puddle of rainwater.

"What do you want from me?" Vane whispered. He cupped her neck, drew her mouth to his and kissed her with a passion reserved only for this woman. Leaving her in no doubt of his intentions.

"We cannot go back to how things were. Too much has happened. Our lives are so different now." She moistened her lips. "But you're the only man I have ever wanted. I would like to know you, Ross, to know the pleasure that comes when two people share a special bond, a deep connection."

The devil on his shoulder rubbed his hands gleefully, eager for an opportunity to sate his curiosity, to know if joining with her would be everything he imagined it to be. The saint in him raised his hands to the heavens and prayed for caution. What if this experience made him want her all the more? If she left again how would he cope? But he was too weak to deny his body, too weak to deny his heart.

Holding her tightly to his chest, Vane leant forward and tugged down the blinds.

"Then kiss me again, Estelle. Convince me this is truly what you want."

She sat up, shuffled to straddle him. "I need you, Ross. Help me to forget every painful memory." She claimed his mouth in a ravenous assault, teased his lips apart and delved inside. It was as though she could not taste him deeply enough, as though she was famished and he was her only sustenance.

The wild, erotic dance of their tongues sent the blood rushing to his cock. He'd never been so hard, never been so eager to consummate an alliance. The sudden urge to feel every inch of her took hold. Frantic hands traced the curve of her hips, gripped her buttocks and drew her against the evidence of his arousal.

A moan escaped her lips.

Good God.

His mind was lost in a heady cloud of lust, of desire. It surrounded him, flowed through his body in pleasurable waves.

"We should be at home in bed, naked," he murmured against her mouth. "Where I can worship your body as you deserve." But in truth, the urgency to fill her full eradicated all thoughts of a more thorough seduction.

"I cannot wait, Ross. If we stop now … I …"

He heard the unspoken words. This might be his only opportunity to have her. The dream to possess her still lived inside him. This was about claiming what he craved, surrendering to the light, admitting she was his only weakness now.

"Just tell me you want me." Vane's voice sounded gravelly, hoarse. He tugged at the hem of her dress, slid his hands underneath, up past the top of her stockings. "Let me hear you say the words."

"You know I want you. It has always been you."

That was his undoing.

"Then forgive me, for I lack the strength of will to prolong this moment." Never had he imagined himself saying those words. "I need to be inside you. Deep inside you. Undo my breeches."

He did not have to ask twice.

She shuffled back as her trembling fingers fumbled with the buttons. A growl rumbled in his chest when her small hand dipped inside. She hesitated, but then her fingers settled around his cock and freed him from his constraint.

"Hurry," she begged.

His mind was too muddled to think. The potent essence of this woman filled his head. The need to drive home obliterated all else.

Estelle dragged up her dress, her erratic movements and laboured breathing a clear sign of her eagerness to join with him, too.

He positioned himself at her entrance. Heaven was but inches away. "I cannot wait a second longer," he panted.

"Do it now, Ross."

With one hand settling firmly on her waist, he pushed inside her in one long fluid movement, up to the hilt.

Time stopped.

Buried deep inside her hot, wet core, Vane held her there and allowed himself a few seconds to appreciate the magic of the moment. His heart sang in celebration.

"Oh, Ross." Estelle's head fell back.

Never had he seen anything more beautiful. She belonged to him. Long before the first time his heart pulsed upon seeing her. Long before they ever met.

He withdrew slowly only to plunge back into her welcoming body. Estelle gasped and arched her back, her breasts rising against the confines of the material. Oh, how he wanted to free them, to tease her nipples to peak, to feast like a king. She ran her hands over his shoulders and balled his shirt in her fists.

Vane could sense she wasn't sure what to do. Hell, her inexperience beguiled him—only made him want her all the more. He would be her tutor from now on, and he would await each lesson with eager anticipation.

And so he settled his hands on her hips, ready for the first exercise in a course that would last an eternity, and guided her movements until she rode him in a unique yet intoxicating rhythm.

"Oh God." Vane watched her come up on her knees and sink back down again and again. "That's it, love. Just like that."

He met her with equal enthusiasm. His measured thrusts became more urgent, more powerful than the last. With Estelle, he didn't need to think of new or novel ways to please her. He didn't have to pretend this was the most erotic experience of his life—for it truly was. All he cared about was watching the look of pleasure on her face as he filled her body.

"Don't stop," she panted.

"Trust me. That is not an option."

Every delicious slide into heaven took him closer to the edge. He reached between them, managed to push two fingers against her intimate place. Estelle responded to his touch, rubbing against him in a delightfully erratic fashion.

"Hmm. Ross." Her tongue skimmed her lips. He wanted to devour her mouth but he would stroke her to completion before taking anything more for himself.

"Come for me, love."

She was the only woman he wanted to come against his fingers, the only woman he wanted to pump his cock with each tremor of her climax.

She reached behind him and held on to the seat, rocked her hips and ground against him, massaging his solid member in the process.

She gasped, shuddered, came apart on a pleasurable sigh.

Vane could no longer keep his passion contained. "Ride me, love."

As her tremors subsided, Estelle did as he asked, taking him deep inside her, raising up, and sheathing him again and again. Her wicked mouth covered his, hot and demanding, every stroke of her tongue sending him wild.

"I need to withdraw," he somehow managed to say. But he

wished he could push her onto her back, cover her body and drive long and hard. "When I do, I need you to touch me."

She raised herself high enough for him to disengage. "What now?" she said, still straddling his thighs.

"Now," he breathed.

Estelle gripped his shaft and he covered her hand with his own and showed her how to stroke him. Every muscle in his body tensed. Vane jerked his hips, pushing his cock through her dainty fingers. He came over the soft skin of her palm—so damn hard he almost choked.

His guttural groan drowned out the patter of rain on the carriage roof. He reached into his coat and gave her his handkerchief, watched in awe as she cleaned herself and then looked at him.

The ripples of pleasure still coursed through his body. Their ragged pants filled the air. Estelle leant forward and touched her forehead to his. A deep sense of satisfaction enveloped him, coupled with a feeling of peace he had never known. This was the only place in the world he wanted to be.

A place he was destined to visit.

A place he was determined to remain.

CHAPTER TWELVE

E stelle closed her eyes and relished the closeness of Ross' body. They sat touching foreheads until their breathing settled. Never had she felt so sated, so blissfully happy. During the moment of intense pleasure, she had almost professed her love, but she knew that her eagerness stemmed from her heightened senses.

Ross sighed contentedly, and his breath breezed over her cheek. At some point, she would have to move. But in the intimacy of the moment, the rest of the world no longer existed. Like this, it was easy to forget they had spent any time apart.

Estelle raised her head and kissed him once on the lips. Oh, his taste was so addictive. "I should straighten my clothes before we reach Whitecombe Street, though I have no idea where we are."

During the wildly passionate encounter, she had been so lost in loving Ross she hadn't considered that they were rattling along in his carriage.

A sinful smile touched his lips. "We were to stop in Whitechapel." He looked so calm, so sated, not at all like the devil who stormed into Mr Erstwhile's shop to demand answers.

She climbed off Ross' muscular thighs and fell into the seat opposite. Embarrassment pushed to the fore, replaced by a flutter of desire when she watched him tuck his impressive manhood back into his breeches and fasten the buttons.

Ross shuffled forward and raised the blind nearest to her. He studied the passing houses for a moment.

"It seems Wickett has run his errand and we are on our way home."

Estelle heard him speak, but her mind was engaged in an internal conversation. After surrendering to her craving for this man, her body felt different. A little sore and tender in places, and blissfully in tune with the universe. But this state of euphoria would fade. And then she would have to face the stark reality that she loved a man she could never have. The intense longing would never leave her and would only be compounded now, having sampled the true magnificence of this man.

Despite his comment to the contrary, Ross would marry eventually. They were both intelligent enough to know that any children born from their alliance would always bear the mark of her shame. And Ross could not beat every member of the *ton* into submission.

Estelle brushed her skirt and tucked the loose strands of hair behind her ears.

Silence ensued.

Ross' intense gaze settled on her face. "What are we to do now?" he said in a rich drawl.

"Do?" Her pulse rose a notch. "Why must we do anything?"

"Then allow me to rephrase the question. Are you still intent on leaving London after what has just occurred?"

How could she answer when she didn't know what to do anymore?

"By your own admission you have had relations with other

women," she said, choosing to be aloof as a means of self-preservation. "How is this any different?"

"How is it different!" he repeated, seemingly unimpressed with her answer. "Please tell me you're joking. Eight years may have passed, but the same raging need flows through our veins."

"What happened brought us both comfort at a time—"

"Trust me. *Comfort* was not what I tasted on your lips. *Comfort* is not what I felt when thrusting inside you, nor when you panted my name and shuddered in my arms."

She shivered at the delicious memory, wishing she could go back to the beginning and relive it all over again. "You're right. It meant more than that." The perfect moment would live forever in her heart. She would embrace it during long, lonely nights. "What do you propose we do?"

For the first time, she witnessed a look of panic mar his handsome features. "Do?" It passed quickly, replaced by a wicked glint in his eyes. "I propose we return to Hanover Square. I propose we spend the next week in bed and take matters from there."

So it was lust, not love, then.

"Have you forgotten that I have work to do in the shop? I cannot abandon the Erstwhiles, not while Mrs Erstwhile is unwell."

She wasn't saying no even though she knew she should.

"Estelle, while I admire your loyalty to them, you no longer need to work for a living."

Anger erupted. Such an intelligent man should know better than to preach nonsense. "Oh, and what do you suggest I do, my lord? Perhaps I should call my man of business and ask him to increase the rents. Perhaps I might sell the family jewels to give me an income while I sit about idle."

"A man is not idle because he owns land," he admonished. "And you would want for nothing if you stayed with me."

The comment robbed her of breath. Good Lord, her worst fears had come to pass. Ross did not see her as a woman of equal status—not anymore.

"So you're proposing I become your mistress."

"Mistress?" He seemed confused.

"That is the name for a woman who has intimate relations with a man who supports her financially."

She should not scoff at the offer. A mistress was all she could hope for should anyone discover the truth about her scandalous time in France. If only she could forget this man, move away to the country and take a husband, raise a family and let society believe she had perished in the shipwreck.

"Are you saying you would accept the offer should I be inclined to make it?" Ross sat forward awaiting her answer with a look of keen interest.

"The fact you have asked the question means you do not know me at all."

Ross snorted. "Forgive me for thinking that the eight years we've spent apart has changed us irrevocably. How am I to know what you think or want when you keep so many secrets?" He dragged his hand down his face and sighed. "The lady I remember would not have permitted me to make love to her in a carriage."

Estelle gasped at the implication that she was somehow loose with her affections. She had given up everything so that this man could sit on his gilded throne.

"You self-righteous ass," she spat. Anger bubbled away inside, but it was merely a reaction to years of hurt. "I permitted you to make love to me because you're the only man I have ever wanted. You're the only man I would ever willingly give myself to, and yet you have to ruin what would have been a beautiful memory."

Ross gulped at her sudden outburst, shock tainting his features. "Estelle, I did not mean it like that. I was—"

"I don't care how you meant it. Clearly, we are different people now, but I do not need you to remind me of my shortcomings." Estelle glanced out of the window, relief flooding through her when she noted the familiar surroundings of Whitecombe Street. "If tonight proves anything it is that we cannot live for the past."

The carriage slowed. The wheels were still rolling when she grabbed the handle.

"You're beginning to sound as philosophical as Mr Erstwhile," Ross mocked. "Why do I get the sense this is all my fault? So I spoke thoughtlessly. Forgive me for being human. Forgive me if I fail to understand what the hell is going on."

The carriage stopped, and she opened the door. Despite the torrential rain, she stepped down to the pavement. Tears welled. The memory of what could have been, pushed to the fore. She could have been his wife not his whore.

"It is not your fault, Ross." Estelle turned to face him. "It is mine. I was too weak to fight for us. I was too frightened to do anything but surrender to those who professed to have our best interests at heart. And I will spend my life living with that regret."

The dam burst. Tears fell. She swung around, rushed to the front door of the apothecary shop and hammered hard with her fist.

"Estelle, wait." Ross jumped down and came up behind her.

"Leave me be." She knocked again. "Go home, Ross."

The soft glow of candlelight appeared and drew closer to the door. Mr Erstwhile peered through the glass pane. He raised his hand in recognition. "Just a moment."

"I should have stayed in France. I should have stayed away."

"Come back to the carriage." Ross gripped her shoulder. His touch almost made her yield. "Talk to me. Tell me what the hell just happened. Tell me how we have gone from sharing a heavenly experience to this."

Mr Erstwhile turned the key and sheltered behind the door as he opened it. "Heavens above, come inside before you catch your death of cold."

Estelle stepped over the threshold. She turned and placed her palm on Ross' chest when he attempted to follow her. "Good night, my lord. Thank you for escorting me home."

"Wait. At least explain what you meant when you said you were frightened," he said as she closed the door. "Estelle!"

Estelle turned the key before Ross had an opportunity to try the handle. She hurried from the shop to the small parlour, aware that Mr Erstwhile traipsed slowly behind.

A cloud of confusion filled her head.

Love was not always perfect—she knew that. Love often required a sacrifice. But she would rather be without Ross than be his mistress. She would rather be without him than be made to feel inferior. She paced back and forth while wringing her hands. Ross called out to her again, his voice but a faint mumble now.

"Would you care for some tea?" Mr Erstwhile, said ignoring Ross' pleas. "Or would something stronger suffice?"

"Do you have sherry?"

"Indeed." He glanced over his shoulder upon hearing Ross rattling the shop door. "His lordship seems rather insistent this evening."

"He will leave in a moment."

"Perhaps he wishes to return your jacket and bonnet."

Estelle ran her hand over her hair and glanced at her dress. In her hurry to leave the carriage she had forgotten her clothes. "We were caught in the rain. They were wet, and I removed them as I did not want to catch a chill."

"A wise decision."

"I'm sure his lordship will return them tomorrow."

Mr Erstwhile pursed his lips. His inquisitive gaze journeyed over her face. "Will you be here tomorrow, Estelle, or will you be on the next mail coach to heaven knows where?"

The insightful comment caught her short. "Why … why do you say that?"

"I may be old, but I am not blind. The day we met aboard the ship it was clear you were running from something." He paused. "Now sit by the fire and warm yourself. Ideally, you should change out of those damp clothes. But I fear that if you go to your room, I might never see you again."

"A lady cannot run forever." Estelle dropped into the seat, picked up the poker and prodded the coal.

Mr Erstwhile smiled. "Then I shall pour us both a sherry before you beat the lumps of coal to powder." He ambled over to the decanters on the sideboard, poured two drinks and returned to sit by the fire.

"To whom or what shall we make a toast?" he said, raising his glass. "To friends and family wherever they may be. To love, for there is nothing finer in this world than two souls who belong together."

With mild enthusiasm, Estelle raised her glass in salute. "To Fate for being a sly, conniving devil."

They both took a sip of sherry. Estelle wanted to drain the contents in the hope it would calm her erratic emotions, but in some things, she was still a lady.

"How is Mrs Erstwhile this evening?" Estelle said by way of a distraction.

"Oh, much better. She should be up and about tomorrow with any luck."

Silence ensued.

They stared at the flames for a while and sipped their drinks.

"Do you know what is strange?" Mr Erstwhile eventually said in the tone of a constable from Bow Street. "For the second time in two days, you have left the shop with Mr Hungerford and returned with Lord Trevane. I trust Hungerford acted the gentleman, and it was his lordship's overbearing nature that led to this sudden change in circumstance."

"You think Lord Trevane is overbearing?" she said defensively. She supposed Ross might appear arrogant, a little forceful of manner, but weren't all deeply passionate men the same?

"He did admit to threatening Mr Hungerford." Mr Erstwhile shook his head. "I cannot help but wonder what poor Mr Hungerford makes of it all. Equally puzzling is why a marquess is willing to brawl in the street for you, Estelle."

Mr Erstwhile never used her given name and yet he'd made a point of stressing it twice now.

"Ah, I see the flicker of surprise in your eyes," he continued. "After tonight, it is fair to assume that while Estelle is your name, clearly Miss Brown is not."

Fear wrapped around her heart like a vine. This kind, honest man deserved to hear the truth.

"It was never my intention to deceive you." She spoke slowly and with reservation. "But I could not return to London without assuming a false identity."

Mr Erstwhile finished the remainder of his sherry and placed the glass on the table next to him.

"Falsehoods occur when one is hiding from the truth." He stroked his white beard. "As an observer, the truth is that you were once in love with the marquess, and he was very much in love with you. From your elegant bearing, clearly you're from *good stock*, as the matrons like to say. And so I must assume a terrible tragedy occurred. One that led to your separation."

"I have lived in a constant state of mourning these last eight years," she said softly. "Losing one's true love evokes a pain deeper than any physical wound."

"In that, we are agreed. I too struggled in turmoil for a while until I followed my heart." He sat forward. "That same turmoil is like a tempest raging through you, shaking your branches. But the time for honesty is nigh. To understand a problem, one must dig down to the roots for more often than not the issue lies there."

Estelle contemplated his comment.

Her problems began the moment she received an ultimatum and invariably made the wrong choice. Everything that happened afterwards was merely a consequence of that one action. It was too late to rekindle what was lost. Even so, she owed it to Ross, to Fabian and to herself to tell the truth.

Estelle stood, and Mr Erstwhile followed. "The time for introductions is long overdue." She inclined her head. "Sir, my name is Estelle Darcy, sister to Baron Ravenscroft, and a lady lost these past eight years."

A smile touched the old man's lips. He bowed. "Miss Darcy. Thankfully, you have found your way home at long last."

The word *home* roused a flutter in her stomach. The odd feeling came to settle in her chest, warm and comforting. England was home. She had lived by many names, had been but a ghost of her former self, but she owned the name Darcy.

Mr Erstwhile gestured to the chair, and they both sat.

"Some might think it an accident that we stumbled upon his lordship in the alley," Mr Erstwhile said. "But I am more inclined to believe Fate guided our way."

Many times since that night, she had pondered the same thing, too.

"Then Fate is cruel, sir, for nothing can eradicate the last eight years. Nothing can take me back to the life I long to live. Circumstance makes it impossible."

Mr Erstwhile tutted. "Though I loathe quoting that blackguard Bonaparte, the man sometimes spouted sense. *Impossible is a word found in the dictionary of fools*," he uttered in a French accent. "And you are by no means a fool, my dear."

This wonderful man had a way of making her feel empowered, of making her believe anything was possible.

"And so we come back to the root of the problem," Mr Erstwhile reminded her. "It is better to speak out than keep your troubles in, as my dear mother used to say, though she put it rather more eloquently. Now, I shall refill your glass while you compose yourself." He stood, took her glass and ambled over to the sideboard.

Other than Maudette, Estelle had never told another living soul what had happened that day. During terrifying nightmares, one was aware of their nemesis, aware of the unbeatable monster sent to wreak havoc with their lives. But in reality, some monsters came in the guise of loving men. Behind their endearing mask, they were greedy, selfish, rotten to the core.

Mr Erstwhile returned with her sherry. She swallowed down the golden liquid and let it soothe her spirits.

"It's a long story," Estelle began as Mr Erstwhile sat down again.

"Then let us start with the fact that you and the marquess are in love."

"*Were* in love," she corrected, now it was more lust than anything else.

With a mild sigh of frustration, he did not correct his earlier statement, but said, "And someone came to tear it asunder."

Estelle nodded. "Lord Trevane's father persuaded my father to invest in what should have been a lucrative venture—silver mining across the ocean in South America."

"And the venture failed, presumably."

"Yes. The mine collapsed. People died. My father lost everything due to a clause in the contract that he had not read properly before signing." She recalled the letter arriving from the solicitor. She had never seen a man cry before that day. "My father was frivolous with money, but he had no reason to distrust the marquess."

"I trust your family home was entailed."

"My father and brother had no option but to break the entailment. The debts were insurmountable. My father took out numerous loans to cover some of his investment, you see. It would have been the end of him had my brother not agreed it was better to pay the debt and begin again."

Mr Erstwhile's eyes flashed with admiration. "Then your brother must be a remarkable man to put his family's needs before his own."

Estelle's heart swelled when she thought of Fabian. She must have hurt him deeply and only hoped he could forgive her.

"By all accounts, he has made rather a name for himself running a fleet of merchant ships."

"Clearly, courage is a family trait." Mr Erstwhile's smile faded, and he frowned. "But surely your dowry was intact. Although Lord Trevane does not strike me as a man who would choose money over love."

Estelle cradled the glass in her lap. "I have no notion what Lord Trevane would choose as I never gave him the option." It was wrong of her to leave without speaking to Ross. She knew that now. But she'd been so confused, so lost and scared.

A heavy silence filled the room.

Mr Erstwhile's shoulders sagged. "But you told Lord Trevane you couldn't marry him?"

"No." Oh, she could never have told him that. "You see his father intentionally ruined my father to make it too difficult for us to marry."

"The marquess would rather see your father bankrupt than have you marry his son? Surely not, child." Mr Erstwhile cleared his throat. "I saw the possessive look in Lord Trevane's eyes when he almost punched Mr Hungerford in the street. No doubt he would have protested should his father attempt to force his hand."

A lump formed in Estelle's throat. Brought to bear by the burden of regret. She struggled to swallow. "Ross knows nothing of the day his father came to see me." It would break him to know the truth about his parents, to know the level of deceit and betrayal. "All he knows is that I left without a word despite promising to marry him."

Disappointment passed over Mr Erstwhile's face. "When we are young, we do not always see things clearly. The lady I know would not intentionally hurt someone she loves."

Estelle closed her eyes briefly. She had made up her mind to tell Ross everything, and would tell the truth now.

"My father would not have prevented the match. But he grew bitter, insisted that I could not know the character of the man I wanted to marry. Indeed, he had decided I should stay with my great-aunt while he and my brother made arrangements to sell the estate. He said time apart might save me from making a dreadful mistake."

"So that is how you came to be so far from home."

"No, I was to go to Yorkshire, not France." To tell him of the shipwreck and her life with the smugglers would be more than his poor heart could take. "But my maid received word that her uncle had come into some money and had bought a vineyard. She contemplated returning to Bordeaux." Estelle's mind had been so heavy with the weight of her burden when all she'd wanted was to be with Ross. "The conversation I had with Ross' father the day before I left persuaded me to flee."

"From the outcome, I imagine it was not a pleasant conversation."

"No."

"And yet I sense *unpleasant* is too mild a word."

"Ross' father came upon me in the orchard one morning. He

made it clear that he had the power to prevent the match. Indeed, he presented a promissory note signed by my father, and said he would call it in unless I told Ross that I couldn't marry him."

Mr Erstwhile stared at her incredulously. "The marquess must surely have had a motive for his despicable behaviour."

"Indeed." The motive stemmed from jealousy and obsession. "Ross worshipped his parents. He often told me that he wished for a love like theirs. But it was perhaps the greatest deception. His father had kept a mistress for ten years. When Ross' mother died, the marquess wanted to marry his lover, but she declined and only agreed to continue the relationship providing Ross marry her daughter."

Mr Erstwhile's mouth fell open. "The marquess wanted his son to marry a courtesan's daughter?"

"No, the mistress was a lady, a widow of wealth and status. The daughter was the legitimate child of a member of the aristocracy. The marquess never mentioned the lady's name. Perhaps he thought that to do so might give me a hand in the game."

To use the word *game* implied a level of amusement—nothing could be further from the truth.

"Dear heaven above." Mr Erstwhile pushed out of the chair. "I believe I need something stronger to drink than sherry." He ambled over to the decanters and came back with a crystal tumbler half-full of brandy. "But you did not tell Lord Trevane that you couldn't marry him."

She could have never looked him in the eye and lied. "No. The marquess threatened to cut Ross off if we married. Said he would see to it that Ross lived the life of a pauper until he inherited. Equally, had he called in the promissory note, my brother would have lost any chance he had of making a decent life for himself."

"And so you ran away to France."

"Yes, with my maid, Maudette." For some reason, she blurted out the tragic events that led to this point. Tears soaked her face. Some words choked in her throat. But it was a cathartic experience—a purging of her guilt and shame, a spiritual cleansing of sorts.

Mr Erstwhile came to his feet. He took her hands and held them tightly. "My dear, if anyone deserves love it is you. It breaks my heart to think of all you have been through. And yet I reserve some pity for Lord Trevane. For the man who has lived for eight years believing you indifferent when the exact opposite is true."

Estelle remained silent for a moment while she tried to suppress the pain in her heart. "I never meant to hurt him. I only meant to give him the life he deserved."

Mr Erstwhile shook his head repeatedly and sighed. "My dear, you have missed the point of life. Love is the only treasure. But it is a treasure without a map. A man may travel the oceans and seas for a lifetime and never find it. For those lucky few who do, well, it is like finding a heavenly island here on earth, and most men would die to defend it."

Estelle came to her feet. "I seem to have made a terrible mess of everything."

"And it is not too late to put things right." He cupped her cheek and smiled. "I would wager Lord Trevane will call tomorrow. And you still haven't told me what happened to poor Mr Hungerford this evening."

Both men would call at the shop. But she needed time to think, time to decide how best to proceed. "Would you mind if I kept to my room tomorrow?"

"Will you keep to your room or board the next mail coach to Edinburgh?" He raised a suspicious brow.

"No. I am so tired of running but I would like a day to myself, without seeing anyone."

A look of recognition flashed in his eyes. "Just remember,

very little is needed to make a happy life. It is all within yourself, in your way of thinking."

Estelle forced a smile. "What would I do without your wise words?"

Mr Erstwhile chuckled. "Oh, they're not mine. They belong to Marcus Aurelius."

CHAPTER THIRTEEN

After spending a sleepless night in Hanover Square, Vane decided to visit Whitecombe Street. Despite replaying the conversation with Estelle over in his mind, he could not fathom what he'd said to enrage her. Perhaps he would never understand the lady. Perhaps that was part of her appeal. Indeed, he could think of no other time in his life when he'd chased after a woman. They always came to him, begging and pleading, offering themselves up as sacrificial lambs.

Vane paused in the hall and gave his butler strict instructions regarding the procedure should any unchaperoned females call. Now he lived alone, some ladies would be keen to receive his hospitality.

The footman followed Vane to his conveyance and opened the carriage door.

"Any news from Mr Joseph?" Vane glanced up at Wickett sitting atop his box. "You did give him our change of direction?"

"No news yet, my lord, and I told Mr Joseph where he could find you."

Vane wondered what his coachman made of the events of the previous evening. Wickett was used to dealing with a devil, not a lovesick pup. "I intend to visit Whitecombe Street, to return Miss Brown's apparel."

Wickett nodded, but from the wary look in his eye, something was amiss. "What is it, Wickett? Speak your mind and let's get it over with."

No doubt the man intended to caution him about languishing over a lost love. Vane dismissed the footman for he did not want all his staff thinking they had a right to an opinion.

"It's just something ain't right, my lord."

Of course things weren't right.

Estelle had closed the door in his face, and he'd spent hours mulling over her cryptic comment. Not to mention having to deal with the all-consuming urge to have her writhing in his lap again.

"Would you care to elaborate?" Vane glanced left and right, pleased to find no one lingering in the immediate vicinity. "In future, I would prefer if we did not discuss your grievances on the street."

"There's something about that fellow from last night that don't sit right."

"Mr Hungerford? The gentleman you conveyed to James Street?"

Wickett nodded. "The man dresses like a duke, but it seems to me it's more about deception than making a good impression."

"He dresses like a dandy, not a duke." The Duke of Bedford would swoon at the comparison. "No sane gentleman co-ordinates beige, green and claret." Vane had taken an instant dislike to Mr Hungerford but presumed it stemmed from jealousy—and yet at no other time in his life had he felt threatened by a rival.

"It's clear to me that he wants Miss Brown to think he has more about him, but his house tells a man all he needs to know."

"Which is?" Vane was more intrigued by the minute. He'd been too preoccupied with his erratic emotions to pay attention to such things.

"I'll wager he's as broke as my granny's teapot." Wickett raised a knowing brow. "In the rookeries, he'd be a cove marked for purse-snatching. But one look at his house and we'd mark it a *deadlurk*—empty, not worth the risk."

"You're mistaken. The Erstwhiles dined there. I doubt they served themselves. Had there been anything untoward, Miss Brown would have avoided Hungerford's company."

"All I can tell you is there are no servants in that house, maybe one if you're lucky. The place was cold, the windows dirty, the frames peeling and rotten. All the curtains were open. He let himself in with a key, but no one came to greet him with a lamp despite the hall being dark."

Vane considered Mr Hungerford's urgency to take a wife. Perhaps the man didn't know how to run a house on his own. It couldn't be that he needed a wife's dowry as he believed Estelle was a mere shopgirl.

"Your insight is remarkable, Wickett. Thank the Lord you're in my employ. Heaven help one of the wolves should catch wind of your mental discernment and try to steal you away."

"Ladies of their ilk don't want a man who tells the truth," he said with a chuckle. "And talking of wolves, a carriage passed by while I was waiting. Happen it was the lady with the ugly pink hat you were speaking to outside the shop yesterday."

"Lady Cornell? Did she see you?"

"I'd say so. She had her nose pressed to the window."

"God damn." The one advantage of moving back to Hanover Square was that it would take the wolves time to find him. "Let me know if it becomes a habit." The sooner he dealt with Lady Cornell, the better.

"Right you are, my lord."

Vane climbed into his conveyance, closed the door and settled back for the short journey.

Estelle's jacket and bonnet lay on the seat opposite. He could almost smell the sweet scent of roses that clung to her skin, mingled with the aroma of sated desire. As the carriage rocked back and forth, his mind drifted to the moment he'd thrust into her body to satisfy his craving, a craving that had plagued him for so long.

Except that he hadn't sated his need for Miss Darcy.

He had temporarily fed his addiction.

Now, the desire to claim her came upon him again. He wanted to see her silky locks splayed over his pillow, wanted to see the heated look in her eyes when she came apart on a bone-shattering shudder. But he wanted more than that. He wanted to unite with her body and soul, to love her and be loved in return.

When they reached Whitecombe Street, Vane was too impatient to wait for Wickett to descend his box. Instead, he gathered Estelle's clothes, opened the door and marched into the apothecary shop.

Mr Erstwhile stood in front of the counter. He wore a monocle as he bent over a man seated on a wooden stool, the pair of tweezers in his hand hovering dangerously close to the fellow's eye.

"I'll be with you in a moment," Mr Erstwhile called out while keeping his hand surprisingly steady. "It looks to be a splinter of wood," he said to the terrified man with his eye held so wide it was almost popping out of its socket. "Now keep still. I think I have it."

Vane couldn't watch and so surveyed the shop by way of a distraction. There was no sign of Estelle or Mrs Erstwhile. Some of the herb drawers were still missing, and only a handful of glass bottles lined the shelves.

"There we are." Mr Erstwhile held up the tweezers.

"Blimey, it felt like a dagger in my eye and yet it's a tiny thing." The man blinked several times in rapid succession.

"It might be sore for a few days." Mr Erstwhile moved behind the counter, spent a minute or so creating a mixture and handed the bottle to the man waiting. "Bathe the eye three times a day for a week. The main ingredient is eyebright. The flower is known for its restorative qualities."

"I'm not sure I can afford the tincture as well," he stuttered.

Vane was about to reach into his pocket when Mr Erstwhile said, "There is no charge today. The eyes are the window to the soul, and I couldn't possibly take a penny to heal something so vital."

The man blinked in surprise. He looked at the bottle as if it were made of rare jewels shipped over from the Orient. "God bless you, sir."

"And may he bless you, Mr Jenkins."

In his excitement, the poor man forgot he couldn't see clearly and fell into the counter before stumbling out of the shop.

Mr Erstwhile met Vane's gaze. "Forgive me, my lord. But such a delicate operation needed my utmost concentration."

"Not at all. I imagine that was not your first good deed of the day."

The gentleman glanced at the bonnet in Vane's hand, and the jacket draped over his arm. "Speaking of good deeds, I see you have come to return Miss Brown's clothes. What a dreadful downpour we had last night. How fortunate you happened upon them in the alley."

"Miss Brown told you what happened with Mr Hungerford?" Vane wondered what other secrets the lady had confided. Mr Erstwhile had witnessed enough of their conversation to know passions ran high.

"Indeed, she did. What a terrible business it is when one cannot stroll the streets for fear of losing their life." Mr Erstwhile pursed his lips. "It is no life for a lady."

The last comment caught Vane short. Something about the

way Erstwhile spoke led him to conclude he knew more about his assistant than he let others believe.

"That is exactly what I have been trying to tell her."

Mr Erstwhile smiled. "Forgive an old man for prying, but might I suggest a different approach—listening rather than telling. When one asks questions, invariably there is always an answer. When a man *tells*, he may never discover the truth."

Vane felt like a schoolboy receiving a lecture from the master, but he knew Mr Erstwhile meant well, and he could not deny the wisdom of his words.

"Is Miss Brown here?" Vane glanced at the door that led from the shop to the living quarters. "I wonder if I might have a moment of her time."

A look of pity flashed across the man's face. He pursed his lips as he came around the counter to stand before Vane. "I'm afraid she feels a little unwell today. Come back tomorrow, and I assure you it will be more than worth your while."

Vane studied the man's kind face. Had Estelle asked Erstwhile to lie on her behalf? He could not tell. Everything about him seemed genuine and sincere.

"Should I be concerned?"

"Not at all." Like a caring father, he patted Vane's upper arm. "Give her time, my lord. Give her time."

One question pushed to the fore. "Has Mr Hungerford called today?"

"First thing this morning. He, too, was informed of her need to rest."

Wickett's suspicions about Mr Hungerford entered Vane's mind. "May I ask you something before I leave?"

"Certainly."

"It might sound odd to you, but when you dined at Mr Hungerford's house did you see any servants?"

Mr Erstwhile frowned. "I saw the maid. Two other staff were

ill, hence the reason he'd been to buy more laudanum. From what I can gather, he treats his staff well and was keen to purchase any medicine they needed."

Perhaps Wickett was right. Something was amiss at Mr Hungerford's house. He should mention it to Mr Joseph.

"Will you tell Miss Brown I called?" Vane handed Mr Erstwhile Estelle's outdoor apparel. "Can you remind her to inform me should she become … restless?"

A knowing smile formed on the gentleman's lips. "Rest assured, the lady is not going anywhere. Call tomorrow. May I be so bold as to suggest you take the day to consider what is important—the past or the present."

This man knew everything it seemed.

Vane resisted the urge to press him for information. Loyalty flowed like blood through Erstwhile's veins. Probing him would achieve nothing other than make Vane look desperate.

Vane inclined his head. "Until tomorrow." He reached the door and glanced over his shoulder. "I used to think that the past defined the present. I have since come to learn that the opposite is true." His current state of mind seemed to have helped old wounds heal.

Mr Erstwhile nodded. "The only thing that matters is how you feel now. After all, what is the past but memories tainted by our imagination?"

Feeling somewhat at a loss at having to wait another day to speak to Estelle, Vane decided to use the time productively. Having received a note to call on Lord Farleigh, he went there first.

Bamfield escorted him into the study where Farleigh sat in a wingback chair reading a book. The hard green cover looked similar to the book Wickett was reading.

"Don't tell me you're reading *Nocturnal Visit*, too," Vane said with amusement. "Are gothic novels not for ladies? Have you not had enough of dark secrets at the manor and mysterious goings-on in asylums?"

"Trust me. No one could pen a novel as suspenseful as the events that occurred at Everleigh." Farleigh turned the book over and glanced at the spine. "But how did you know?"

"Know what?"

"That the book is entitled *Nocturnal Visit*."

A cold shiver passed through Vane. "Please tell me you're joking. Has Wickett spoken to you?"

Farleigh frowned. "Your coachman? Why would he seek my counsel?"

"Lady Cornell gave Wickett a copy of that book in order to convey a message," Vane admitted. "The title is not a coincidence, and my man enjoys jokes at my expense."

He was beginning to wonder if Lady Cornell would ever overcome her obsession. She had pestered him long before he left for Italy. Two years had not cooled her ardour. Still she pressed her advances.

"That explains it." With his mouth curled into a mischievous grin, Farleigh flipped to a page. "'Knowing of your interest in exploration and that you're a man who admires courage, perhaps we might have a little adventure of our own.'" Farleigh chuckled. "The words are Lady Cornell's, not mine."

"And here, I thought you held me in the highest regard."

"Oh, I do. Most men would struggle to resist such a blatant means of seduction. Indeed, you wouldn't believe the risks the woman took to find her way into your bed."

"Into my bed?"

Farleigh spoke as though the event had already occurred.

"Lady Cornell had her maid deliver this last night." Farleigh

159

gestured to the book. "Sometime around midnight, Rose heard a noise coming from the bedchamber you were using."

A sense of dread took hold.

Surely Lady Cornell wasn't bold enough to force her way into the house. "Please tell me someone had left the window open, and that was the source of the disturbance."

"If only that were true. Imagine my shock when I crept into the room to find Lady Cornell naked in your bed. In the dark, the daft dolt thought I was you. Suffice to say, her bedroom banter leaves a lot to be desired."

God damn.

Vane covered his mouth with his hand. Had he heard this tale in his club he would have found the incident highly amusing. But he needed to do something about the lady's obsessive nature, and soon.

"What I would like to know is how the hell she got in here."

"That is a puzzle I am determined to solve," Farleigh said, waving for Vane to sit in the chair opposite. "Although I am told her maid once had a dalliance with my footman."

Vane declined the offer of a seat. "I'm afraid I can't stay. I have an errand to run across town." He would instruct Mr Joseph to have a man watch Lady Cornell until such a time as he could deal with the matter. "I trust Lady Cornell's failed attempt at seduction is the reason you asked to see me."

Farleigh nodded though his expression turned grave. "The lady's desperation is bordering on dangerous. Cornell has already proved to be a man of cunning and deception. Just because you could beat him in the ring or put a ball in his chest from two hundred yards, doesn't mean the man is not to be feared. And you know how besotted he is with his wife."

Vane dragged his hand down his face and sighed. "I shall deal with it. This business with Miss Darcy demands my utmost attention. Consequently, I have not had the opportunity to decide what to do with Cornell."

"As much as I believe Miss Darcy should be your priority, you must make a decision, and quickly. Cornell has already hurt one woman you love. What if he learns the truth about Miss Darcy?"

"He won't." There was every chance Vane would arrive at the apothecary shop to discover she'd left on the late-night coach. "Besides, Miss Darcy is no wallflower, and is more than capable of taking care of herself."

A frisson of doubt crept into his mind. Just because she'd lived with smugglers, did not make her an expert in human nature. She believed Mr Hungerford's intentions were honest. And Vane had been so interested in Estelle's story that he had told her next to nothing about what a blackguard Cornell turned out to be.

"I hope you're right," Farleigh said in a grave tone.

Now Farleigh had him worried.

Lady Cornell knew where to find Estelle. It would not take much for the woman to incite Lord Cornell into a jealous rage, and the snake always wrought vengeance on those incapable of fighting back.

Vane inclined his head. "Thank you for your counsel. Perhaps I have misjudged the threat Cornell poses. Have no fear, I shall deal with the matter promptly."

He would visit Mr Joseph and have someone watch the premises on Whitecombe Street. At this rate, Joseph could rent a house in Mayfair as well as hire a carriage.

Farleigh smiled. "I shall be here if you need me."

Mr Joseph was not at his table in The Speckled Hen tavern.

Despite offering the landlord a bribe, Fred refused to say anything about Joseph's whereabouts though he offered Vane a mug of ale and suggested he sit and wait.

Vane declined the offer. A man of his ilk did not linger in the slums of Whitechapel when alone. Instead, he had Wickett park outside Mr Hungerford's house so he could observe the comings and goings.

Wickett was right. As daylight faded, no one came to draw the curtains. Not the faintest flicker of light could be seen glowing from within. There was something eerie about the place. A disturbing silence that left an uncomfortable feeling in Vane's chest. Despite the bitter chill in the air, Hungerford's was the only smokeless chimney.

Something was most definitely amiss.

Vane returned to the tavern, relieved to find Joseph at his table. The rumble in his stomach persuaded him to order supper. And the smell of stew wafting past his nostrils was preferable to the stench of the streets.

Vane sat down opposite Joseph. "Any news on Hungerford?"

"I've just come back from seeing his maid."

"So he has servants," Vane said, surprised. "I've been watching his house for the past two hours and didn't see you there."

"That's because he's given the maid notice. He sent her packing this morning." Joseph picked up his notebook, which lay amongst a pile of tatty paper, and flicked to the required page. "Biggs followed her to the Servants' Registry. He gave me the nod as I'm better at dealing with those of a delicate disposition."

Vane knew enough about scoundrels to know the glint in Joseph's blue eyes meant he'd received more than information from the maid.

"And what did you discover?"

"That she's the only person who works for him. That his wife fell ill within the first two weeks of marrying him. So the maid said."

"Did she say why he's given her notice?"

"She said he's leaving. Seems the house is rented." He scanned his notes. "Her story rings true when you consider he's planned to take the coach to Bath tomorrow."

"Bath?" None of it made any sense. Why court Estelle if he was planning to leave London? "Did the maid say why he needs to leave so soon?"

The landlord appeared at Vane's side and plonked the bowl of stew on the table. Steam rose from the vessel like a ghostly apparition—a good sign, he decided.

"Can I get you anything else, my lord?"

Vane shook his head.

As soon as the landlord shuffled away, Vane repeated his question. "Did she say why?"

"Oh, she was more than free with her tongue when the mood took her." The runner grinned. "She said that now his wife had died he wanted to move. By all accounts, he was married before but lived in Dartford. Seems she died, too."

"Did you find any record of his last wife at St Clement Danes?"

"No. I tried other churches in the district but found no record of anyone by that name. I know the maid said they were married, but it wouldn't be the first time two lovers lived as man and wife."

Hungerford seemed too principled to live in sin.

"He could have lied to maintain appearances, I suppose."

Joseph shrugged. "I do have a list of the places he visited this morning."

Vane beckoned for the list with some impatience. "May I see it?"

"Happen it's best I read it. When a man writes in a hurry, it can look like an ink stain." Joseph checked his notes. "He went to see a fellow in Spitalfields. A French silk weaver, so my man Simmonds said."

After the attempted robbery in the alley, it was not a coincidence. Perhaps it was not a coincidence that the intruder entered the Erstwhiles' shop on the night they dined with Mr Hungerford.

"Did he go anywhere else?"

"He hired a yellow bounder from Mr Drummond on Compton Street. He told Drummond that he didn't want collecting from the house but wanted to travel from the yard."

So he'd hired a post-chaise rather than travel by mail coach.

"Told him there'd be two passengers," Joseph continued.

"Two passengers!" Vane stopped himself from shooting out of the chair.

Surely Hungerford didn't expect Estelle to go with him?

A knot formed in Vane's throat, so big it almost blocked his airway. Perhaps he was wrong, and Estelle was using the man to help her run away. He wanted to trust her, but not knowing what had driven her from Prescott Hall all those years ago left him with a flicker of doubt.

Vane coughed to clear his throat. "Do you know what time he'll be leaving?"

"Six o'clock. Hungerford wanted to leave after dark, but Drummond convinced him it was better to navigate the city streets before the fog descended. I had to slip Drummond a couple of sovereigns to get him to spill his guts."

Vane snorted. "I'm sure you will add it to my bill."

Joseph glanced at the door briefly. "There's not much to tell about the lord you wanted watching. He comes to and from the museum, mostly. Often late at night, though I can't help but think he's hiding something."

"Concentrate all your efforts on watching both Lord and Lady

Cornell." Vane gave the runner a brief recount of the lady's obsession. "And post a boy outside Mr Erstwhile's apothecary on Whitecombe Street. Leave Hungerford to me."

"I'll see to it right away, my lord." Joseph eyed the bowl of stew as though he'd not eaten for a week. "Are you having that?"

Vane had lost his appetite. He pushed the bowl across the table. "You're welcome to it though I might stay for a while and order a drink." It was too early to go home and sit alone.

Joseph was already tucking into the meal. "Happen you could help me with a few questions, then."

"Certainly."

"I'm investigating the theft of items from a gentleman's club —watches, snuff boxes and the like. But I can't go into the club to question the members."

Vane relished the distraction for it took his mind off the urge to call on Estelle and ask if she was leaving with Mr Hungerford. Every fibre of his being told him she was not. Perhaps the man had made an offer to more than one woman. Still, Vane would wait until five o'clock to call at the apothecary shop.

If Estelle had left, then he would not chase after her. He would leave London and start afresh somewhere new. Perhaps visit Lillian, head out to a faraway place on one of Fabian's merchant ship.

If Estelle remained in London, then the time had come to ask the one question branded into his heart. What the hell had prompted her to leave him all those years ago?

CHAPTER FOURTEEN

Estelle woke to the sun beaming through her bedchamber window. It was so bright she blinked numerous times before she could open her eyes sufficiently to see who was busying about in her room.

"Are you awake, Miss Brown?" Mrs Erstwhile's voice penetrated Estelle's drowsy mind. "I've brought you some tea. Mr Erstwhile says you're starting with the sniffles and we don't want you taking ill on us."

Estelle shuffled up to lean against the pillows and drank in the welcome sight. "You look as bright as a button today. I know the stomach pains have subsided, but I didn't expect to see you looking quite so cheerful."

Mrs Erstwhile placed the cup and saucer on the side table and moved to the window to fuss with the curtains. "The restorative Mr Erstwhile made perked me up no end."

Perhaps the tonic contained a secret ingredient, though Estelle knew it wouldn't be anything sinister. Mr Erstwhile would never force his wife to consume anything without her knowledge.

"I can't tell you how pleased I am to see a rosy glow to your cheeks." Had anything untoward happened to Mrs Erstwhile,

Estelle would have felt compelled to remain at the shop indefinitely.

"I'm convinced it was something I ate, and yet we've all dined together this week, and I was the only one taken ill."

"Except when we dined with Mr Hungerford," she reminded Mrs Erstwhile. Estelle had told the gentleman of her dislike for macaroons, and yet he had presented them with a tower of biscuit treats. "You were the only one to eat from the plate of macaroons."

Mr Hungerford had done his utmost to persuade Mr Erstwhile to try one. Feeling under pressure to please his host, Mr Erstwhile had taken a macaroon from the plate and nibbled on the corner. As soon as Mr Hungerford nipped out of the room, Mrs Erstwhile offered her assistance and gobbled it down.

Mrs Erstwhile slapped her hand across her mouth.

"From what I recall, you definitely had two," Estelle said.

Guilt flashed in Mrs Erstwhile's eyes. "It might have been more like five or six." She shook her head. "But I've never known anyone become ill after eating a macaroon."

Perhaps they were ill if they ate too many, Estelle thought.

"Thankfully, you're better now and should not dwell on it anymore." Estelle reached for the teacup and cradled it between her cold hands. "Can I ask you something? It is of a personal nature."

With a proud smile, Mrs Erstwhile hurried over and sat on the edge of the bed. "My dear, we speak openly and honestly here. Ask away."

Estelle wasn't sure how to phrase her question without it seeming rude. "Did you ever have any doubts about your relationship with Mr Erstwhile? Was there ever a time when you felt … when your positions in society made you doubt if things would work?"

Mrs Erstwhile did not look the least bit offended. "Oh, many times. Even when we married I still feared the pressure might affect him. I never cared about myself." She screwed up her nose and gave a funny wave. "It takes courage for a man to go against everything he's been taught to believe."

Ross possessed the courage of a whole battalion.

"Love finds a way." Mrs Erstwhile patted her hand. "Is this about Mr Hungerford or the marquess? I hear both men called to see you yesterday, and both promised to return today."

"It's about the marquess." And her ridiculous notion that she was unworthy of his affection. "I care nothing for Mr Hungerford and desire only to make my position clear."

Mrs Erstwhile's expression grew solemn, and she cast Estelle a look usually reserved for starving match girls. "Most gentlemen are not as understanding as Mr Erstwhile. Don't expect too much." She leant forward and rubbed Estelle's arm gently. "It's not for me to tell you what to do. But if you're set against Mr Hungerford, you must tell him so at once."

Estelle nodded. "I shall do so today, without delay."

"Good. Now finish your tea and take a moment to clear your head. You'll find eggs and toast on the table if you have a stomach for it."

Her stomach rumbled at the mere mention of food. "I'll dress and come straight down."

Mrs Erstwhile stood and made for the door. "Take your time, dear. I have a strange feeling it's going to be a hectic day."

The hours from ten until one o'clock dragged. Customers came and went, with their wracking coughs and odd skin complaints. Every tinkle of the bell had her eyes fixed on the door. Every five minutes, Estelle glanced at the clock. Every half an hour, the chime from the one in the hall set her more on edge.

Who would call first?

She knew exactly what she would say to Mr Hungerford. But where on earth would she start when it came to Ross?

The answer to the conundrum appeared a little after one o'clock.

Mr Hungerford entered the shop, dressed elegantly in mustard trousers and a forest-green coat. Such a garish combination spoke of extravagance and a preoccupation with French fashion. Ross did not need grandiose displays to make a point. Power and wealth radiated from every fibre of his being.

"Miss Brown," Mr Hungerford said after paying his respects to the Erstwhiles and asking after Mrs Erstwhile's health. "May I say how marvellous it is to see you up and about. After getting caught in that dreadful downpour, I feared you would be abed for a week or more."

"Not at all." Estelle forced a smile. She imagined telling him that she worked with smugglers and was used to spending hours in the water helping to haul in stolen goods. "It was nothing more than a little sniffle."

"Excellent. Then perhaps a stroll might do you a power of good. The sun is shining, and there's not a cloud in sight." He turned to Mr Erstwhile. "I trust you're able to spare her for an hour."

There was a time when to walk the streets without her maid would have been tantamount to a scandal. Now, her position came with a freedom she found equally constraining.

"Miss Brown is free to spend time outdoors if she so wishes." Mr Erstwhile cast her a reassuring grin. "Indeed, I'm sure you have things to discuss."

Was that a covert way of telling her to put the gentleman out of his misery? It had to be done, and now. A short stroll would make the task easier. He could hardly protest to any degree whilst out in public.

"A walk would be beneficial. Give me a moment to get ready." An hour at most would suffice. Should Ross call, Mr Erstwhile would keep him entertained until she returned.

"I hope you can forgive me for my complete lapse in judgment the other night," Mr Hungerford said as they walked along Whitecombe Street. "I should have stayed and taken supper, as you suggested."

"There is nothing to forgive. I was just as foolish and should have insisted we return home."

Estelle found his affable manner nauseating. If she were to marry, she wanted a man who made her feel safe without being controlling. He would need to be strong, exude a level of raw masculinity that made her knees tremble. In short, she wanted a man like Ross Sandford.

"Well, there is one consolation I suppose."

"And what is that?"

"It gave me an opportunity to make a declaration. I can only put my lack of caution down to my pining heart."

Oh, heavens. Someone pass her a chamber pot for she was liable to cast up her accounts.

Estelle stopped walking as they reached Princes Street. "Perhaps we should take a slow stroll back."

"Why when it is but a short walk to a coffeehouse?" His childish pout made her want to hit him over the head with a chamber pot let alone use one to contain the evidence of her suffering. "At least let me buy you a hot beverage, to make amends for the dreadful events in that alley. And it will help to ward off a chill."

"Sir, I fear there is something I must tell you."

Mr Hungerford raised a hand to silence her. "If it is as I suspect, then at least let us sit down rather than discuss such a personal matter here in the street. I know of a tasteful establishment a little further ahead."

Estelle suppressed a snort. The man was adept at speaking too intimately in public. Why the sudden change of heart now?

"Very well." She sighed. "But I must return to the shop within the hour." She hoped to be there when Ross called.

"Rest assured. I shall endeavour to ensure your needs are met."

Estelle sighed inwardly. She would never get used to his odd phrasing.

They continued until Mr Hungerford directed her to a coffeehouse on Compton Street. He placed a hand at the small of her back—sending an icy shudder straight through her—and guided her into the premises. Every table was occupied. People huddled around the stone hearth, their drinks balanced on the mantel. Others crowded into every available space.

"And I thought Brandersons had the monopoly," she said, hovering near the door. "Let us return to Whitecombe Street."

"Never fear. I know the proprietor, and he will secure us a table."

They shuffled and pushed their way up to the serving counter. The pungent smell of sweat-soaked bodies, mingled with the bitter scent of coffee, irritated her nostrils. As did the thick plumes of tobacco smoke lingering in the air.

Mr Hungerford summoned the proprietor and leant across the wooden surface to whisper something into the man's ear. After accepting a few coins by way of a bribe, the man wandered out and headed to one particular table. He spoke to the group of men, who vacated their seats without so much as a cross word.

Mr Hungerford escorted her to the table and pulled out her chair. "I shall wait at the counter for our drinks else it will take an age to be served."

He hurried away leaving her alone.

Being in the cramped place reminded her of the times she'd sat in the tavern in Wissant with Madame Bonnay simply to keep watch on the revenue men. Sometimes they approached and made lewd suggestions, but in the madame's company, Estelle always felt safe.

And yet now, every instinct told her to run.

But was that not the tactic she used to avoid all awkward conversations?

Estelle spent five minutes contemplating whether to stay or leave before finally deciding to remain at the coffeehouse for ten minutes in order to decline the gentleman's marriage offer.

Mr Hungerford came towards her carrying two pewter goblets. A gentleman nudged his arm as he passed, causing the liquid to slosh over the rim of one vessel, but Mr Hungerford said nothing.

Ross would have demanded an apology, but then she imagined one look at the marquess' broad shoulders and men gave him a wide berth.

"The wait for coffee would have seen us sitting here for another hour, and I know how desperate you are to return to the shop." Mr Hungerford placed the goblets on the table. "I ordered wine instead. Do you mind?"

"No, not at all."

If anything, the potency of the beverage would give her the courage to get this matter over with, and so she took a sip straight away. It tasted a little sour, but she had long since given up being a connoisseur of fine wine or insisting she only take a drop with dinner.

Mr Hungerford spent ten minutes rambling on about the weather and about the benefits of inhaling the country air. Whenever she tried to speak, he mumbled about the merits of Bath, and she got the impression he was stalling.

"Sir, I believe we should get to the matter at hand," she said, and then took another few sips to bolster her confidence.

"Can we not enjoy our drinks first?"

While some might imagine her plight had given her a level of self-assurance aristocratic misses struggled to possess, every role she'd played since leaving Prescott Hall had been a submissive one. Then, it suited her to remain inconspicuous. But now she was tired of playing the naive fool.

"No, sir, we cannot." Estelle straightened. "I must tell you that I cannot possibly accept your offer of marriage. I do not love you, you see. And regardless of my position, I could not marry for anything less."

She brought the goblet to her lips to mask a relieved sigh. Mr Erstwhile was right: the truth was better spoken aloud than left festering within.

Mr Hungerford fell silent.

"Will you not say something, sir?"

His features twisted into a sinister sneer, but the ugly expression faded. "I didn't know you suffered from romantic delusions, Miss Brown. I hoped you might find me congenial, someone with whom you might have a comfortable life."

Estelle shook her head. After giving herself to Ross in the carriage, she could never conceive doing so with any other man.

"You make love sound like a dream for fools."

"In my experience, feelings change. Love comes and goes like flowers in spring. Marriage should be based on so much more. Do you not think?" His abrupt tone marked another change in him. Perhaps these conflicting emotions stemmed from frustration or disappointment.

"Infatuation is fleeting. True love lasts a lifetime," she countered before finishing what remained in the goblet so she could be free of this difficult conversation.

He scoffed at that. "So, you intend to be the mistress of a marquess."

"Mistress? What makes you think that?" The comment stung. It brought her mind back to Ross' secret exchange with Hungerford outside his house in James Street. "Is that what Lord Trevane told you?"

"Why else would the marquess be interested in you?" he said with a level of contempt she had never heard in his voice until now.

Who was this man?

She thought she knew, but doubts surfaced.

"Is that what he told you?" She demanded an answer. The wine had given her a heavy head and more than a little courage. Indeed, she felt rather peculiar. "I want to know."

"As a matter of fact, he did. In any event, I pointed out that you were far too principled to consider the position."

And yet, like a naive fool, she had given herself to Ross in the carriage. For all intents and purposes, she had already embraced the role. "I must admit to being somewhat surprised. Lord Trevane is an extremely private man, not one who airs his business to all and sundry."

Her world suddenly swayed, and she struggled to focus. The odd sensation stemmed from more than Mr Hungerford's shocking revelation. Bright lights flashed in the corner of her eye. Everything seemed distant. It was as though she stood outside her body looking at herself seated at the table.

"What else did you expect?" he said, looking at her rather oddly. "He is a member of the aristocracy. When he marries, it will be to a lady of position and wealth."

She possessed neither of those things and was desperately trying to think of a retort when a sharp shooting pain in her stomach drew her to her feet. Dizziness forced her to sit back down.

"You don't look well," Mr Hungerford said. He drained his goblet and stood. "Come. I shall see you safely home."

"Just let me sit for a moment. It might pass. It's rather hot in here, and there are so many people."

Mr Hungerford studied her face and peered into her eyes. He checked his watch numerous times and glanced towards the door. Estelle thought about standing, but all she wanted to do was lay her head on the table and sleep.

"We should leave before your symptoms worsen," he said.

"You're right. We should go now." If she did not move soon, she feared she might not be able to walk.

He rounded the table and brought her to her feet. "Take my arm. Grip it tightly."

Estelle had to clutch his arm with both hands just to keep her balance. Her head pounded. She could hear voices but no words of clarity. Once outside, the blinding sun hurt her eyes, and she squeezed them shut as they ambled along Compton Street.

While his manner had been abrupt, stern almost, Mr Hungerford's temperament suddenly reverted to the considerate gentleman who made her nauseous. As they continued, he whispered to her in a comforting voice.

"We will be home shortly," she heard him say. "Hold on to me, and I shall steer you in the right direction."

When Estelle finally opened her eyes, she was in a busy courtyard. Her vision blurred, but she saw horses, men carrying saddles and a row of yellow coaches.

A tall, scrawny man addressed Mr Hungerford. "We've loaded your luggage. Are you ready to leave now, sir?"

"Indeed. We are in somewhat of a hurry. My wife is unwell."

His wife?

In a daze, she looked up at him. "You must take me back to Whitecombe Street. I need to go home."

He patted her hand and gave a little chuckle. "You must forgive my wife," he said. "I fear she is growing delirious." Mr

Hungerford met her gaze. "My dear, we are going home, home to Bath."

Bath?

When the man moved out of earshot, Mr Hungerford whispered, "I enjoy a challenge, Miss Brown. I like a wife to be submissive. Once we're in Bath, you will learn to do what I tell you and show respect and gratitude to your husband and master."

CHAPTER FIFTEEN

V ane was lounging in the copper tub recalling the delicious memory of the moment he plunged into Estelle's warm, welcoming body. In his licentious years, he had never craved the same woman twice. As soon as they proved inferior, as soon as they failed to raise a flicker of emotion in his chest, he moved on to the next one. It was a fool's game; he knew now. A ridiculous plan to deal with rejection and grief.

He had allowed his life to be steered off course by one woman. Love truly was as powerful as the poets proclaimed—and he was still deeply in love with Estelle Darcy.

A knock on the door dragged Vane from his reverie. Pierre entered. The petite Frenchman came towards him in the effeminate way he did when in a state of panic.

Pierre's hands flapped as he clutched a letter. "My lord, I must give you this at once. Wickett, he says it cannot wait."

Vane reached for the towel on the floor and dried his hands.

Pierre stepped closer and presented the letter with trembling fingers. "It is urgent, my lord, urgent indeed."

"Yes, Pierre, you have told me twice." The absence of a wax seal told Vane it was from Mr Joseph. The scrawled words were a little difficult to decipher. Upon the second read, the gravity of the situation gripped him by the throat and forced him to charge up out of the water. "God damn. Fetch my clothes. I must leave at once."

"*Mon Dieu*!" Pierre grabbed the towel and dabbed the floor as water cascaded over the sides of the tub.

"Leave it," Vane commanded. "There is no time to lose." He climbed out, crumpled the letter in his fist and hurled it into the hearth. He snatched another towel from the chair and dried his body. "Hurry."

Pierre ran to the dressing room, stopped and turned back. "But you have not said what you wish to wear, my lord."

"Does it matter?" Vane paused. Knowing Pierre's taste for foppish fashion perhaps that was not a good idea. "I'll wear black." They were the clothes he wore when out on the hunt. And by God, murder was the only thing on his mind.

Wickett had readied the carriage and was waiting atop his box when Vane raced from the house, followed by a footman.

"I thought you'd want to leave right away, my lord."

"When did you receive the note from Mr Joseph?"

"Minutes before I sent it up with Pierre. Hungerford is on the move. Seems the gentleman asked for the post-chaise to be ready to depart at three o'clock instead of six. Mr Joseph said he dropped his luggage there earlier."

Vane dragged his watch from his pocket. "It's almost two. Get me to Whitecombe Street as quickly as possible."

"Aye, my lord. The Devil himself won't stop me when I'm in a mind to hurry."

Vane climbed into his conveyance. As soon as the footman closed the door, the vehicle jerked forward. Wickett's cries to the team of four rent the air. The tension mounted.

What was Hungerford about?

Was it a case of him growing frustrated by the competition

and so he'd decided to leave? Or would Vane arrive at Whitecombe Street to find Estelle clutching her valise?

He pressed his fingers to his closed lids to relieve the pressure.

Would there ever be a day when life was simple?

Would he ever wake in the morning with a clear mind?

The carriage raced at breakneck speed, jolting, swerving around corners. Vane sat forward and clung to the leather strap overhead to steady his balance as he watched for the familiar buildings of Whitecombe Street. Wickett's curses reached Vane's ears as the coachman weaved around handcarts and dodged crossing sweepers.

The vehicle creaked to a halt opposite the apothecary shop. Vane composed himself. After all, the stories he had concocted in his head were just that—figments of his wild imagination. Until he spoke to Estelle, he knew nothing of her true intentions.

He strode up to Mr Erstwhile's door and pasted a smile. Good God, his heart was beating so hard against his ribs he feared the organ might burst from his chest.

The bell tinkled as he entered. Mr Erstwhile stood behind the counter grinding a sweet-smelling herb with a mortar and pestle. With a steady hand, Mrs Erstwhile decanted liquid into a blue bottle. They both looked up to greet their customer.

"Good afternoon, my lord." Mr Erstwhile smiled. "I hoped we might see you today."

Why? Did he plan on putting Vane out of his misery once and for all?

"I did say I would return to see Miss Brown." Noting the lady's absence in the shop, he added, "I trust she is well."

"Indeed, she is."

"It was just a little chill," Mrs Erstwhile said. "Nothing that a day in bed couldn't cure."

They stared at him for a moment as if waiting for him to speak.

Mr Erstwhile wiped his hands on the brown apron tied around his waist. "Would you care to come through to the parlour and take tea, my lord?"

Vane's racing heartbeat pounded in his ears. "Will Miss Brown be joining us?" Or was this the part where he discovered she had already left.

"As you know I am a man of truth, my lord. It pains me to call the lady Miss Brown when we both know that is not her name."

So, he knew everything.

"Miss Darcy told you about our history?"

"The lady has been through so much. We all need someone in whom we can confide, someone impartial." Mr Erstwhile gestured to the hall. "Come. Let us sit for a while and wait for Miss Darcy to return."

Vane's heart sank to his stomach. "You mean to tell me the lady is not here?"

Panic gripped him by the throat. She promised she would inform him should she be inclined to run again.

Mr Erstwhile must have sensed his despair for he gave a reassuring smile. "She has not left on the mail coach if that is what you fear. No, she has gone out with Mr Hungerford for an hour, merely to decline his offer of marriage. After all, a lady cannot marry a man when she is in love with someone else."

Vane heard the words, but his mind struggled to process the information. So Estelle had left with Mr Hungerford.

"Did she tell you where they were going?"

Mr Erstwhile frowned. "For a stroll, I think. Why? What has you in such a fluster?"

Anger flared. If Estelle had taken him for a fool again, the entire world would feel the Devil's wrath. The lady was more than capable of deceit. So why did his pained heart scream for him to trust her? Perhaps because he was a lovesick fool.

"Mr Hungerford has hired a post-chaise," Vane said bluntly. "He is to take receipt of the vehicle at three o'clock today. I'm told he's going to Bath, that the coach was hired to ferry two passengers."

Mr Erstwhile glanced at the wall clock. "Then I must assume he will return with Miss Darcy promptly if he wishes to be at the yard in time to satisfy the contract."

"Indeed," Mrs Erstwhile began. "Miss Darcy promised to be no more than an hour."

Were they naive, too trusting, or was he suffering from an overactive imagination?

"You're both missing the point. What if Miss Darcy decided to leave with him?"

"Leave with Mr Hungerford?" Mrs Erstwhile shook her head and looked at him as if he'd said the sky was falling. "No, my lord. She told me this morning that she cares nothing for the man. I imagine the other passenger is his valet."

No valet worth his weight in gold would dress a man so tastelessly. Well, Pierre might, which was why Vane kept him on a tight leash.

Vane removed his hat and thrust his hand through his hair. "Then I shall head to Compton Street to discern the truth for myself."

"Then you must come back and let us know all is well." Mrs Erstwhile hastened around the counter to open the door. "There is every chance Miss Darcy will be here when you return."

Mr Erstwhile met his gaze. "A man must reserve judgement until he has determined the facts."

Vane nodded, but it was far easier to spout wise words than to live by them.

Deciding that navigating conveyances and carts would only hinder his progress, Vane opted to walk. He instructed Wickett to meet him outside Mr Drummond's yard on Compton Street. After a few long strides, a sudden sense of urgency took hold. It niggled away in his chest forcing him to break into a run.

People stopped and stared as he barged past, confusion marring their brows. They scanned the length and breadth of the street. Was there a fire or robbery? Was a drunken lord running amok to avoid a constable?

When he reached Princes Street, the compulsion to hurry developed into a mild panic and then into an intense fear that consumed him mind and body. He had lost Estelle once. Twice if he counted the shipwreck. A deep sorrow had lived in his heart ever since, and he wasn't sure what he would do if he lost her again.

As predicted, Vane reached Mr Drummond's yard before Wickett.

The large wooden gates were wide open. Stable hands were out in the courtyard, taking receipt of hired horses. Boys as young as ten led fresh horses from the stables to those gentlemen waiting for an exchange. Other boys had the sorry task of sweeping up after the muscled beasts.

A row of yellow bounders lined the back wall. One man was securing the harness on a post-chaise. Two coachmen, both dressed in boxcoats and gripping whips in their hand, stood conversing next to the vehicles.

There was no sign of Mr Hungerford or Estelle.

Another man, with a thick neck and flat nose, appeared from a small wooden building to Vane's left. He scanned Vane's attire as he approached. "Can I help you, sir? I'm Drummond, the proprietor. Do you need a horse or a bounder?"

"Neither. I'm looking for someone," Vane said, his tone conveying his impatience. "A gentleman by the name of Hungerford, and I believe he hired a coach to take him and his … his passenger to Bath." It would not do to assume anything at this point. "Are they here, or have they left the yard?"

Perhaps sensing a dangerous undertone in Vane's voice, Mr Drummond jerked his head to a coachman. The burly fellow sauntered over to stand behind his employer.

"I'm afraid it's bad business to discuss a client's plans with a stranger. Now either you want to hire a coach or you don't."

No doubt he preferred to sell the information. The man had already taken two sovereigns from Mr Joseph and could quit with his holier than though attitude.

Vane gritted his teeth, flexed his fingers and stared down his nose. "You will tell me what I want to know. And you will tell me now."

The coachman made a point of firming his grip on the whip.

"Gentleman or not," Drummond said, assessing the quality of Vane's clothes once more. "My livelihood depends on discretion."

"Has Hungerford left the premises?" Vane reiterated. Wrestling with these men might relieve some of his frustration. "I would like to speak to him that is all."

"You say that, but you look like you want to tear the man's head from his shoulders. You're not the first to ask after him. It's one thing giving out information in exchange for coin. But I'll not have men brawling in the yard. All it takes is one kick from a skittish horse and I'll have my licence revoked."

So, Hungerford was on the premises. Why else would Drummond be concerned with men brawling?

Vane glanced at the line of parked carriages. The stable hands were busy checking the buckles on the bridles. Only one vehicle looked ready to depart and the time was quickly approaching three o'clock.

"Perhaps I do want to hire a coach," Vane said more calmly. "How long will it take to ready the horses?"

Drummond eyed him suspiciously. "That depends on how much you're willing to pay."

Vane retrieved a calling card from his coat pocket and thrust it at Drummond. "I'll pay whatever it takes."

Mr Drummond took one look at the embossed crest and his eyes grew wide. He gave a toothless grin and gestured to the door of the wooden building. "Follow me into the office, my lord, and we can discuss the terms."

Presuming the threat had diminished, the coachman ambled back to his associate. Vane waited for Drummond to lead the way and followed him for a few steps before turning abruptly and taking flight.

Vane darted towards the carriages, dodged men and horses, went skidding on straw-covered manure.

"My lord," Drummond called out.

A coachman tried to block his path but Vane was agile enough to duck and swerve past him. Wrapping his fingers around the handle of the carriage door, Vane yanked it open.

Two people lounged back in the seat.

A knot formed in Vane's stomach.

Anger burst to life in his chest.

Hungerford had his arm draped around Estelle's neck. Her eyes were closed as she rested her head on his shoulder. The intimacy of the moment caused bile to burn in Vane's throat. He felt nauseous, sick to his stomach, and so bloody enraged he was liable to end up in Newgate before the day was out.

"What's the meaning of this?" the fop said. "Can you not see that this coach is occupied?" It took a few seconds for recognition to dawn. Hungerford's mouth fell open and an odd whimper escaped. "Lord Trevane." Gulping, he added, "Wh-what do you want?"

"What do I want?" Vane repeated incredulously. He wanted to knock the man's teeth down his throat. He wanted to shake Estelle and demand to know how the hell she could kiss him while carrying on with this craven dandy.

"You lost," Hungerford said, managing to find courage from somewhere. "Miss Brown is coming away with me. She decided she would rather be a wife than a mistress."

Vane was about to reply when Drummond caught up with him.

"My lord, what's this about? Step away and let's talk about it inside, away from prying eyes."

Vane glanced back over his shoulder to find at least ten men rooted to the spot, watching and waiting. "Go away, Drummond. I have business with Mr Hungerford."

"You have no business with me, my lord." Hungerford flapped his hand as a king did when he'd had enough of being pestered by peasants. "Mr Drummond, please remove his lordship so we may be on our way."

Vane grabbed hold of the door. "I'm not leaving until I have spoken to Miss Brown."

"As you can see, she is resting."

Drummond sidled up to Vane. "If you've got a gripe with the man, you'll have to take it up with him elsewhere, or I'll be forced to call for a constable."

"Call the damn constable. Rouse the cavalry for all I care." No one could hurt him now. "I'm not leaving without an explanation." He could not foresee living another eight years wondering what the hell had gone wrong. Didn't the Erstwhiles deserve an explanation, too?

"It's almost three o'clock, Mr Drummond," Hungerford shouted in a smug tone. "We must be away to Bath. You promised a reliable service."

Vane glanced at Estelle. Her eyes fluttered open and then closed again. "Miss Brown, may I speak to you for a moment?"

"I don't know who you've come to see, my lord," Drummond said. "But the lady's name is Mrs Hungerford, not Miss Brown."

Vane could feel the blood draining from his face. He shot Hungerford a hard stare. "You're married?"

"Indeed." Hungerford gave a satisfied grin. "This afternoon by special licence. Now, as you can see, my wife is unwell. We must be on our way."

A cloud of confusion filled Vane's mind. None of this made any sense. Was Estelle so adept at deception she'd feigned the depth of her affection? Did she despise his father for her father's losses in the mining venture? Was she so aggrieved she would take her vengeance out on him?

Vane released his grip on the door and stumbled back. "Have no fear, Drummond. I'll leave as soon as I've heard the lady say she is happy. I want her to tell me this is the life she has chosen."

"Ross?" Estelle's croaky voice reached his ears.

Vane stepped forward and studied her. Estelle tried to open her eyes, but it was as though her lids were too heavy. "Estelle? Can you hear me?"

"Will someone close the damn door!" Hungerford cried. "His lordship is determined to put my wife in an early grave."

"I'm going to have to ask you to step back, my lord." Drummond shuffled around to stand at Vane's right shoulder. "It's not right to trouble a lady when she's ill."

The burly coachman came to stand on the left. Without warning, both men grabbed Vane's arms and attempted to pull him back.

"Get your blasted hands off me, else there'll be hell to pay."

"H-help ... help me, Ross." Estelle's weak plea sounded genuine.

Drummond and his lackey dragged Vane back as Mr Hungerford leant forward and slammed the door.

"Good God, did you not hear what she said?" Vane writhed and struggled against their hold. He kicked the lackey in the shin. The man groaned but was far more robust than the rogues Vane had fought in the alley.

"Someone fetch a constable," Drummond shouted.

No constable with an ounce of sense would dare arrest a marquess without consulting a magistrate.

"Go get your constable and be quick about it." Vane twisted and squirmed in a bid to break their hold. "I swear I shall raze the place to the ground if that carriage leaves this yard. Estelle!"

"Happen you care for the lady, but it's not up to me to meddle in personal business." Drummond jerked his head at a man in the crowd. "Climb atop your box, Albert, and you can be on your way."

Vane focused his mind. He dropped his weight suddenly, forcing the lackey to release his grip. With his free hand he swung for Drummond, catching him on the jaw though the punch lacked the strength to put the man on his arse.

Amid the mayhem, the coachman flicked the reins.

A click of a hammer brought a gasp from those gathered around. "Happen you didn't hear his lordship clearly the first time," Wickett said, breaking through the crowd while wielding a pistol in each hand. He aimed one at the coachman, the other at Drummond. "If his lordship has cause to speak to the lady, you'd best let him."

A tense silence ensued.

Drummond stepped forward and opened the carriage door. "Beg your pardon, sir, but I can't let you leave just yet."

"Damnation!" Hungerford cried. "This is lunacy. Is there not a law about disruption on the highway?" He poked his head out of the carriage and called out, "Make ready to depart." But the coachman refused to budge with a pistol aimed at his chest.

While Vane appreciated Wickett's timely intervention, the last thing he wanted was to see his coachman swing from the scaffold. "Lower the weapons, Wickett. Drummond can see something is amiss."

Wickett did as Vane commanded, but every man in the courtyard gave him a wide berth.

Drummond fell silent as he looked at Estelle. "Mrs Hungerford, would you mind stepping out for a moment? His lordship wants to know that you're well before you leave."

"Of course she's not well," Hungerford snapped. "Any fool can see that. Have you not listened to a word I have said?"

While Vane tried his utmost to remain calm, Mr Hungerford's brash manner ruffled Drummond's feathers.

"Now you listen here," Drummond began. "I've had a fist to the face and a pistol to the head because of you. I'll lose business when people hear of this ruckus. And all because you won't let his lordship speak to the lady."

"Ross?" Estelle's voice sounded weak, helpless.

"Who's Ross?" Drummond said to no one in particular.

"That would be me," Vane said.

Drummond turned, waved him forward and stepped aside.

Vane cast an assessing gaze over Estelle. Her eyes flickered, her head lolled forward. Hungerford sat next to her. Amid all his bravado, panic flashed in his eyes.

"Estelle, can you hear me?" Vane reached for her hands but Hungerford slapped him away.

"You do not have to say anything to him, Miss Brown," Hungerford whispered.

Unable to control himself, Vane punched Hungerford on the jaw. The sharp jab served as a warning. "The lady's name is not Miss Brown," Vane whispered through gritted teeth. "Her name is Miss Darcy, and she is the sister of Baron Ravenscroft."

Hungerford gulped in surprise as he clutched his cheek.

Vane caught Estelle's hands and pulled her forward. "Touch her again, Hungerford, and I'll break your nose." Her body was limp, and she flopped into his arms like a cloth doll. "Estelle, please speak to me."

Her eyes fluttered open. "Ross," she breathed. "Help me. Don't … don't let him take me."

All those standing nearby heard her words.

Estelle's head fell back and her eyes closed. What the devil was wrong with her? Vane bent his head. He could smell wine and something sweet, almost spicy.

"Someone run and fetch a doctor," Vane cried as a deep sense of dread consumed him. "I fear the lady may have ingested something. I fear she may have been poisoned."

"Don't be ridiculous." Hungerford climbed out of the carriage. "Miss Brown may have taken a drop of laudanum to help settle her stomach for the journey. That is all."

"Miss Brown?" Drummond raised a suspicious brow. "So this lady is not your wife?"

Hungerford's cheeks flamed and he pushed his fingers down between his neck and cravat as if struggling to breathe. "The paperwork is a mere formality. We intend to marry once we reach Bath."

Mr Drummond beckoned his coachman. "Step down, Albert. This coach isn't leaving the yard until I've cleared this matter with the constable."

"But you've no right," Hungerford protested.

"I have every right." Drummond stepped closer to the fop and stared down his flat nose as if ready to throttle the man. "I'll not have folk say I came to the aid of a criminal."

"Will someone get a blasted doctor!" Vane wanted to beat

Hungerford to a pulp, too, but his only concern was for the helpless woman in his arms. He looked down at her. "Estelle, please try to keep your eyes open."

She blinked again, lifted a weak hand to his cheek. "You … you came for me."

The muscles in his throat grew tight. "Keep talking. Don't close your eyes."

A man lingering near the gates waved his hands and cried, "Here comes the constable."

"But this is preposterous," Hungerford complained. "Let me speak to him." Hungerford stormed through the crowd as if ready to berate the constable for taking the complaint seriously. "We shall have this misunderstanding sorted out in no time."

But it seemed Hungerford had no intention of confronting the constable. As soon as he reached the gate, he turned on his heels and fled in the opposite direction.

"Someone apprehend that man," Drummond shouted. "Albert. Connor. Go after him."

Both coachmen jumped upon hearing their names called and charged after Hungerford. What with the weight of their boxcoats and their stout figures they would be lucky to spot Hungerford let alone catch the fellow. Wickett, on the other hand, raced off like a whippet.

"Is there somewhere the lady can lie down?" Vane asked Drummond.

He didn't care what happened to Hungerford. If he didn't pay for his crime today, Vane would see to it that he paid eventually.

"Bring her into the office. There's a trundle bed I use when waiting for late arrivals."

Vane carried Estelle to the small wooden building. He was about to cross the threshold when a chorus of cries and high-pitched screams pierced the air. A cacophony of other noises accompanied the din: splintering wood, the squeal of frightened horses, a blood-chilling shriek.

Albert returned. "Mr Drummond, come quickly." The man couldn't catch his breath. "The … the carriage ploughed right into him."

Fear rattled in Vane's chest.

Don't let it be Wickett.

Drummond hurried off after his coachman.

Vane kicked the open door and entered Drummond's office. He placed Estelle down gently on the bed, knelt at her side and clutched her hand.

A boy knocked the door and stepped into the room. "Doctor's on his way, my lord, said he'd be a few minutes."

Vane nodded.

He sat staring at Estelle, brushed strands of silky hair off her face and stroked her cheek. Memories of the past surfaced, images that pained him even now. He had been too late to save her from the disaster on *The Torrens*, too late to save her from eight years of hell. But Fate had blessed him today.

"Ross." Estelle opened her eyes and looked at him. "Don't … don't go. Stay with me."

Vane forced a smile. "Nothing could tear me away."

CHAPTER SIXTEEN

D octor Hanson spent thirty minutes examining Estelle. Vane suspected Hungerford had given her an overdose of laudanum and prayed to God he was right, and that no permanent damage was done.

While Vane stood waiting for the results of Hanson's observations, Wickett returned and explained how Hungerford had darted across the street, dodged one carriage but fell into the path of another. The poor coachman failed to stop in time and now had the death of the foolish fop on his conscience.

The constable spoke to Vane and Mr Drummond, but as Hungerford had already met his end, the only thing left to do was fetch the coroner.

"The constable witnessed the incident himself," Drummond said as they waited in the courtyard for the doctor to finish tending to Estelle. "He agrees it was an accident though I had to explain why my men were chasing him. One word from you should please the coroner when he arrives. I'd hate for him to think it was a witch hunt."

"Trust me. Hungerford is the only one guilty of a crime, and I shall inform the coroner of all the facts." Including details of the assault in the alley by a Frenchman from Spitalfields. Perhaps he might suggest they investigate the recent death of Hungerford's wife, too.

Vane spent another two hours at Drummond's yard. The doctor explained it would be beneficial to leave Estelle to rest for a while before moving her. And it gave Vane an opportunity to deal with the coroner.

"Good Lord," Mrs Erstwhile said, rushing into the courtyard with Mr Erstwhile in tow. Vane had sent Wickett to speak to the couple, knowing they were awaiting Estelle's return. "Where is she? Please tell me everything is all right. What on earth happened? Your coachman said Mr Hungerford is dead. Is it true? Is he to blame?"

Mr Erstwhile placed a hand on his wife's arm. "My dear, at least let his lordship answer the first question before you bombard him with the rest."

"Miss Darcy is sleeping in Mr Drummond's office." Vane gestured to the wooden building. "You may go inside and sit with her. Doctor Hanson said she requires rest but is certain she'll make a full recovery."

Mrs Erstwhile scurried off while her husband hung back.

"Wickett said Mr Hungerford drugged her in order to spirit her away."

"Based on her constricted pupils the doctor believes she has ingested laudanum. And yes, the dose was given by Hungerford to subdue her while he made his escape." One did not need to be a constable to reach that conclusion.

Mr Erstwhile shook his head. "Estelle avoids taking any medicine and always refuses my offer of a restorative." Water flooded his eyes, and he inhaled deeply to keep his emotions at bay.

"Along with her slight frame, that might explain why she reacted so badly." Vane put a reassuring hand on the old man's shoulder. "You weren't to know of Hungerford's intentions." Indeed, Vane struggled to fathom the fop's rationale. "The coroner seemed so interested in the case, he decided to speak to the magistrate. When a man is confident enough to abduct a lady, the consensus is he may well have committed a similar crime before."

Mr Erstwhile closed his eyes briefly. "And to think I left her alone with him, entrusted her to his care. The lady was out of her depth, and I didn't see it."

A pang of guilt hit Vane squarely in the chest. For a second, he had doubted Estelle's loyalty. "The lady has been out of her depth for eight years, battling one criminal attack after another. If it is any consolation, I did not see it, either."

They exchanged consolatory smiles.

"She deserves so much more from life," Mr Erstwhile said. "Do you not think?"

Two weeks ago he would have refuted the claim. Eight years ago, he would have said she deserved a grand house and a prestigious position in society. Now, she deserved the only thing that mattered—love.

"Come." Vane patted Mr Erstwhile on the back. "Let's see how she's faring. And then I shall escort you all home."

Once back at Whitecombe Street, Vane carried Estelle up to her chamber. Mrs Erstwhile followed and settled her into bed. The effects of the laudanum were wearing off. And so, Mrs Erstwhile agreed to give them a few minutes' privacy.

Vane dropped into the chair next to the bed. "How are you feeling?"

"The urge to sleep does not feel so great now," she said.

"Doctor Hanson assured me I should feel more like myself tomorrow."

They stared at each other. So many words filled his head. But where should he start?

"At what point did you suspect Mr Hungerford's motives?" he said.

Estelle took longer than usual to reply, no doubt her mind was still hazy. "I knew nothing until we arrived at the yard, but by then it was too late." She sucked in a breath. "While I have found myself in many precarious situations over the years, I am just a naive country girl at heart."

"You're not naive, Estelle. Hungerford had everyone fooled." Thank heaven for Mr Joseph. "Were it not for the fact I hired a man to follow him, you would be on your way to Bath now." Bile bubbled in his stomach at the thought. "And I—"

"Would have believed I had left you once again."

He tried to swallow down the lump in his throat. "Yes," he whispered. "You would have been the devil who betrayed me twice."

A tear trickled down her nose. "I am too weak to talk at length now. But know that I never betrayed you, Ross. The only person I betrayed was myself."

He didn't know what that meant. Despite wanting to ask a myriad of questions, he knew now was not the time to pester her for information. She would tell him when she was ready, and somehow during the last week he'd learnt patience.

Vane captured her cold hand and pressed a kiss on her knuckles. He lingered there for longer than necessary. "Rest now." He stood and straightened the coverlet. "I shall call again tomorrow to see how you fare."

Estelle smiled. "Thank you. I dread to think where I would be without you."

Her remark hit him like a lightning bolt to the heart. That was all he'd ever wanted. To be her protector.

"Have no fear," he said in a rich drawl. "I'm sure I can think of a way you might repay me for my efforts. Pleasure is as good a currency as any."

A blush touched her cheeks, bringing life to her pallid countenance. "I'm afraid you might be disappointed. I lack your experience in such matters."

"How wrong you are. You're the only one with the skill to please me." He inclined his head. "Now, I must leave before I'm tempted to draw back the bedsheets and sidle in beside you." He could feel a stirring in his loins at the mere thought. "I doubt Mrs Erstwhile could take another shock today."

A weak chuckle left her pale lips. "You would be most welcome, though I can't promise I won't mumble and mutter incoherently. Then again, I imagine I'm not the first woman to fall asleep with you in bed."

There was a touch of amusement in her tone and a hint of jealousy.

"It may surprise you to learn that I have never fallen asleep with any woman." There was something intimate about the act, something deeply personal. "You would be the first."

The energy in the room shifted. Desire sparked in the air between them. He imagined a host of delicious ways he might wake her in the morning: a gentle suck of her earlobe, nimble fingers wandering down to a warm haven, pressing his erection against her soft buttocks.

"You should know I'm an early riser," he added just to fan the flames of lust a little more.

"I shall bear that in mind as I am full of vitality in the morning, too."

"Then you should most definitely get some rest." With a wide grin, Vane bowed. "Until tomorrow, Miss Darcy."

"Until tomorrow, my lord."

After spending an hour taking tea with the Erstwhiles, Vane returned to Hanover Square. He went straight to the drawing room, poured a glass of brandy and downed the entire contents.

Hungerford was dead—and he was not sorry.

Estelle had no intention of leaving—and he was elated.

Soon, he would have the answers he desired, and then eight years' worth of suffering would be buried in an earthy grave, never to see the light of day again.

Excitement sparked in his chest when he considered a life filled with love, not bitterness and resentment. Reuniting with Estelle had wrought a change in him. The urge to fight rogues in the back alleys had abated. Though one man still needed to feel the full force of his wrath.

Vane contemplated stalking to the museum and creeping through the cold corridors until he found Lord Cornell. From what Vane had read, the explorer Belzoni had brought an Egyptian sarcophagus to London, and he imagined lifting the lid, gagging Cornell and depositing him inside.

A chuckle left Vane's lips. There would be stories in the broadsheets of ghosts and curses, of strange mumbles coming from the ancient tomb. The museum would never be more popular as people stared at the gold coffin unaware that a man had slowly suffocated inside.

Or he could just march to Bedford Square, roll Cornell out of his bed and beat him into submission. But Vane refused to fight a weak man. And so that brought him back to Fabian's plan to ruin the lord financially, to cause him great humiliation.

With his mind made up, Vane called Marley and informed the butler he was going to bed.

"But it's ten ... ten o'clock, my lord?"

"I know what time it is, Marley." No doubt the man recalled the days when his master left the house at ten and retired at dawn. "It has been a long day." And he'd not slept well these last few nights.

Marley inclined his head. "Of course, my lord, I did not mean to be impertinent."

Vane noted the dark circles under his butler's eyes. "You look as though you need rest, too. I have sent word to Sandford Hall, and you should be back to a full complement of staff in a few days."

Almost three years had passed since Vane left this house and swore never to return. Consequently, he'd sent most of the maids and footmen to his country estate. With a house as large as Sandford Hall the staff were never short of work.

"Thank you, my lord. I know Mrs Barton will appreciate help in the kitchen and Pierre is distressed about the time it takes to launder your clothes."

"Pierre is only happy if he is complaining."

"He decided that all your cravats needed pressing, and that Lord Farleigh's staff were unskilled when it came to keeping your linen white."

"I shall speak to him in the morning."

"Thank you, my lord, and may I take this opportunity to welcome you home."

"Thank you, Marley. Now, let us both retire."

Vane ventured up to his bedchamber. Pierre arrived to undress him, but Vane had no time for dramatics this evening, not when his mind was the calmest it had been in years. After dismissing his valet, Vane washed, stripped off his clothes and settled into bed.

Sleep came upon him in a matter of minutes.

He woke an hour later to the creak of a floorboard. With

awakened senses, he listened for another sound but heard nothing more and so closed his eyes as he lay sprawled on his stomach.

His mind was slowly drifting when he caught a whiff of jasmine in the air. The scent irritated his nostrils. A gust of cool air breezed over his bare buttocks, and the boards near the bed creaked again.

Vane turned over and sat up.

It took a moment for his eyes to grow accustomed to the dark. A figure stood but a foot away, gripping the corner of the bedsheets. He would have reached for the blade hidden under his pillow, but from her clawing scent and the flare of her hips, evidently the intruder was a woman.

"What the hell do you want?" And more to the point how the hell did she get in?

From the golden locks draped over her bare shoulders, it was not Estelle. Anyone else could go to the devil.

"Don't play coy, Vane." She slipped beneath the sheets. "You like to taunt me. You like to make it difficult as that is how you judge a woman's worth."

Lady Cornell!

As well as having an obsession with gothic novels, Lady Cornell had taken to inventing fairy stories. "Don't presume to know me. You don't have the first clue what I want or need."

The harpy—for the labels *ravenous* and *predatory* did most certainly apply in this case—moistened her lips as her hungry eyes scanned his bare chest. "Oh, thou dost protest too much. Now lie back and let me show you why we belong together."

Vane shook his head. Why the hell was he still sitting in bed with this woman? He threw back the coverlet and came to his feet.

"How in the devil's name did you get in here?"

A smile touched her lips as her gaze shot to his cock. "Impressive. Let me see what I can do to get his attention." She came up on her knees and palmed her full breasts. "Come to bed, Vane. I did not come here to talk."

"I shall ask again. Who let you in?"

He strode over to the chair, grabbed his breeches and thrust his legs inside swiftly. Sometimes his cock had a mind of his own, and while flaccid now, he'd not give this woman even a twitch of encouragement.

"No one. I simply broke a pane of glass in the door leading to the servants' entrance, reached inside and turned the key."

"Then I shall be sure to send your husband the bill." Vane found his shirt and dragged it over his head.

Unperturbed, Lady Cornell stretched out in the middle of his bed, her legs spread wide in invitation. "I know you've not bedded another lady since you returned from Italy."

"And how could you possibly know that?" Vane considered how he might get her out of his house without using force.

She giggled. "Oh, please tell me you're teasing. Surely you know that your conquests compare notes. How else would I know that you have a fetish for dominance? That you like it hard and rough."

"I fear you have been ill informed on both counts."

Her confident smile faltered. "You mean you don't have a preference when it comes to dalliances in the bedchamber?"

"I mean I have no need to slake my lust for I am already satisfied beyond measure. And what I choose to do in any aspect of my life is no concern of yours." Vane rounded the bed, scooped up the pile of clothes on the floor and threw them at her. "I shall wait outside while you dress."

He had almost reached the door when Lady Cornell made an odd mewling sound. "So you have taken up with that strumpet from the apothecary shop. I did not include her in your conquests as it is clear she is of a different class. It's amazing what a shilling can purchase these days."

Vane stopped and clenched his teeth. He was a man who cared nothing for other people's opinions. Yet he would not permit anyone to slander Estelle Darcy.

"That lady has more dignity and grace in her little finger than you could ever hope to possess. And when it comes to you, Lady Cornell, do you honestly think I would entertain the woman who played a part in my sister's ruination?"

Uncertainty flashed in her eyes. "Your sister's ruination? Why would you think I had anything to do with that?"

"You mean you don't know?"

"Know what?"

"Did you not tell your husband that we were intimate?"

Guilt flashed in her eyes. "I did not tell him directly. I … I might have mentioned to a few gossipmongers that you admired me, that you had suggested I be your mistress."

"To make him jealous?"

She shook her head. "No! In the hope you might warm to the idea and make the offer. But in any event, was Lord Martin not to blame for what happened to your sister?"

This woman thought she had all the answers, thought it was all a silly game.

"Your husband believed your tales and blackmailed Lord Martin to ruin my sister, purely as a means to hurt me."

Lady Cornell appeared genuinely shocked. She gathered the bedsheets up to her chest to cover her modesty and sat there with slumped shoulders as the gravity of what she had done brought tears to her eyes.

"Had I known my husband was capable of such a vile thing I would never have said anything. It was just gossip. I didn't know anyone would get hurt."

"When it comes to deception, there is always a victim."

A tense silence filled the room.

Vane's thoughts drifted to the countless times Lillian had cried in his arms. No lady should have to deal with such heartbreak. And what of Estelle: the smuggler's lackey, the injured maid? She had borne her shame better than most—with a disguise and a level of acceptance he admired.

Lady Cornell suddenly gasped. "What if I was seen coming here?"

"Then your husband will soon learn of it and perhaps I may get the opportunity to punish him for what he's done." Vane pushed the thought from his mind. Cornell was weak and cowardly, and would never challenge him to a duel.

She blinked rapidly. "Do you want me to tell him? Do you want an opportunity to seek revenge? I will do anything for you, you know that."

What he wanted was to take Estelle and go far away from these hypocritical fools. Yes, the burning need for vengeance still flowed through his veins, but revenge did not keep a man warm at night. And after shooting Lord Martin, Vane knew that satisfaction was fleeting.

"I don't care what you do. But you need to leave." He gestured to the mound of material. "Get dressed, and I shall escort you out. I trust you've brought your carriage. If not, I shall rouse my coachman."

She nodded. "Yes, my carriage is waiting in the mews."

Vane thrust his feet into his boots and left the room. He paced the hall to distract his mind. Lady Cornell finally emerged. Her mussed locks hung about her shoulders and she looked like she'd been tumbled in a haystack.

"Are you certain you don't want me to warm your bed?" she said in a seductive lilt. "It's not too late to change your mind."

How many times must he explain his lack of interest? "For fear of sounding like Lady Hamilton's parrot, I think you know the answer."

They descended the stairs and took the door from the hall that led down to the servants' quarters.

"I'm afraid there's glass on the floor," she said as they approached the back door.

"I shall have someone clean it up in the morning."

"Will you not carry me to safety?"

"Certainly not."

They dodged the fragments of broken glass. Vane escorted her to the waiting carriage. Merely because he wanted to ensure she didn't hide in the broom cupboard and sneak upstairs while he slept.

He opened the door, and she stopped before him. "I'm sorry for whatever pain Cornell has caused. With any luck, he is not long for this world, and then we can both celebrate." Without warning, she kissed him on the cheek.

A gasp from behind drew Vane's attention.

Another figure approached—smaller in height and frame. The woman had the hood of her black cloak raised, the gold lining framing her face like a halo.

She stepped closer, the light from the coach lamp illuminating her features.

"Estelle? What are you doing here? I didn't expect to see you this evening." Why was it his tone carried a guilty edge when he had done nothing wrong?

"I … I came because I had something important to say that couldn't wait until tomorrow."

"Then come inside."

Lady Cornell gave a sly snigger.

Estelle looked at him, pain swimming in her eyes. "No. It's not important now. It can wait until another time." She noted Lady Cornell's state of dishabille. She looked at his open shirt hanging out of his breeches. And then she swung around, picked up her skirts and ran.

CHAPTER SEVENTEEN

"Estelle, wait!"

She could hear the clip of Ross' boots on the cobblestones. He would catch her, of that she was certain. Still, she would not make it easy for him, and so she pressed on even though she wanted to crumple to the ground and sob until there were no more tears left to shed.

Perhaps she was still suffering after the harrowing events of the day. Perhaps the laudanum Mr Hungerford had used to drug her only added to her feelings of fragility.

"Estelle!" Ross pleaded. "At least give me a chance to explain."

She ignored him, knowing that soon she would have to stop running. The pounding in her head had returned and the tears filling her eyes made it hard to see in the dark.

Ross grabbed the back of her cloak and swung her around to face him. She slipped on the damp cobblestones. One knee buckled, but she did not fall.

"Hold on to me." Ross' muscular arm slid around her waist, and he pulled her to his chest. "You should not have left your bed."

"Why? Because you wish I'd not caught you cavorting with Lady Cornell?"

"I was not cavorting with Lady Cornell."

"Then why did she kiss you? Why are you both half-dressed?" Her tone conveyed anger and disappointment, and yet being held by him was so comforting.

Damn these confounding contradictions.

"It is a simple misunderstanding. If you come inside, I shall explain."

Lady Cornell's carriage rattled past. She watched them from the window, a smug grin playing on her face.

"Look at her," Estelle snapped. "The lady looks thoroughly satisfied to me."

Ross dropped his arm, and she felt the loss instantly. "Do you honestly think I would entertain that woman while paying court to you?"

It was a trick question.

If she revealed her doubts and fears, she was admitting she didn't trust him. Life in France had given her cause to trust no one. And yet, she desperately wanted to believe the best of him.

"I don't know what to think, but I know what I saw." For some bizarre reason, she wanted to be angry with him, too.

Ross took hold of her upper arms, not as firm as Philipe Robard had done, but in a gentle way that spoke of affection. "You saw a man roused from his bed by a madwoman intent on seduction. You saw me escort her to the carriage to ensure she did not return."

"You must have invited her inside. You must have given her some indication that her efforts would be rewarded."

Ross glanced up at the night sky and thrust his hands through his hair. "God, the woman needs no encouragement, and she happened to force her way into my house. Take a look at the broken door if you don't believe me."

Surprisingly, she did believe him. In her heart, she knew he would never lie to her. And yet her faith in him only served to accentuate the depths of her own deceit.

"It doesn't matter now," she said with a resigned sigh as she took a step back. "It was foolish of me to come."

"What possessed you to walk the streets alone at this time of night? This is not a smugglers' haven. Mrs Erstwhile would have a fit of apoplexy if she knew."

"Mr Erstwhile brought me here in a hackney cab, but I asked that he leave me just outside the square."

Mr Erstwhile had caught her sneaking downstairs. She couldn't lie to him and had revealed her plan to visit Ross. He was not her father and could not forbid it, but having his respect and approval meant the world to her.

"Are you telling me he permitted you to come to a gentleman's home in the middle of the night?"

Mr Erstwhile was an advocate of true love. He was a man who rose above petty judgements, a man disillusioned with Society's rigid rules. She'd told him she loved Ross with all her heart and that was a justifiable reason for her to come.

"For a wise man, he can be extremely naive," Ross added.

He could say what he liked about anyone else, but she would not stand for him belittling Mr Erstwhile.

"I think you'll find he is exactly the opposite. Everything he says and does is based on experience and sound judgement. His motives are free from jealousy and spite, unlike your father."

The last few words fell from her lips without thought.

"Unlike my father?" Ross blinked in surprise. "What do you mean?"

Estelle bit back a curse. She had come to tell him everything, purely because she wanted tomorrow to be a new day, a fresh start. Now she was not so sure.

"Just that some men act in their own best interests regardless of the cost."

"And you think my father one of those men?" His frown conveyed suspicion.

She turned away from him. "I must go. The cab will be waiting." The hackney had taken Mr Erstwhile back to Whitecombe Street. The gentleman assumed Ross would convey her home. "One lady has kept you from your bed. I should hate to do the same."

"Then why come?" Ross grabbed her arm to prevent her hasty retreat. "Did leaving Prescott Hall have something to do with my father?"

Estelle tried to tug her arm free, but without warning, Ross grabbed her around the waist and hauled her over his shoulder.

"What on earth are you doing? Put me down."

"Forgive my masterful approach, but you will come inside, and we will have it out."

She knew what he meant by the comment, but still, images of them writhing naked in his bed flashed into her mind.

"Then put me down and let me walk."

"No." A large hand settled on her buttocks as he held her in place. He strode through the door leading from the mews to the garden. "For eight long, painful years you have left me in the dark. But it stops here, tonight." He marched through the broken door, fragments of glass crunching beneath his feet. "You will tell me exactly why you ran, why you left me and permitted me to believe you were dead."

She tried to wriggle free, but one strong arm held her there.

"I think I have been more than patient, Estelle."

His boots clipped on the marble floor as he stormed through the hall. Estelle expected him to turn into the drawing room, but he headed for the stairs.

The butler appeared, his clothes a touch less than perfect. "Is everything all right, my lord. I heard raised voices."

"Go to bed, Marley. Everything is in hand."

"Y-yes. Good night, my lord."

Ross mounted the stairs with ease, marched into his chamber and locked the door. Four long strides and he was at the bed. He threw her down onto the mattress and stood above her.

"Now," he began, drawing his shirt over his head. "You will answer my questions. I think after all that has occurred you owe me your cooperation."

Estelle nodded. She might have formed a reply, but her hungry eyes feasted on the muscular planes of his chest. The rippling muscles in his abdomen made her mouth water. As did the enticing line of dark hair drawing her eyes to a point below the waistband of his breeches.

"Let us get a few quick questions out of the way first. I'm told that is the best way to discover the truth." He threw his shirt onto the chair behind him. "Did you ever love me?" He reached for her leg, unlaced her boot, tugged it off and let it fall to the floor.

"Yes," she breathed. "I loved you with all my heart. I swear to you that is the truth."

Ross removed the other boot. "Did you leave Prescott Hall under duress?"

She hesitated. "Yes."

From the sudden rise and fall of his chest, his breath came quickly now.

"Did you want to marry me?" He took hold of her foot, his hands venturing up under her dress to undo the ribbon on her stocking.

"Yes," she whispered as his warm hand settled on her bare thigh and rolled the stocking down to her ankle. As he removed it, he bent his head, kissed and nipped her toes. Heat flooded her body, burned in her core.

"Will you permit me to make love to you again?" He repeated the process with her other stocking, his heated gaze searing into her as he sucked the tip of each toe. "Right here. Right now."

"You know I will," she panted.

With a wild, sinful look in his eyes, he stared at her while unbuttoning his breeches. "Loving you has never been a problem for me. Trusting you, on the other hand, has proved infinitely more difficult."

"I understand."

With an arrogant grin, he pushed his breeches off his hips to reveal his solid shaft. Heavens above. Her nipples ached at the sight. The pulses in her intimate place grew more profound.

"Then you will answer the next question honestly. But first, believe me when I tell you that you're the only woman I have pleasured these last two years." He took her hands and brought her to her feet. "You're the only woman I will pleasure until the day you say you no longer want me."

"That will never happen."

After removing her cloak, Ross turned her around and unthreaded the ties on her dress. Once undone, his hands settled on her shoulders, and he pushed the garment free until it fell to the floor. He did the same with her petticoat.

She wore front-fastening stays and so he would need to turn her back to face him. Instead, he stood behind her, the heat of his body penetrating the thin fabric. His hands traced the curve of her hips and the fullness of her breasts as he pressed his erection against her buttocks.

"Do you like that, Estelle?"

"Yes." Her body ached for him, craved that which she had been denied for so long.

"Later, you can tell me what my father did to make you doubt me," Ross said, pressing his lips to her neck, nipping the sensitive spot with his teeth, gently sucking. "You can tell me the reason you felt you couldn't speak to me."

Ross drew her round to face him, proceeded to work on her stays, tugging at the ties, pulling them free, watching her with a hot, intense gaze that made her knees weak. Her breasts jiggled as he continued with his ministrations. The sensual curve of his lips forced her to swallow hard.

Once he'd freed her of her stays, he stepped back. "Remove your chemise."

She wasn't sure she had the strength to lift the flimsy garment.

"Do it slowly. Tease me, Estelle. Reveal yourself to me in such a way that I can barely contain my excitement."

Oh, heavens!

Not knowing how to tempt a man, all she could do was listen to the demands of her body, embrace the fierce passion flaming within. She closed her eyes briefly and let lust take her.

"Do you want me, Ross?" she whispered, reaching up and removing the pins from her hair. Raven black locks tumbled down over her shoulders.

"Good God, I want you so badly, I'm struggling to stand."

His reply bolstered her confidence.

She skimmed her hands down the front of her chemise intending to reach for the hem. But her aching nipples relished the light brushing, and so she cupped her breasts and fondled them as she wanted him to do.

Ross blinked, gulped, his breathing grew heavy, and she found she rather liked playing the temptress.

"Minx," he said.

Excited by his response, she ran her hands over her hips, dared to venture to the intimate place that throbbed for his touch. When her fingers skimmed down between the apex of her thighs, a pleasurable moan left her lips.

His hard shaft jerked in response, and he took himself in hand

and stroked back and forth as if it eased the pressure building inside. Gripping the hem, she slid the material up inch by inch, aware that he was biting down on his bottom lip, that a hum resonated in his throat when she exposed her breasts.

"I knew you would be beyond beautiful," he said, his heated gaze devouring every inch of her body as she dropped her chemise on the floor. "I cannot tell you how many times I have imagined it in my mind. But still you take my breath away."

"I too have thought of you many times. I have stared out at sea and dreamed that a wave would come and scoop me up and carry me back home to you."

He closed the gap between them, bent his head and kissed the brown birthmark he'd last looked upon with disdain. "You are home now. This is where you are supposed to be." His arm snaked around her back as his tongue traced the outline of her nipple, teasing her, tempting her.

She pushed her hands into his hair, inhaled the intoxicating scent of bergamot, of something unique, totally masculine. "Tell me how it would have been on our wedding night."

He straightened and looked at her, his blue eyes sparkling. "I would have been gentle and tender. I would have taken you slowly, stared into your eyes as I filled your body. I would have given you everything of myself, held nothing in reserve."

Oh, it sounded so perfect. "Will you not do so now?"

He kissed her, a slow melding of mouths that tugged at the muscles deep in her core. Their tongues danced in a sensual, erotic rhythm. The taste of him fed her addiction, soothed her soul.

"I will do whatever you ask," he said, breaking contact. "But you must answer one question first."

She had nothing to fear anymore. This man made her feel strong and invincible. "Ask me anything."

"Do you love me, Estelle?"

The directness of his question made her catch her breath.

"I am not speaking of how you felt years ago," he continued. "Or how you felt while living in that hellhole in France. I am speaking about how you feel now. Here. In this moment."

She did not have to examine her thoughts. The answer lived within in her. Indeed, she heard it before he asked the question. "I have loved you for as long as I can remember. Yes, I love you now as much as I did then."

One corner of his mouth turned up into a wicked smile. He took her hand, pulled the coverlet back to the end of the bed and gestured for her to lie down.

She sank down into the mattress, gloried in the sight of him rising above her. He lavished her body with tender kisses, tasted her intimately in a place she never imagined he would. His actions were slow, yet she could feel an intense passion barely contained.

He did not bring her to that glorious place where she cried out his name and shuddered in his arms, but it was not far away. Indeed, the feel of him entering her body, of him pushing deep, sent a pleasurable shiver racing to her toes.

Ross cupped her face and kissed her as he withdrew and entered her again.

"Oh, Lord," she panted for the sensation was beyond anything she had experienced before. It was beautiful, highly arousing. Heavenly. "Do it again."

Their eyes locked and the power of it touched her soul. "With pleasure."

He closed his eyes on the next deep, measured thrust. A groan left his lips.

"Give yourself over to me, Ross." She wrapped her legs more firmly around his waist as he rocked in and out of her.

"Do you like the feel of me inside you?" he breathed before

moving to kiss her lips, her chin, to suck her lobe. "Do you like it when I fill you full?"

"Like it? It's divine."

Her words brought a slight shift in energy, he quickened the pace, angled his hips in such a way that he rubbed against the intimate place begging for release.

"Oh, Ross," she gasped as the bed creaked and he drove harder.

"I need to withdraw soon."

"Don't." The foolish word left her lips unwittingly, for common sense played no part in it.

He stopped and looked at her, his eyes heavy with desire. "If I don't withdraw, you know what that means should there be a child?"

Oh, she knew. Nothing in this world would make her happier. "I know."

He pushed inside her again. "Then you will swear it before God."

She didn't know if he meant to marry her or make her his mistress. "What am I to swear to?"

"That you will marry me. What else?"

"I swear."

He plunged inside her. Four strokes and they were both hovering on the brink of their release. Her body exploded first, and then he stilled above her, flooding her with the essence of the man she loved, as he would have done on their wedding night. A guttural groan left his lips. They gasped each other's names. She felt whole, blissfully happy. Surely nothing could come between them now. Surely nothing but happiness lay beyond this night.

CHAPTER EIGHTEEN

They lay wrapped in each other's arms, their legs entangled, their souls entwined. Vane stroked her hair, caressed her cheek, ran his hand over her bare shoulder because he could not stop touching her.

"When you came here, you said you had something important to tell me," he reminded her. They were on the verge of falling asleep, but he knew Mr Erstwhile wouldn't settle until she returned home.

Her warm brown eyes searched his face. "I came because it is time you learnt the truth. It was wrong of me to keep it from you, and now I can see that not knowing caused more pain than disappointment ever could."

"Why not wait until tomorrow?"

"I hoped we could put the past behind us, that tomorrow could be a fresh start, a new day."

Vane came up on his elbow and gazed down at her. "Then tell me everything. Leave nothing out. Let us have no secrets anymore." He suspected the truth would be unpleasant. After all, it had given her cause to leave him and flee to France.

"I'm not sure where to begin."

"Begin with what this has to do with my father." He was desperate to know.

After a moment's hesitation, Estelle told him about his father's deliberate effort to ruin her father. Vane discovered the extent of his father's betrayal, of the vile threats, of the ultimatum given to a young woman so torn she had not known what to do.

Tears flowed as quickly as her words.

Water filled his eyes, too. Not for his poor mother, for her father or brother, but for the innocent woman cornered by a tyrant. Vane pictured Estelle standing in the orchard, wringing her hands, gazing up at the sky and pleading for the Lord's help. He could feel the gut-wrenching pain that accompanied leaving those you loved behind.

Were it not for the love filling his chest now, he would rage through the house in a destructive frenzy. He would smash his fist through the portrait of his father hanging in the hall, chop it into small pieces and use it for firewood. But nothing could change what had happened in the past. And all he wanted now was to bask in this beautiful state of bliss.

"I'm sorry I left without telling you."

Vane sighed as he wiped her tears away. He understood her motive now. "I cannot imagine how hard it must have been for you, but I wish you had trusted me. We could have eloped. Together, we might have found a way to help your father."

"Mr Erstwhile would say that hindsight is the Devil tormenting our minds. That no one can foretell what might have been." She gave a weak smile. "But I do have one question."

"What is that?"

"If your father went to great lengths to ensure you married his mistress' daughter, why did you not wed?"

He fell silent for a moment while he gathered his thoughts. Those months after he believed she'd drowned in the shipwreck were the most painful of his entire life.

"Everything makes more sense now," he said with an air of melancholy. "I became withdrawn after you left, then angry, then rebellious. My father tried to console me, control me, but I refused to listen. He made many attempts to persuade me to marry, threatened me, even came up with a list of prospective brides, the current Lady Cornell being his favourite."

"Lady Cornell?" Estelle snorted. "That confirms his logic was flawed."

As the words left her lips, recognition dawned. The veil of secrecy slipped away and he saw the truth for the first time.

"Good God. Lady Trent was my father's mistress." Vane sat up and dragged his hand down his face. "Lady Cornell's mother was known for her conquests. Everyone spoke of a secret lover though no one knew his name. That's why my father insisted her daughter would be a perfect match."

Vane had been given an ultimatum—marry her or suffer eternal damnation. His father's weak heart meant he was denied an opportunity to carry out the threat.

Estelle sat up. Vane's gaze fell to the soft curve of her breast, and he draped his arm around her, drew her close and settled back against the pillows.

"Perhaps that's why Lady Cornell is so obsessed with you," she said as her fingers twirled the hair on his chest, traced the numerous scars he'd received from brawls in dark alleys.

"It certainly explains why she thinks we might be well suited." Vane chose that moment to explain again how the lady happened to be in such a state of dishabille as she left his house. "My friend, Lord Farleigh, believes the woman is dangerous."

"Well, she is not afraid to take risks." Estelle paused. "You told me she wanted you to kill her husband. Do you think that's her motive or is it that she still hopes to marry you?"

Vane shrugged. "I would say it's both. After tonight, she

knows I would like nothing more than an excuse to ruin Lord Cornell, whether by legitimate means or not."

"What grievance do you have with him?"

"Cornell orchestrated Lillian's ruination." Vane went on to tell Estelle about the events two years ago, about how Lord Martin offered marriage, took what he wanted and then boarded the next ship to France. "Fabian threatened Cornell when he discovered the truth about his involvement."

Estelle fell silent.

"I have hurt Fabian, too, haven't I?"

Vane refused to lie to her. "Yes, but he believes you left because of something I did. He's blamed me for years. We fought about it only a few weeks ago." Fists had flown. Threats were exchanged.

"Then I shall have to correct his misconception."

"We could travel to the island. Your brother deserves to know you're alive and well." And time away from London would give them an opportunity to make plans for the future. "Though I should warn you, his men are somewhat brash and unconventional."

"You forget I've spent four years with a gang of smugglers." She chuckled, but the sound lacked any genuine amusement.

It was his turn to fall silent. Vane pushed all thoughts of her time in Wissant from his mind, lest it torment him.

"What will you do about Lady Cornell?" Estelle asked. "You cannot permit her to continue in this outrageous manner."

In truth, he didn't know. When he married Estelle—and he would marry her—perhaps it would bring an end to her obsession.

Vane was about to answer when a knock on the door commanded his attention.

What the hell did Marley want at this hour? Perhaps the butler had discovered the broken glass on the floor and feared an intruder.

"I should attend to that," he said.

In spite of his nakedness, Vane strode to the door, opened it ajar and peered at his butler. "What is it, Marley?"

"Forgive the disturbance, my lord, but Wickett insisted I give you this at once." He handed Vane a letter. The burgundy wax seal meant it wasn't from Mr Joseph.

Vane took the letter. "Wait here a moment." He closed the door, broke the seal and strode over to the lit candelabra to read the missive. He read it twice. Not because it was illegible, but because he couldn't quite believe what he was reading.

"Is there something wrong?" A frown marred Estelle's brow.

"Here, you may read it for yourself."

She took the letter and muttered as she absorbed the words. "Lord Cornell wants to meet with you at this hour? Do you think he discovered his wife came here this evening?"

"I doubt it is a coincidence." Vane cursed inwardly. After their earlier conversation, no doubt Lady Cornell told him where she had been and what she had discovered in the process.

"Why would he ask to meet you at the museum? Is it not closed?"

"Cornell works closely with the curators. Quite often he sources new pieces and rearranges displays. When it comes to antiquities and the study of ancient cultures, there is not a man in London more knowledgeable." He hated paying the scoundrel a compliment.

"And he works there this late?" Her voice held a nervous edge.

"He's been known to work through the night on many occasions." Vane returned to address his butler. "Have Wickett ready the carriage. I shall be down as soon as I'm dressed."

"Shall I wake Pierre, my lord?"

"No. I'll see to things myself." The last thing he wanted was the Frenchman stumbling upon the naked woman in his bed.

Vane closed the door. He could sense Estelle's anxiety before he turned to face her.

"You're not going?" She climbed out of bed and came to stand before him in all her wondrous glory.

He drank in the sight of her soft breasts, of the gentle flare of her hips. He stared at her in awe, in lust, in love. "I must."

"But why? Has he not already caused untold damage to your life?"

"Which is why I must put an end to it once and for all."

She placed her warm hands on his chest. "Don't go. Forget about them. I cannot imagine he simply wants to talk."

"Estelle, the man is a menace, as is his wife. I shall not have either of them ruining things for us now."

Her breathing grew ragged. "Then I'm coming with you."

"The hell you are. I don't trust either of them."

She ignored him, moved to the pile of discarded garments and found her chemise. "Either I come with you, or I'll make my way there alone." The thin chemise slithered over her body to distract him momentarily. She continued dressing, the firm set of her mouth and determined stare a sign he should not challenge her.

Vane was unused to being defied. But then he would rather have Estelle with him than sit wondering when she would appear.

"Then you're to remain in the carriage," he said as if he was in control of this situation.

"If that is what you wish."

Vane entered his dressing room, rummaged around in the armoire and returned dressed in his usual black garb. Estelle sat on the edge of the bed, her boots fastened, her cloak tied around her shoulders and the hood raised. She'd plumped the pillow and straightened the coverlet. He'd forgotten she was accustomed to making her own bed.

"Are you ready?" she asked, and he thought he saw a guilty glint in her eye.

"I was born ready."

Wickett drove past the museum and brought the carriage to a stop on Russell Street, some three hundred yards away, as Vane instructed.

Shrouded in her black cloak, Estelle sat opposite, staring at him with wide eyes and an open mouth. "This is madness."

"Yes, but it is necessary." Since the embarrassing incident with Fabian, Cornell had hidden in the shadows. But that didn't mean he wasn't planning his revenge.

"So necessary you're willing to risk your life?" she mocked.

"There is nothing to fear. The night you stumbled upon me in the alley I'd been brawling with two rogues."

"And look how it ended. You were practically unconscious when we found you."

Only because the wolfhound sought to distract him. "I am more than capable of defending myself against Cornell."

Estelle glanced out of the window at the dimly lit street. "But you don't know the museum as he does. The smugglers always outwitted the revenue men because they knew every hiding place."

"Don't worry about me. Thirty minutes and I'll be back." Perhaps with an appointment to meet at dawn on Hampstead Heath.

She crossed the carriage and fell into his lap. "I cannot lose you now. Not after all we have been through."

Vane kissed her: a slow, languorous affair that stirred his loins and teased his senses. "Only when we've dealt with the past, can we think about the future."

"Mr Erstwhile would disagree."

"Mr Erstwhile is not here. And in this instance, I'm confident of his support." He kissed her again for good measure. "Now, promise me you will wait here until I return."

She shook her head. "I cannot do that."

"You cannot wait, or you cannot promise?"

"Both."

"God damn, Estelle, must you be so stubborn? How can I deal with Cornell if I'm worried about you?" He lifted her up and deposited her on the seat opposite, then he opened the door and dropped to the pavement.

"Will you not at least take a weapon?"

The museum was full of ancient swords and spears. One of those would suffice. "I can always hit him over the head with a marble bust." When she failed to find it amusing, he added, "Should anything untoward happen, I'll not have the magistrate believe I entered the building with intent."

She huffed and then thumped the seat.

"Wait for me," he said before closing the door. He glanced up at Wickett. "No matter what happens, the lady is not to leave the carriage. Is that understood?"

"I can't promise I can keep her in there, but I'll not let her out of my sight. You have my word on that."

"If you see Cornell leave before me, I suggest you send for a constable."

Wickett's expression turned grave. "Just have a care. Your mind's not as focused as it used to be."

Vane raised a brow. "As long as there are no hounds roaming the corridors I shall be fine."

"Hounds or wolves?"

"Both."

As per the instructions in the missive, Vane followed the wall until he came to the wooden service gates. He slipped inside, walked through the garden and entered the building.

Cornell asked Vane to meet him in the basement. It was where men spent hours huddled around the desks beneath the vaulted ceiling, examining relics from a bygone era. Should he meet anyone patrolling the corridors all he had to do was give Cornell's name and his own calling card and no one would question his presence.

That fact made him doubt Cornell had sinister intentions.

Vane stepped stealthily down the stairs. Lord Cornell may have summoned him, but he would not put himself at a disadvantage by warning the lord of his approach.

He crept past the row of glass cases, past the table where someone had been taking rubbings from stone tablets, towards the glow of candlelight in the far corner. Cornell sat slumped over a desk, numerous implements laid out in front of him, while he used the pointed end of a tool on a decorative necklace.

Vane cleared his throat. "You wanted to see me?"

Cornell jumped up from his seat and bumped into the table. He dropped the tool, and it clattered on the floor. It took him a moment to find his voice.

"Trevane?" Blood crept up Cornell's neck to flood his cheeks. The man's bottom lip trembled. "You're not allowed down here. It … it is strictly off-limits."

Vane snorted with contempt. "Did you not send for me?"

"Send for you?" Cornell seemed confused. "No."

"Don't play games. I received your letter. The wax seal bore your crest. How else would I have known where to come?"

"There must be some mistake," he said, draping a cloth over the gem-encrusted necklace he'd been working on. His hands were shaking, and he refused to meet Vane's gaze. "What reason would I have for asking you here?"

"Oh, I don't know," Vane said arrogantly. "Perhaps you want to offer an apology for being the conniving bastard responsible for ruining my sister. Perhaps you want to explain why you paid a man to follow her to Raven Island. Or why you seem to think I'd be remotely interested in bedding your wife."

Cornell fell silent, though he seemed more concerned with the items on the table than he did Vane's accusations.

"Look, I acted out of spite and jealousy." Cornell shivered visibly. He held up his hands in mock surrender, and yet he would not move from the table. Clearly he was hiding something. "Lord Ravenscroft made his position clear. Should I venture to injure the lady again that damn pirate will put a ball in my chest."

"Yes, but not before I stuff your head up your horse's arse."

The man's saggy jowls wobbled in fright.

"And so you didn't summon me here to call me out?" Vane continued.

Cornell blinked rapidly. "Good Lord, no. Why on earth would I do that?"

Vane stared at the craven oaf. Perhaps he should give the lord a beating. Teach him a lesson. "If you didn't send the letter asking I come here, then who did?"

A feminine chuckle sliced through the air. Lady Cornell stepped out of the shadows and aimed a pistol at her husband. "I think you'll find that was me."

CHAPTER NINETEEN

Five minutes had passed since Ross entered the museum, yet every second felt like an hour. In her mind, Estelle concocted a host of scenarios. Lord Cornell, a jealous, obsessed husband, lay in wait ready to blow a hole in Ross' chest. Or would Ross creep up on the man, punch him for his past misdeeds, deliver a fatal blow that would see him swing from the gallows?

Was it a trap?

An ambush?

With heightened anxiety, she opened the carriage door and stepped down to the pavement. Wickett climbed down from his box and was at her side before a word left her lips.

"I know what you're thinking, miss, and his lordship will have my hide if I don't persuade you to step back inside the carriage."

"Something is wrong, Wickett." Whether it be intuition or the bitter chill in the air, a shiver raced from Estelle's neck to her navel. "I can sense it."

From the flash of alarm in his eyes, she knew he sensed it, too.

"His lordship knows how to handle himself. I know I shouldn't say this, but he enjoys a good fight."

Estelle recalled tracing her finger over the scars on his arm and chest though she had been too preoccupied to ask how he came by them.

"Lord Trevane told me he was fighting in the alley on the night we met."

Wickett pursed his lips. "That was one night out of many. He likes to prove no one can hurt him. Wounds heal. Scars fade. Still, nothing seems to calm the torment raging inside."

Was she to blame for that? she wondered.

"Then we must go after him before he does something he may live to regret." Something that might see them separated for far longer than eight years.

Wickett shook his head. "He's calmer this last week. Happen he'll think twice before taking any unnecessary risks."

Estelle was about to protest when a figure appeared from the shadows. The man was tall and dark with a menacing aura which she attributed to the beaver hat concealing his eyes and the broad shoulders accentuated by the capes of his greatcoat.

Wickett straightened at her side, his hand sliding covertly into his coat.

The man approached them, pushed up the brim of his hat with a walking cane which she considered was more a weapon than an aid to help with one's balance. "What the hell are you doing here?"

"Mr Joseph?" Wickett relaxed his shoulders and sighed. "I could ask you the same."

Mr Joseph glanced back over his shoulder before stepping closer. "I'm waiting for the constable and the chief magistrate. But there's no time. You'd best get his lordship out of there."

Panic flared.

"Where? The museum?" Wickett frowned. "Lord Trevane is meeting Lord Cornell."

"God damn." Mr Joseph hit the ground with his walking cane. "Sorry, miss, for cursing."

"Pay it no mind." She had heard far worse from Faucheux. "If you summoned the magistrate, then you must know Lord Trevane is in danger." How could this man know of Cornell's letter when they had received it less than an hour ago?

"Lord Cornell is a crook. After Lord Trevane asked me to watch him, I followed Cornell to St Leonard's in Shoreditch. He met a man there, a jeweller named Morris, and they made an exchange. Turns out it's one of many."

"An exchange?" she said, wondering what on earth he was talking about and what this had to do with Ross.

"Seems Cornell is doing more in there than studying old relics," Mr Joseph said. "He's swapping priceless gems for paste."

Estelle might have been shocked, but she'd heard of titled men involved in smuggling. Why not theft on a grand scale? "And you're worried because the magistrate will want to know why Lord Trevane is in the museum meeting a jewel thief."

"You have the right of it, miss," Mr Joseph said. "I know his lordship well enough to know he's not involved. What I don't know is why the hell he's in there."

"He received a letter to meet Lord Cornell," Estelle said. "I read it myself."

Mr Joseph rubbed his bristly chin. "You're sure it was from Lord Cornell? I'm asking because his wife entered the building five minutes before you got here. I hear she's been hankering after Lord Trevane for some time."

The sense of panic grew stronger now as if every new snippet of information tore another breath from Estelle's lungs.

"How long has Lord Cornell been at the museum?" she said though was somewhat reluctant to hear the answer.

"My man followed him here at eight o'clock and kept watch until I arrived."

Which meant that Lord Cornell could not have sent the letter. Estelle stood for a few seconds, trying to decide what to do. Was Ross oblivious to the fact Lady Cornell was inside? Had it been the lady's motive all along to have Ross kill her husband? They were certainly ill-matched, most definitely ill-suited.

"So the magistrate knows Cornell is the one stealing the gems?" Wickett asked.

Mr Joseph explained how he caught Morris with the real gems and forced a confession. "Morris makes the imitation paste based on Cornell's measurements and drawings. It might take three or four attempts until it's right. Morris sells the gems to his contact abroad and they share the funds. That's what the magistrate seems to think."

While Wickett went on to probe Mr Joseph about how they would get his lordship out without alerting Lord Cornell, Estelle shrank back furtively. Both men were so engrossed in plotting and planning that they failed to notice her sneak behind the carriage and race across the road.

She opened the service gate and slipped inside, stole through the garden to the door leading into the museum. The one that Cornell assured them was open. As she reached the narrow flight of stairs leading down to the basement, she heard voices.

Skilled at tiptoeing lightly on her feet, Estelle plastered her back flat against the wall and crept downstairs.

Three figures stood at the end of a room crowded with display cases, tables and broken statues. The dust in the air clawed at her throat. It took every effort not to cough and sneeze.

"So that is your plan," Lord Cornell said, shaking his head at his wife.

Lady Cornell stood with her back to Estelle. She wore a long black cloak and held something in her hand.

"Trevane comes here with a story to distract me," Lord

Cornell continued, "so you can creep up behind and commit murder."

Lady Cornell chuckled. "Vane knew nothing about my plan and merely took the bait, as I intended."

Estelle hated it when Lady Cornell called him that. While *Vane* was derived from his title, it meant disloyal, fickle, and in no way conveyed the character of the man she knew.

"Trust me," Ross said. "I am as much in the dark as you are."

"Then allow me to shed a little light on the situation." Lady Cornell moved closer to her husband. "You see, I was always supposed to marry Lord Trevane. My mother dedicated ten years of her life to make sure it happened. But as you know, when she died I had no option but to marry a blubbery mammal stupid enough to put Colonel Preston's odd creatures to shame."

"Now listen here," Lord Cornell protested. "I've given you everything. You want for nothing."

"Other than a virile man in bed," Lady Cornell countered. "And everyone knows Vane is the epitome of sexual prowess."

Estelle could not argue with that.

Lord Cornell looked astounded. "Marriage is about more than a quick romp beneath the sheets."

Ross cleared his throat. "I think you'll find the word *quick* may have led to the problem."

"Precisely," Lady Cornell agreed. "And so, as Vane and I were meant to wed—"

"That may have been your mother's plan," Ross interjected, "but it was most certainly not mine. There is only one woman I hope to marry, and it is not you." Ross snorted. "You can shoot me, and still I will not change my mind."

Estelle slapped her hand over her mouth to stifle a gasp. Was it a pistol Lady Cornell held in her hand?

"Oh, I have no intention of shooting you, Vane. And I'm

certain when you've heard what I have to say you will change your mind about marrying me."

Lady Cornell was suffering from some sort of mental imbalance. Either that or her arrogance knew no bounds.

Without warning, the lady raised her hand, pulled the trigger and shot Lord Cornell. The sharp crack echoed through the room, shaking the glass doors in the display cases.

"Good God!" Ross cried as the lead ball ripped into Cornell's chest, taking the man clean off his feet. "Have you lost your mind?"

Lord Cornell grabbed the cloth on the table and dragged it with him as he landed with a thud on the tiled floor.

"Lost my mind!" Lady Cornell screeched. "Do you know what it has been like for me? Watching you cavort with other women, hearing their lewd tales. Having to go home to that monstrosity." She waved the pistol at the man groaning and writhing on the floor.

"If we don't help him, he will die." Ross knelt down over Lord Cornell's body.

Estelle took the opportunity to creep closer. At any moment, Wickett and Mr Joseph would appear. What if the lady had a knife and stabbed Ross amid the confusion?

"That is my intention. When he's dead, we will be free to marry."

"You're deluded if you think there is any chance of that happening." Ross shrugged out of his coat, rolled it into a ball and placed it under Cornell's head.

"We are in this together now. If caught, we'll both hang."

"I highly doubt it." Ross sounded so confident. "Enough people know of your obsession, of your silly notes, and I have the letter inviting me here."

Lady Cornell snorted. "You think I don't know who she is. My mother described her to me many times. You gave it away when you called her Estelle. Such an unusual name. It certainly explains why you're so besotted with a shopgirl."

Ross glared at Lady Cornell, his eyes dark, dangerous. "Be careful. Be very careful."

Lady Cornell shrugged. "Once the world knows Miss Darcy survived the shipwreck and is so free with her affections that she whores about in coaching inns, she will be shunned. Imagine the humiliation. Imagine the torment. Imagine how people will treat your children."

Estelle's stomach grew hot, so hot it burned as bile bubbled and rose to her chest. She was set to burst, to hail fire and brimstone down upon this pathetic creature.

But Ross shook his head and laughed.

"Do your worst. You may be governed by society's rules, but I am not. And I can assure you, neither is Miss Darcy."

Lady Cornell fell silent for a moment. "She doesn't love you. If she did why has she only recently returned to town?"

"That is no business of yours." Ross turned back to look at Lord Cornell. He pressed his fingers against the man's wrist. "It's not too late to call for help. I'm sure you can think of something to account for firing the shot."

Without warning, she threw the pistol on the floor, darted forward and grabbed a sharp implement off the table. She jabbed it at Ross. "Step away from him. I'll not suffer his presence another minute."

Estelle slid her hand into her boot and drew the hunting knife that she had found beneath Ross' pillow. She moved closer.

"How do you hope to account for his death?" Ross said. "You'll not get far before you're apprehended. Have you ever heard someone's neck crack when they fall from the gallows?"

"Oh, that pistol isn't mine," she said with an air of arrogance. "I think you'll find that the initials engraved on the plate are yours. Indeed, your coachman should know better than to leave your carriage unattended. I managed to sneak back and take it while you were busy with your whore."

Ross jumped to his feet. "My God, if you were a man I'd break every bone in your blasted body."

"I'm simply showing you that I am just as strong as you. Together, we would make an invincible pair. You've no choice but to work with me now."

Ross sighed. "Move aside. I must find help."

Lady Cornell slashed at his shirt, cutting through the linen. Ross staggered back. He pressed his fingers to the skin visible through the slit in the material. Spots of blood tainted the tips.

Estelle was but a few feet away and could not wait any longer. As she crept forward, she met Ross' gaze. His eyes widened in horror.

"Oh, you're right to be scared," Lady Cornell said. "I have been so patient. I've let you cast me off and humiliate me. I've played the simple-minded coquette, but no more. Either we concoct a story together, or I shall blame you for what's happened here."

"May I offer another suggestion?" Estelle said, coming behind the lady and pressing the blade to her throat. "Scars can look so ugly on a woman. Do you not think?"

Lady Cornell gulped and stuttered.

Ross' gaze moved to a point beyond Estelle's shoulder, and fear flashed in his eyes.

"Drop the knife, miss." The man's voice was firm, eloquent.

Estelle heard the clip of numerous booted footsteps. A man with spectacles and a pointed ginger beard stepped into her field of vision, accompanied by Mr Joseph.

Estelle lowered her arm and let the knife fall to the floor.

Lady Cornell stumbled forward, panting and clutching her throat. "Thank heavens you arrived when you did." She swung around and pointed at Estelle. "That woman attacked me and shot my husband out of some misguided sense of spite and jealousy. She wants locking up in Bedlam."

Wickett approached along with two other men. He inclined his head to Ross, and somehow the silent communication wiped the look of fear off Ross' face.

"I'm Sir Malcolm Forston, chief magistrate"—the gentleman drew his fingers down the length of his beard—"and I must inform you that we heard everything from our position on the stairwell." He waved his hand to one of the men hovering behind and pointed at Lord Cornell. "Attend to the victim, Withers."

Lady Cornell's countenance turned deathly pale. "I don't know what you think you heard, but I can tell you—"

"I saw you shoot the gentleman," Mr Joseph said. "I read the letter you sent to Lord Trevane asking him to meet you here."

Ross had left the letter in the carriage. Wickett must have shown it to him.

"I drew the knife because I thought Lord Trevane's life was in danger," Estelle said, feeling the need to explain her aggressive actions. "I was waiting outside with Mr Joseph when I grew fearful for his lordship's welfare."

Sir Malcolm's gaze drifted to the decorative necklace on the table. He ventured over and ran his fingers over the gems.

"Take Lady Cornell into custody, Johnson."

"No! Wait!" Lady Cornell cried. "Do you know who I am? You can't do this."

Johnson came forward. "Yes, Sir Malcolm."

But Lady Cornell punched and kicked out until he had no choice but to restrain her.

"If the devil won't keep still put her in chains," Sir Malcolm said with an air of frustration.

Wickett offered his assistance, and after another violent scuffle, Johnson finally led Lady Cornell away amid a cacophony of blasphemous curses.

"Well, Withers?" Sir Malcolm said, staring at the body on the floor. "Will he live? Can we question him?"

Ross coughed into his fist. "While I have no regard for Lord Cornell, the man has been shot. Must you take his statement now?"

Sir Malcolm raised a brow. "I'm afraid the law is intolerant when it comes to showing compassion to criminals, my lord. The man is a jewel thief. Evidence of his crime is there on the table. Forgive me, but I would like to know details of any accomplices if he's not long for this world."

Ross' mouth fell open. "A jewel thief? Lord Cornell?"

"That is what the facts suggest. Your man, Mr Joseph, is the one who made the discovery and so the Crown is indebted to you." Sir Malcolm inclined his head. "Now, I will require a statement regarding the events of the evening. But for now, you're both free to leave."

A look of suspicion marred Ross' features. "Do you not need me to fetch a doctor?"

Sir Malcolm shook his head. "Withers here was trained by the Surgeon General during the Peninsular War when the medical teams were severely understaffed. It was enough to deter him from the profession, but he can be called upon on occasion to remove a lead ball if need be."

Clearly, Sir Malcolm wanted them out of the way. The thefts appeared to be more important to him than attempted murder.

Ross inclined his head. "Then we shall leave you to your work."

Ross offered Estelle his arm, and they walked out of the museum with Wickett in tow.

"We should have a doctor look at the knife wound to your stomach," Estelle said.

"It's nothing. Just a scratch." He cast her a sidelong glance.

"You can tend to it for me." From his blunt tone, and stone-like countenance, he was not himself.

"Are you angry with me?"

"Angry? No. Livid? Most definitely. One mistake and that woman would have taken your life."

"Where to, my lord?" Wickett said as they approached the carriage, unaware of their little spat.

"I imagine Miss Darcy is keen to return to Whitecombe Street," Ross said. "I'm sure the people who care about her would like to know she is safe."

"I shall tend to his lordship's *scratch* before we set off." It would leave more time on the journey home to work on soothing his temper. Else he might seek to take his frustration out on rogues in an alley. "And then you may head to Whitecombe Street."

"Right you are, miss." Wickett opened the carriage door and gave a knowing grin. "Shall I take the scenic route? Happen there's a lot to discuss, considering what happened in the museum."

"Yes, Wickett," Estelle said, trying not to look at Ross as she could feel her cheeks flame. "His lordship has a voracious appetite for conversation."

CHAPTER TWENTY

Their amorous antics in the carriage on the journey home went some way to calming Ross' temper. Though it wasn't anger that gripped him when he recalled the memory of Estelle creeping up on Lady Cornell while wielding the knife—it was fear.

Being inside Estelle's warm body banished all irrational thoughts of losing the only thing that mattered. But as he could not keep her prisoner in his bed, he knew he had to get his erratic emotions under control.

After a day spent giving statements and answering Sir Malcolm's questions until the magistrate was satisfied, Vane suggested it was time to put Fabian out of his misery, and Estelle agreed.

"You're quiet," Estelle said as they sat in his carriage rattling along the coastal road on the way to Branscombe in Devonshire. "You've hardly spoken since we stopped to change the horses in Weycroft. Have the events of the last week finally taken their toll?"

Vane had pushed thoughts of Mr Hungerford's nefarious deeds from his mind. Cornell was dead, and his wife would hang for his murder. It should have brought an element of satisfaction —but it did not. So many lives destroyed, and for what?

Greed?

Obsession?

Certainly not love.

The suspicious part of his nature wondered whether Sir Malcolm wanted Lord Cornell to die. Five days had passed since the incident in the museum and there had been no mention of the jewel thefts in the broadsheets. If people were to learn that a lord stole from the Crown, it would only shake stability amongst the ranks. Now it was but a simple case of a marital disagreement escalating to murder.

Not that it mattered. Their part in it was over.

Vane glanced at the woman he loved with every fibre of his being. She was nervous. He could tell. The tears she'd shed upon leaving the Erstwhiles had long since dried, but her lips were drawn thin. She nibbled the inside of her cheek and fiddled with the hem on her jacket.

"I was just thinking about Fabian," Vane said, hoping it would prompt Estelle to reveal her troubles. "Eight years is a long time. I know he will be waiting on the dock, eager for your arrival."

"That is if he received your letter."

Estelle had taken to inventing problems in her mind. Fabian would be away on a long voyage. The inclement weather would prevent them from crossing to the island even though there wasn't a cloud in sight.

"Fabian received the letter," he reassured her, "and we will be with them in a matter of hours." The thought of seeing Lillian brought a warm glow to Vane's chest.

"Does he look the same?" Estelle glanced out of the window at the calm sea stretching out to the horizon. "I keep picturing the young man with hope in his eyes and so much love in his heart."

Vane could hear the silent words lingering within the

comment. What she really wanted to know was if Fabian had been tainted by his experiences. Had grief stripped away all that was good and left him bitter, resentful.

"He looks every bit a pirate." Vane chuckled, hoping to lighten the mood. "His hair is far too long, and he exudes a devil-may-care attitude that frightens most men. But his eyes carry the same look of hope. His heart is still full of love."

She smiled, and a contented sigh breezed from her lips. "I wonder if it will be awkward between us, strained even, if he might struggle to suppress his disappointment in me."

Vane crossed the carriage and settled beside her. "Please stop worrying." He took her in his arms and kissed away her fears. "You survived four years with a gang of smugglers. You can survive a reunion with a stubborn pirate."

"I know," she said, cupping his cheek. "But this means so much to me. Once we are reunited, I can finally move beyond the past and embrace life. And I have missed him so much, Ross."

"I understand." He was close to his sister, too. But Estelle was wrong to think they had nothing else to fear.

Guilt surfaced, accompanied by a flicker of doubt. These uncomfortable sensations had nothing to do with her brother. Vane was confident Fabian would welcome Estelle as if the last eight years had never existed. But while the problems in London were behind them, there were a few matters in France that needed addressing.

"You've hardly slept these last few days," Vane said, stroking her hair in a slow soothing rhythm. "Close your eyes and I shall wake you when we reach Branscombe."

She shrank down in the seat and huddled closer to him. "I shall try."

❀

They arrived in Branscombe at noon. Vane booked Wickett a room at the coaching inn so he could catch a few hours' sleep. Fabian's men were already waiting on the beach ready to ferry them across to the island.

"Remember, the sailors are somewhat unconventional," Vane said as they walked across the shingle.

The Scot, Mackenzie, strode over and slapped Vane on the back. "Och, it's good to see you've not lost that brooding expression. It's a look that makes men quiver in their boots."

"Most men, but not you, Mackenzie," Vane said with a smirk. He wondered what Estelle made of the large red-haired fellow.

"When a man's been swamped by giant waves, there's not much that can frighten him after that. Och, and I've seen wind whip clothes off a man's back."

Estelle stiffened at Vane's side. "I agree, Mr Mackenzie. There is nothing more terrifying than a storm at sea."

Vane turned to Estelle. "That doesn't stop Mackenzie diving into the water at any given opportunity."

"Did your mother not tell you that the best way to deal with fears is to tackle them head-on?"

"I believe we ran into each other before, Mr Mackenzie," Estelle said. "In Paris."

"Aye, one look at my ginger beard and you raced away as fast as your legs could carry you." Mackenzie bowed his head. "Miss Darcy, I cannot tell you how it warms my heart to know you're well. There'll be ale all round tonight, that's for sure."

"Thank you, Mr Mackenzie."

"Come now." The Scot took their luggage and ushered them towards the boat. "His lordship has been waiting on the dock all morning. His toes are probably frozen in his boots."

"Could you just give us a moment alone before we depart?" Vane said. This would be their last opportunity to speak privately for some time.

"Aye," Mackenzie said with a grin. "We'll wait for you in the boat."

"What is it?" Estelle turned to him and placed her hand on his chest. "Your heart is racing."

Vane took her hand. "Do you remember when you came to Hanover Square, and I asked you if you loved me?"

A smile graced her lips. "How could I forget?"

"You didn't ask how *I* felt and so I want to tell you now, before ... well, before Fabian captures you and refuses to let you go." Any trace of amusement in his voice was fleeting.

Estelle gazed deeply into his eyes. "Then let me reaffirm what I said. I love you, Ross. There is no one in this world for me but you."

Vane swallowed past the lump in his throat. "You are the love of my life, Estelle. I love you more now than I ever have. You're strong when you need to be, daring even when you shouldn't be. You're not afraid to show your vulnerability and I admire that." He couldn't help but smile. "Have I told you I love you?"

"Twice, I think." Her beaming smile warmed his heart.

"Then never forget it." Vane kissed her quickly on the lips and then gestured to the boat. "Fabian has lived for eight years thinking he would never see you again. Let us go and put an end to his torment."

Vane helped her into the boat and they set off for Raven Island.

Mackenzie hummed a tune as he took to the oars. "From what I remember, my lord, your rowing skills would put any seafaring man to shame."

Fighting with men in dark alleys had given him a tremendous amount of upper body strength. "At the time, we were rushing to rescue my sister," Vane said. "Panic does that to a man."

Estelle sat silently beside him, staring at the dot of land on the horizon. Her countenance grew more subdued with each stroke of the oars. When the island came into full view, she sighed.

"It looks beautiful here."

Vane had been so enraged the day he'd first come to the island, he'd failed to notice the true magnificence of the landscape. The sun shone down upon hills of flourishing green vegetation. Gulls swooped in the sky. The water sparkled. The fresh, briny scent of the sea air calmed the mind.

"It truly is a haven away from the world." He turned to Estelle and noticed a tear running down her cheek. Without saying a word, he simply held her hand.

"Not long until we reach the dock," Mackenzie said. "Happen we'll find the men hanging from the top-sail just to get a wee look at you."

There were a handful of sailors on the dock. Amongst them Vane saw Fabian standing with his arm wrapped around Lillian, holding her close. Vane's heart swelled at the sight of his sister. She looked so happy, so carefree, and for that he owed Fabian a debt so huge it could never be repaid.

They drew alongside the landing pier. Mackenzie threw a line and one sailor rushed forward, tied a knot and slipped it over the piling.

Vane climbed out onto the wooden walkway. He held out his hand and brought Estelle up to join him. For a few seconds, Fabian and Estelle just looked at each other and then she picked up her skirts and ran. Fabian took flight, too, the thud of his boots on the planks obliterating the squawks of the gulls.

Estelle jumped into her brother's arms and he hugged her tightly. They both dropped to their knees, still hugging, and yet laughing at the same time.

While the pair held each other close, Vane met Lillian's gaze. She smiled and hurried towards him, took his hands and squeezed.

"I cannot tell you how thrilled I am to see you." She released one hand and touched his cheek tenderly. "I cannot tell you how much this means to Fabian."

"It seems your husband was right all along." And Vane was the blind fool who refused to listen.

"Love brings hope does it not?"

"Indeed."

"How on earth did you find her?" Lillian's eyes widened in her eagerness to hear the tale.

"I didn't." Vane couldn't help but smile. Even Mr Joseph had struggled to locate her. "She found me. I would like to take the credit, but it was purely accidental."

"Or perhaps Fate played a part," Lillian said.

He didn't know how things happened as they did. Occasionally, he wondered if one's destiny was already decided. If all events, good and bad, were merely lessons in one's development. Perhaps one couldn't understand the lesson because it was part of an infinitely bigger picture.

"When Estelle left, I lost my faith in life, in love, in everything. So I'm inclined to think you're right. I've lived without faith and I've learnt to trust in it again."

Lillian searched his face. "You seem different. Have you and Estelle reconciled your differences?"

"We have." Vane nodded. Oh, they had done so much more than that. "I love her, Lillian, and she feels the same way."

Lillian gave a contented sigh. "It is what I have always known. It is what I have prayed for."

Behind them Fabian took Estelle's hand. He placed it in the crook of his arm and escorted her away from the dock to the path leading up to the castle.

Estelle glanced back over her shoulder and Vane's heart lurched. The look she gave him conveyed the depth of her devotion. He smiled back and hoped she would understand what he had to do.

Mackenzie dabbed his eyes as he prepared to climb out of the small vessel. "Och, it's a sight to behold. I can tell you that. The drink will flow tonight."

"Wait." Vane held up his hand to prevent Mackenzie from climbing up onto the landing pier. "Do not disembark yet."

Lillian frowned. "Is something wrong?" She looked at Vane and then at the boat. "Why do you want Mackenzie to remain in the boat?"

Vane's tongue grew thick in his mouth as he struggled to find the right words.

"You're leaving, aren't you?" Lillian blurted.

"I'm afraid, I must."

"Is it because of Estelle? If you love her why can't you stay? Talk to me."

"Lillian, I will if you stop bombarding me with questions. I have important business elsewhere. That is all."

Lillian fell silent though her eyes flitted back and forth as though trying to make sense of it all. "Does Estelle know of these business plans?"

"No." He reached into his coat pocket and handed Lillian a letter. "Will you give this to Estelle? Tell her I pray she understands. Tell her to wait for me."

Lillian shook her head repeatedly. "But I don't understand. Why can't you stay and explain?" Two deep lines appeared between her brows.

Good God, he wanted nothing more than to spend a week in a castle with the woman he loved.

"Because Estelle needs time alone with Fabian without a distraction. And there is something I must do for her if she's ever to be free of the nightmare she's lived these last eight years."

"Then leave tomorrow. Come up to the castle and dine with us. Have a good night's rest before you embark on your journey."

"Lillian, stop it. You're only making it more difficult."

Vane closed his eyes briefly.

One word from Estelle and he would never leave her side. They had a future together, years to spend living the life they'd dreamed. But she could not live in peace while fearing the smugglers. He could not permit their children to suffer for someone else's mistake.

"You know Estelle will beg me not to go," he continued. "You know she will insist that my reasons don't matter. But our father was to blame for what happened to her and I will at least attempt to put it right."

Vane took Lillian by the arms and kissed her on the cheek before she said something to change his mind or questioned him about the past.

"Why must you always be so stubborn? Why must you feel as though you're to blame for those things beyond your control?" She sucked in a breath. "What happened to me was not your fault. What happened to Estelle was not your fault, either. Stop blaming yourself and be happy."

Vane stepped away. "If you care for me at all, you will support me in this."

"Support you? I will stand guard at your back until the day I die."

"Then let me go. And promise me you will reassure Estelle that I am doing this for the right reasons."

Silence ensued.

Lillian sighed. It was the sound of surrender.

She threw her arms around his neck and hugged him tightly. "Then promise me you'll take care. Promise me you will return to us soon."

"I swear it." Vane kissed her on the temple, then pulled away and climbed back into the boat. "Can you take me back to Branscombe, Mackenzie?"

"Aye, my lord," Mackenzie said. The sorrow in the Scot's voice was nothing to that in Vane's heart. "Happen I need the exercise if I'm ever to outdo you with the oars."

Vane did not look at Lillian as the boat moved away from the pier. He knew she watched him, knew that he had left her with an unbearable task and it was wrong of him. To distract his mind, he took up the spare oars and helped Mackenzie row.

"Och, there's no need to offer assistance," Mackenzie said. "I once rowed the length of the River Tay without even stopping to drain the dragon. Not as fast as you'd do it mind."

Vane chuckled. Mackenzie had a way of bringing a man out of the doldrums.

"You're welcome to come with me to France," Vane said, pulling on the oars and propelling them through the water.

"Had you told me earlier I might have run it past his lordship." Mackenzie stared at him for a moment. "Not that I've taken to prying into other people's affairs," he said, changing the subject, "but I admire what you're doing."

"I imagine you're the only one who does."

"Have no fear. The lass will understand. I knew the moment you stormed into the castle with a pair of duelling pistols that you were a man who followed his heart no matter the cost."

"I'm not entirely sure whether I'm following my heart or my conscience."

"If you're doing it for the lass, then it's your heart for sure."

Vane nodded. "I've not had an opportunity to thank you."

Mackenzie chuckled. "We're not on dry land yet. I may still dive overboard and take a dip if the urge takes me."

"I mean for having the sense to notice that the woman in Paris bore a striking resemblance to Miss Darcy. Had you pushed it from your mind we would not be here today."

Fate again, Vane thought.

"His lordship always brought her picture out whenever his mind was hazy with drink. And a good job he did, too. The lass' image is ingrained in my memory."

"Then we'll drink to that when I return. Make sure the men save at least one cask of ale for me."

Mackenzie shook his head. "For you, I'd promise most things, but I cannot promise that."

"What made you want to purchase a castle?" Estelle gripped her brother's hand as he led her through the bailey and into the great hall. She stared up at the array of weapons on the wall, at the long table stretching the length of the dais. "I can't help but feel as though I have been transported back in time."

"It suits me to live here with the men," Fabian said. "And I cannot abide the hypocrisy of London Society." He sighed. "I'm grateful Lillian loves it here, too."

Estelle glanced back over her shoulder, wondering when Ross and Lillian would appear. She supposed they had plenty to discuss. At some point he would have to tell her about the depth of their father's betrayal.

"Ross said you married for love. I cannot tell you how happy I am for you, Fabian."

"Lillian is a remarkable woman. She is everything I ever wanted." Fabian brought Estelle's hand to his lips and kissed her knuckles. "You cannot know how it warms my heart to know you're alive and well. After learning of the sighting from Mackenzie I had to search for you. I still have men in France."

"It was wrong of me to stay away." There were so many things to tell him. No doubt he had many questions of his own.

"We must find somewhere quiet where we can sit and I can tell you all that has occurred these last eight years."

Having told Ross everything about her time away, telling Fabian would prove somewhat easier. She glanced back over her shoulder again, looking for the man she loved with all her heart.

"Shall we eat first?" Fabian said. "You must be famished after the long journey."

"We stopped numerous times en route. And Mrs Erstwhile prepared a basket and we've been nibbling on the contents since we left." Oh, how she wished the Erstwhiles were here, to meet her brother, to see the castle, to give their support.

"So, you're familiar with Vane's staff?" There was another question hidden behind Fabian's words. Surely he knew that it was too late to worry about her virtue or reputation.

"The Erstwhiles own an apothecary shop and I worked as their assistant."

"You worked for them?" He turned to her and cupped her cheek. "Come, perhaps you should explain everything now. For I fear the rest of the day will be spent with me besieging you with questions."

Fabian led her up to the top of the keep. The weather was warm, the sky clear and she could see the surrounding heathland, could even make out a small boat in the distance.

They remained up there for three hours.

Estelle told him everything about her time with the smugglers, about Faucheux's threats to find her, even about her terrible time at the hands of Philipe Robard.

"You're telling me this Hungerford fellow drugged you, and that if Vane hadn't arrived in time you would be living with a lunatic in Bath?"

"Yes," she said, aware that her poor brother suffered greatly from hearing her stories because he'd not been there to help her. "But must you call him that?"

"Forgive me, Estelle, but any man who attempts to abduct a woman is most definitely not of sound mind."

Estelle sighed. "I am not speaking about Mr Hungerford. I am speaking about Ross."

Fabian frowned. "You don't like the name Vane?"

"It implies a weakness of character that is far removed from the truth."

Fabian narrowed his gaze and studied her for a moment. "You still love him."

"Oh, yes." Estelle put her hand over her heart. "More than ever."

"Does he feel the same way?"

"He does," she said confidently.

"Then I must hope he will do right by you, despite all that has occurred." Fabian came to his feet and gestured to a point in the distance. "There's a small church on the island. You can marry there if you both so wish."

How easily her brother skimmed past all the trauma and scandal to concentrate only on her future. But how could she ever be accepted as the Marchioness of Trevane?

"And you think it is possible for a lady like me to marry a marquess?"

He looked at her and smiled. "I think it is possible for a lady like you to do whatever her heart desires."

Estelle came to her feet and hugged him. His biased comment still gave her hope. "Oh, I have missed you so."

"I would have never stopped looking for you."

"I know."

He stepped back. "Let's go and find Lillian and Trevane. They must have grown tired waiting for us to return. And then I can take you on a tour of the island."

Estelle nodded, though hoped she would have some time alone with Ross before they headed out on an adventure.

"And then you will tell me where I might find Philipe Robard, and Faucheux," Fabian said.

Oh, heavens, Fabian was as determined as Ross when it came to avenging a lady's ruined reputation.

"Why? What will you do?"

"Exactly what you think I might do."

"It's all forgotten now, and I want to keep it that way." At least for the time being. Dread the day Faucheux ever came looking for her. But with Ross at her side she could cope with anything.

"I shall discuss the matter with Trevane." Fabian took her hand and helped her descend the narrow flight of stairs leading down to the first floor. They eventually found Lillian reading in the drawing room: an intimate space with oak-panelled walls and a huge stone hearth.

Lillian stood as they entered. She smiled weakly.

"I'm sorry I didn't get a chance to welcome you earlier." With her book in her hand, Lillian crossed the room to greet them. "I know you both had so much to talk about."

"It's lovely to see you, Lillian. One way or another, I believe we were destined to be sisters." Estelle glanced at the empty sofa wondering what had happened to Ross.

"Indeed, we were."

"Where's Lord Trevane?" Fabian said with a grin. "In case you're wondering, Estelle prefers I use his full title."

Lillian pursed her lips, distress evident in her eyes. She opened her book, removed a letter and handed it to Estelle. "This is for you. My brother told me to tell you that he loves you and asks you to be patient and wait for him."

"Wait for him?" Estelle felt the blood drain from her face. She gripped the letter. "What do you mean?" She glanced behind her. "Where is he?"

Lillian shuffled uncomfortably on the spot. She looked at Fabian. "He has returned to Branscombe."

"Branscombe?" Estelle shook her head. Perhaps he'd forgotten something. But the hollow feeling in the pit of her stomach said otherwise. "Then he is coming back?"

"Of course," Lillian said. "He told Mackenzie he would return as soon as he's done what he needs to do in … in France."

"France!" Estelle's world swayed. She felt nauseous. Dizzy. It was as though sharp talons pierced her chest and gripped her heart ready to squeeze the life from it. "France?" she whispered, looking down at the letter in her hand. A tear dropped onto the paper. "Why?"

"I think you know," Lillian said softly.

Fabian put his hand on Estelle's shoulder. "After what I have just heard, it is what any man who cares about you would do. It is a good sign. A sign of his lasting devotion."

"No!" She swung around and with one hand grabbed her brother by his shirt and shook him. "Fetch a boat. Bring him back."

Fabian covered her hand with his own. "He loves you, Estelle. He will return. But he is worldly enough to know that you cannot live happily in fear. He is honourable enough to want to seek vengeance on those who have hurt you."

"No. The past doesn't matter. He knows that." Oh, where was Mr Erstwhile when she needed him? Estelle stepped away and hurried to the door.

"Wait!" Fabian cried. "Where are you going?"

"To find Mackenzie. To get a boat. To bring him back."

Fabian grabbed her around the waist and pulled her against his chest. "He will return. You must wait for him as he asked you to do. The time will pass quickly. I promise you."

No!

Estelle crumpled to her knees and Fabian followed. "I lost him once, Fabian. I cannot lose him again."

"I understand."

They remained there for a few minutes until she found the strength to stand. Lillian took her hand and led her to the bedchamber allocated for the duration of her stay. Of course, Fabian presumed the arrangement would be permanent, but Estelle's life was with Ross wherever that might be.

Lillian reassured her of Ross' affections and then left her alone to read the letter. Love poured from the page, dripped from every word. She was his life, his love, his everything, he said. But he could not let her live under a cloud of fear for the rest of her days.

Wait for me. She read those words repeatedly. *Marry me*.

Estelle slept clutching the letter. Every day she ventured to the top of the keep and stared out at sea searching for his boat, wondering when he would come home to her.

CHAPTER TWENTY-ONE

Twelve days had passed since Ross took Estelle's hand and hauled her out of the small boat. Compared to eight years it should have been nothing. He'd said he was coming back. But she could not shake the deep sense of loss. Every night she prayed for him. Every day she awaited his return only to retire feeling drained, lovesick and alone.

She had used the time productively, rebuilding her relationship with Fabian and Lillian. Witnessing the depth of their love only made her miss Ross all the more.

Every day, she wandered down to the secluded cove, paddled her feet in the sea, sat and watched the waves break on the sand.

Today, a thick blanket of cloud obscured the sun. Sharp gusts of wind whipped her hair loose from its knot. But she enjoyed the peace and solitude, and it gave her time to daydream about Ross.

She put her hands over her ears as another gust howled past. Mr Erstwhile would caution her about being outdoors in such harsh weather. He'd treated plenty of people with a chill in their chest, mostly from going out in all elements.

She groaned inwardly when she sensed someone approach. Perhaps Fabian had come to keep her company, or Mackenzie with wild tales to make her laugh. For as the days dragged on, her mood grew more melancholic.

Whoever it was draped his coat over her shoulders and dropped down beside her. In an instant, she knew it was not Fabian or Mackenzie. The alluring scent that clung to the coat belonged to only one man.

Her head shot to the right, and her heart almost leapt out of her mouth.

"Did you miss me, Estelle?" Ross looked out at sea before turning to face her. A lock of ebony hair hung rakishly over one brow. The sight of him stole her breath. "Are you angry I went away?"

It took a moment to speak. "Angry? No. Livid? Most definitely."

He smiled at that.

Relief flooded through her, starting in her fingers and racing to her toes. "So you took a trip to France without me."

"I wouldn't call it a trip exactly. More a mission to right the wrongs of the past."

"And did you succeed?"

He raised an arrogant brow. "What do you think?"

She scanned his face and body. Her gaze fell to the marred hand resting on his knee. "How did you come by that bruise on your knuckle?"

"Oh, that." He examined the bruise and flexed his fingers. "My hand collided with a gentleman's nose and then smacked into his jaw."

"Was it anyone I know?"

"As a matter of fact, he is the son of a merchant who lacks manners when it comes to maids."

Estelle couldn't help but feel a frisson of satisfaction. "Is he dead?"

"No, though I fear he may need to recuperate for some time."

"I see."

Another gust of wind forced her to suck in her breath. Ross reached over and drew his coat more firmly around her shoulders.

"And what else were you up to on your secret mission?" Surely he'd not gone off in search of the smugglers.

"I spoke to the magistrate who showed an interest in what happened at Drummond's yard. It seems Hungerford did hire the Frenchman to attack you in the alley. He also hired him to break into the shop. When questioned, the man waffled on about the Erstwhiles eating poisoned macaroons, about Hungerford wanting to take advantage of you when you were at your most vulnerable."

"Good Lord. The level of deceit is astounding." Now she knew why Mr Hungerford insisted on serving macaroons when he knew she hated them.

"Oh, and I spent a night in Wissant," Ross continued. "You'd be surprised what you can learn when you ply the locals with wine and ale."

"Wissant? You have been busy." Estelle inhaled to calm the nervous flutter in her stomach. "And ... and what did they tell you?"

"Faucheux is dead. That is the name of the smuggler you fear?"

Estelle's heart thumped hard against her ribcage. "Please tell me you didn't kill him."

Ross shook his head. "The band of smugglers were caught and hung years ago. Faucheux was hung for the murder of Monsieur Bonnay. The group fought without a leader and were caught with contraband some months later."

Faucheux was dead.

A sense of peace settled in her chest, one she'd not felt since the carefree days of her youth. She had been so angry with Ross for leaving, and yet no words could express her gratitude. Never again would she worry whenever she heard a gruff French voice.

She turned and clutched his arm. "Do you know what that means?"

"It means you have nothing to fear. It means no one can ever testify to the part you played all those years ago."

The love she felt for this man burst through her. She flew into his arms, causing him to fall back onto the sand.

Her mouth closed over his instantly. She devoured him, thrust her tongue wildly against his. Twelve days' worth of anguish ignited into a passion she could not contain. She kissed his cheek, his chin, nibbled the spot just beneath his ear, bit down on his lobe.

"So you have missed me," Ross panted as he grasped her buttocks.

Consumed by lust, Estelle straddled him, gathered up her skirts and fumbled with the buttons on his breeches. "Take me now, Ross. Take me here. I need you."

Freeing himself from his constraints with ease, he gripped his manhood.

"Hurry," she said, aware that they were alone on the beach but at any moment someone might appear. But she could not wait to take this man into her body. "Quickly, Ross."

With a moan of intense pleasure, she took him into her core, *deep* inside her, as *deep* as their position allowed.

Ross lay back on the sand. "Oh, God, Estelle. You don't know what it's been like for me these last twelve days."

She clasped his hands and held them above his head, sheathed his solid shaft, rode him as if her life depended upon it, until her ragged breathing obliterated the sound of the wind.

It was rough, heart-stoppingly wonderful. He was so hard she could feel him swelling inside her. She enjoyed playing the temptress, and so she clutched his waistcoat in her fists and ground against him again and again.

"We need to share a bed tonight," he said between short gasps of breath. "I don't care if it's in the blasted stable." He closed his eyes. "Lord above."

He came apart, groaning her name, flooding her body.

Estelle stilled and waited for Ross' breathing to settle.

But without warning he flipped her onto her back. "I'll not leave you unsatisfied."

She did not need to reach the dizzying heights of release, just being close to him was enough for now, but he moved to kneel between her legs and buried his head between her thighs.

"No, Ross. No."

He gripped her thighs as his wicked tongue flicked back and forth over the sensitive bud. The mounting pressure banished all embarrassment. She thrust her hands into his hair, tugged and pulled at the roots, wanted to shout a host of licentious things as the world fractured into hundreds of glittering pieces.

Ross rolled onto his back, and they both lay there panting, looking up at the sky.

"Well, that was a rather nice homecoming," he said, catching his breath. "Perhaps regular trips to France might be in order." He tucked his manhood away and came up on his elbow. "Marry me, Estelle."

"You know I will."

"At this rate, there will surely be a child, and so I want us to wed soon. Let us have a lavish celebration. Let us marry in St George's. Would you like that?"

Estelle sighed. "Ross, such extravagance is unnecessary." She did not want to disappoint him, but clearly, he had not thought this through. "We cannot afford to draw attention to the event. People will ask questions. How will I explain where I've been these last eight years?"

"Reach into the pocket of my coat and remove the letter."

Intrigued, she sat up and did as he asked.

"Open it," he said, "the seal is already broken."

Estelle peeled back the folds and read the letter. Her gaze drifted to the embossed mark at the top. She shook her head. "How on earth did you come by this?"

The letter was written by the Reverend Mother of a convent in Brittany. It stated that a lady had been brought to them having been found unconscious on the beach. Due to the trauma, she suffered memory loss, and she remained with them until snippets of her memory returned some eight years later. At the bottom of the page she saw her name written in ink.

"The convent is crumbling down around them, and they are in dire need of funds. I happened to have the finances available to pay for a new roof, a new prayer room and for other things besides."

Estelle looked at him and then looked at the Reverend Mother's signature. "You bribed a servant of God?"

"Not bribed exactly but suggested they offer a helping hand to an innocent woman forced to act against her will. When she heard your story, she wanted to help."

"Is this true?" She waved the letter at him. "Did you really speak to the Reverend Mother, because I find it hard to believe a woman of such grace would lie."

A smile touched Ross' lips. "Does it matter? Someone as holy as the Reverend Mother would never disclose the personal information of those given sanctuary. And should anyone search for proof, I have the receipt to show I donated a substantial amount of money out of gratitude."

Estelle shook her head. "Your cunning astounds me."

"I would do anything for you, and to secure the future of any children we may have."

Estelle put her hand on her stomach. The thought of carrying his child brought a lump to her throat. "Then I shall treasure this letter because it shows the lengths you will go to for those you love."

"So will you choose St George's?"

While Ross had done everything to eradicate the past, she was as much a product of her mistakes as her successes. Being true to herself was what mattered now. "Fabian suggested we might marry here. It's a small church but rather quaint. Would you be terribly disappointed?"

Ross grinned. "I'd marry you on the beach if it were possible, and so Raven Island it is. Though I wonder if you know the full extent of what you're committing to."

She was to marry a man who made her heart soar, her pulse race. "Oh, I'm committing to a man who is the epitome of sexual prowess." Not that she had any complaint.

Ross raised a brow. "I wasn't speaking about me. Mackenzie will want to host the wedding breakfast, and I hear he excels when it comes to picking the entertainment."

"It is not the entertainment of the day that I shall concern myself with," she said, returning to straddle his lap once again, "but more how you plan to please me on our wedding night."

"You want your pleasure to come in slow, rippling waves, I seem to recall."

Estelle fought to suppress a grin. "Do I? How strange that my memory seems to have failed me."

Ross' hands settled on her hips. "Then perhaps another demonstration is in order."

CHAPTER TWENTY-TWO

T*hree weeks later*

"Come," Lillian said, grabbing Estelle's hand and pulling her towards the bailey. "Mrs Brown spent the whole day yesterday preparing the cart."

Estelle needed a distraction to calm her nerves. In an hour, she would be the Marchioness of Trevane. More importantly, she would be married to the man she loved for the rest of her days. "I'm sure I shall love it no matter what she has done."

When Estelle entered the bailey, it wasn't the sight of the pretty rose garlands or the reams of pink ribbons that stole her breath. It was the sight of Mr Erstwhile sitting on the seat gripping the reins in his hand, a beaming smile illuminating his face.

"Are you ready, my dear? We do not want to keep his lordship waiting."

She had Ross to thank for making the day special before it had even begun. He had arranged for someone to tend the

Erstwhiles' apothecary shop in their absence. He'd arranged their transport to Branscombe, and Fabian had found them a room in the castle.

"I wouldn't want to be late," she said. Mackenzie appeared and offered his hand so she could climb up onto the seat. "His lordship might think I've left on the mail coach."

Mr Erstwhile smiled. "I believe his lordship would chase you to the ends of the earth."

"Aye," Mackenzie said, helping Lillian up to the seat, too. "And he'd swim there in just his breeches if he had to. Now give me a moment to scoot into the back, and we can be on our way."

Mr Erstwhile looked proud seated at the helm. Mrs Erstwhile had gone ahead to the church, the maid in her needing to make certain everything was clean and in order.

"I cannot tell you what it means to be here," Mr Erstwhile said, "to see you so happy and about to wed the one you love."

Estelle touched him lightly on the arm. "It would not have been the same without you here."

"And I wouldn't have missed it for the world."

The wedding party consisted of a small gathering of close friends. Ross invited Lord Farleigh, Rose and the children. He'd also extended an invitation to the Earl of Stanton, Lord Farleigh's brother-in-law, and his wife, Nicole. When one made a stand against the sticklers in society, it was best to do so with an army of peers guarding your back.

They rattled along the narrow road towards the church on the hill. Estelle's stomach flipped. She couldn't wait to see Ross. But another surprise had her buzzing with excitement, too.

Fabian was waiting for them outside the church. He strode towards them looking so smart in his cravat and waistcoat, though she preferred seeing him in the more relaxed garb of a would-be pirate.

Mackenzie came to help them down from the cart. Fabian

kissed Lillian on the cheek and whispered something in her ear that brought a blush to her cheeks.

"You look beautiful," Fabian said, taking Estelle's hand and bringing it to his lips. "Trevane arrived an hour early. The man is eager to claim you as his wife. Indeed, I feared he might sleep in a pew last night."

In that moment, Estelle did not know if it was possible to be any happier.

"Well," Mr Erstwhile began. "I had best go inside and find a seat."

"Your wife has saved a seat for you," Fabian said, casting Estelle a covert grin. "But you've no need to go inside just yet."

"Is the Reverend Sykes not ready?"

"He's ready," Fabian said, "but you cannot enter the church without the bride."

Mr Erstwhile looked at Estelle, a little confused.

Estelle turned and hugged him. "My brother must give me away," she said, "but I would like you to assist him."

"Me?" Mr Erstwhile covered his heart with his hand. "Oh, but I could not intrude."

"Sir, Estelle would like us both to escort her to Lord Trevane."

Tears welled in the man's eyes. "You would?"

"I would," Estelle said, struggling to hold back her own tears.

A look of pride and joy brightened Mr Erstwhile's countenance. "Then it would stand as one of the greatest honours of my life."

A few tears did fall, and they all took a moment to compose themselves before heading into the church.

Ross looked immaculate in a dark blue coat and gold waistcoat. Their gazes locked, and he mouthed *I love you*. His eyes held a look of promise that warmed her core and left her anticipating what the night would bring. There was a glimpse of the younger man about him. The happy, carefree lord who'd chased her about the orchard and swore to love and protect her until his dying day.

Afterwards, they dined in the great hall in what proved to be rowdy celebration organised by Mackenzie. Fabian's men joined them, as did Wickett.

"Look at Wickett," Ross said, leaning in and whispering in Estelle's ear as they sat at the long table on the dais. He took the opportunity to kiss her cheek, pressed another on her jaw. "Fabian's men are plying him with drink. I might see if one of them can get him to sing or dance. It will give me ammunition when he attempts to tease me."

"You have rather an unconventional relationship with your coachman," Estelle said, sliding her hand under the table to grip his muscular thigh. She found she could not keep her hands off her husband.

Ross sucked in a breath as her hand edged higher. "The man has saved my life on more than one occasion though I would never tell him that."

Estelle's fingers settled on the fall of his breeches and caressed him in slow, sensual strokes. "Perhaps he's not the only one with the ability to tease you."

"Then you should know I'm a man with a hunger for revenge." He met her gaze and whispered, "Would you like me to make you come in front of all these people?"

Had she been sipping her wine, she might have choked. "How would you do that?" She had to admit to being a little excited.

"Trust me. No one would know."

"That is simply not possible."

Ross raised a brow. "Is that a challenge, Lady Trevane?"

Estelle loved this playful side of him. He looked so different from the dangerous devil who had dragged her into a coaching inn and forced her to tell her tale. "I cannot see how you would have an opportunity."

Ross gestured to the men setting up the music stands in the far corner. "In a minute, Mackenzie has arranged for Fabian to play his fiddle while everyone dances. We don't have to join them on the floor straight away."

"I highly doubt our guests will let us sit out."

Ross placed his napkin on the table, stood and moved to speak to Fabian. Her brother looked at her and then nodded.

"What did you say?" she said when Ross returned to his seat.

"I said you were feeling a little hot, a little overwhelmed by the events of the day, and we would sit out for the first dance and join them for the second."

Ross proceeded to tell her exactly what he wanted to do to her in bed that night. The precise details fired a heat between her thighs that was soon a blazing inferno. How was it she was panting with arousal and he'd not even touched her yet?

When Mackenzie stood, banged his gavel and instructed them the dancing was to commence, Ross placed his hand on her thigh.

"Cross your legs," he said with supreme confidence in his ability.

She did as he asked, and the sensation only heightened her need to find her release. Good Lord. She was liable to stretch out on the table and let him take her there and then. That thought sent another pulse of desire shooting to her core.

Fabian stepped down from the dais to join two other men. They played a country tune and their guests piled to the floor. Everyone danced, though the Erstwhiles were lauded for their stamina when they managed to keep pace with Mackenzie's jig.

The music was loud. The crowd were laughing and singing as Ross' fingers delved between her thighs and played her through the fine material of her dress as easily as Fabian stroked the strings on his fiddle.

Estelle struggled to sit still.

Ross' gaze never left her face. "I'll not wait until tonight to be inside you."

That was it. She came apart then. The muscles in her core clamped down, missing the feel of having him to grip on to, though still sending pleasurable shivers to her toes.

Ross waited until the tremors subsided and then sat back with a huge grin on his face.

"So," she began, a little breathless. "It seems you have found yourself another opponent as well as Wickett. Now, I shall have to think of new and novel ways to tease you."

"Then I shall look forward to the event with bated breath. Perhaps you may get your first opportunity in an hour or two. Mackenzie has hidden a chest of coins with clues how to find the treasure. I imagine most people will go on the hunt."

Estelle smiled. "But not you?"

Ross took hold of her hand. "No, not me. I have the only treasure I want right here."

THE END

Thank you!

Thank you for reading *The Daring Miss Darcy.*

If you enjoyed this book please consider leaving a brief review at the online bookseller of your choice.

You can sign up for my newsletter and receive a free digital copy of
What Every Lord Wants at:

www.adeleclee.com

Coming soon!
At Last the Rogue Returns

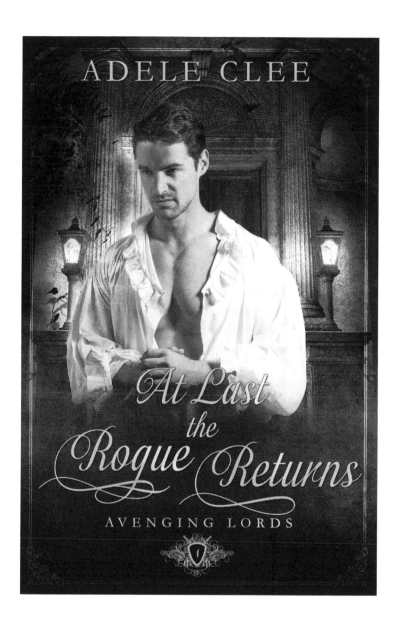

ADELE CLEE

At Last
the
Rogue Returns

AVENGING LORDS

A lady discovers that the monster of her nightmares might just be
the hero of her dreams.

Books by Adele Clee

To Save a Sinner

A Curse of the Heart

What Every Lord Wants

The Secret To Your Surrender

A Simple Case of Seduction

Anything for Love Series

What You Desire

What You Propose

What You Deserve

What You Promised

The Brotherhood Series

Lost to the Night

Slave to the Night

Abandoned to the Night

Lured to the Night

Lost Ladies of London

The Mysterious Miss Flint

The Deceptive Lady Darby

The Scandalous Lady Sandford

The Daring Miss Darcy

Avenging Lords

At Last the Rogue Returns

Printed in Great Britain
by Amazon